SCARLET KING

Thieves and Thorns

This novel is entirely a work of fiction. The names, characters and incidents portrayed in it are the work of the author's imagination. Any resemblance to actual persons, living or dead, events or localities is entirely coincidental.

Cover design by Monique Hemme at Cover2Cover Author Services

First edition

ISBN: 978-1-7399387-1-0

This book was professionally typeset on Reedsy. Find out more at reedsy.com

Dear Chad(s),
Fuck you.
Sincerely, all the spicy book girls x

Contents

Preface		iii
Prologue		iv
1	Rory	1
2	Rory	7
3	Rory	14
4	Darius	20
5	Rory	25
6	Ezra	33
7	Darius	38
8	Rory	46
9	Conan	53
10	Rory	57
11	Ezra	64
12	Darius	68
13	Rory	73
14	Conan	79
15	Ezra	83
16	Rory	88
17	Ezra	94
18	Rory	107
19	Rory	113
20	Conan	118
21	Darius	123
22	Conan	126

23	Rory	132
24	Rory	137
25	Ezra	146
26	Ezra	150
27	Conan	154
28	Rory	159
29	Ezra	165
30	Conan	172
31	Rory	177
32	Rory	183
33	Darius	189
34	Darius	200
35	Rory	203
36	Conan	211
37	Rory	218
38	Ezra	224
39	Rory	233
40	Darius	240
41	Rory	246
42	Rory	252
43	Conan	257
44	Rory	267
45	Darius	277
46	Ezra	284
47	Rory	292
48	Darius	297
Acknowledgements		303
About the Author		304
Also by Scarlet King		305

Preface

This is an ADULT, DARK REVERSE HAREM fantasy novel. This means the main character does not choose between love interests. This book is written in British English. There is a cliffhanger at the end of this book, but a HEA at the end of the duology.

Content Warning: This book contains explicit sexual content, including group sex and M/M content. This book is NOT meant to represent safe sex or kink. This is a work of fiction and fantasy. It is not meant to represent realistic BDSM activities, nor should it be taken as such.

This book contains content that may be triggering for some readers. Please read with care.

Trigger Warnings:
  Graphic sex
  Dubcon and CNC
  Mentions of (past) rape and sexual assault
  Graphic violence
  Blood
  Death
  (Past) abuse and trauma
  Panic attacks and PTSD symptoms

Prologue

I was covered in blood and only some of it was mine. It was dark and sticky and glistened every time the moonlight caught it. My legs burned as I ran, every damn muscle in my body aching with the effort it took to keep myself moving.

The torn skin on my neck stung as the freezing night air aggravated it.

"You won't get away from us!" Eryx called after me, his voice far too close for comfort. Fear had my steps faltering. The panic fuelled adrenaline coursing through me was the only thing keeping me upright.

My only answer was to push on, unable to cast any spell to help me. I'd drained my magic in my escape. No, all I had left in my arsenal was sheer stubbornness and a broken, battered body.

"We will find you!" he screamed, voice more distant now. I'd given myself a head start when I fucked with his asshole friends, and the distraction had likely saved my life. I refused to answer him, not that I could have even if I tried. My throat was raw, dry and scratchy, and I badly needed water. And food. More than that though, I needed shelter. Somewhere, anywhere safe.

The last time I'd ever felt safe was years ago. Sitting in front of the fire at my grandmother's house, helping her with spells, in the cottage she'd owned for years in the woods. A flash of her dark hair, her quick fingers tying herbs together with twine, the flicker of firelight creating long shadows across her face raced through my head. I was so far from there. So far from home. And yet, there was nowhere else I could think to go.

Of course, she wasn't there now. Nobody was. She'd burned with her house, leaving nothing but a pile of ashes and razed ground. Perhaps the village then. What the fuck was it called again? I tried to remember but thinking felt like running through mud. Thick and painful and so damn tiring.

I was so damn tired.

I ran until my legs buckled beneath me and my breaths were heaving gasps that burned my lungs. It was late, the sun long set and the sky an inky black, and still the trees were tall and thick around me. I'd always loved the forest but now it felt more like a trap than a home.

I collapsed at the roots of a tree, tucking myself as close to the trunk as I could. How had it come to this? Running from the man who'd sworn he loved me. Running from the fucking cult he'd dragged me into, from the addiction he'd cursed me with, from the death I knew was waiting just around the corner.

Eryx had never loved me. In truth, I'd never loved him either. But fuck had I wanted to. So desperate for a fucking morsel of affection that I'd let him ruin me for six years, drive me into a haze for most of them, drink my blood until I was high on the feeling of not feeling at all. He'd made me numb and I'd thanked him for it.

Never again.

I was shaking, both with exhaustion and adrenaline, but there was nothing I could do for it. The strips of cloth that barely passed for clothes were pasted to my skin with dried blood. I held my hand against the wound on my neck, tracing the puncture marks with my finger and grimacing at the sharp spark of pain.

I hoped to all the false gods that it wouldn't scar. I couldn't bear it.

Soon, I promised myself, I'd go home. Back to Haven - *that was the name* - and the kind woods and the ground my grandmother had died on. I'd rebuild, myself and the home, and I'd survive. Fuck, I'd survive.

And then I'd make him wish he hadn't.

Soon.

But now, I needed rest. Just a few minutes. Just to catch my breath. Just until the shaking subsided and I could feel my limbs again. Just…

1

Rory

Museums at night were fucking creepy. Being in this one at night, with nothing but old bones for company, had every nerve in my body on edge. The small corridor smelled of disinfectant and dust - a combination that made me wonder whether someone had just sprayed cleaning solution instead of actually washing anything. It was nearly silent. The only sound was my too-loud breathing and the soft squeak of my trainers on the linoleum. I badly wanted to cast the noise away - perhaps throw a protective bubble around myself - but whispering the spell under my voice would only serve to attract attention and drain me of energy. I'd blacked out the security cameras of course, a large spider conveniently covering the lens of the one closest to me.

Ahead, a faint green glow spilled across the floor, beckoning me. I was so close now. The safety light they'd installed beside the most valuable exhibits only added to the anxiety curling in my gut and the sensation of bugs crawling on my skin. Sweat beaded on my brow as I eased forward, unable to hear any tell tale signs that the room was occupied. If I'd timed it right, the security guard was still three exhibits away in the shifter room - with the grotesque, clearly fake, stuffed wolves and bears the humans liked to claim were 'real shifters hunted by the bravest defenders of our towns'.

I snorted then immediately cursed myself. My feet paused their advance as I waited with bated breath, hands clenched at my sides in case I had to resort to physical violence if anyone heard me. But there was nothing except the low, persistent buzz of electricity as I finally turned the corner.

It was dark save the eerie glow of the blinking light near the door, and I knew from the time I'd spent studying this place that the camera in here had lost its power a month earlier. No one had bothered to fix it - perhaps they hadn't noticed, or perhaps they were too arrogant to think anyone would take advantage of it.

My eyes quickly found what I'd come for and for a second, I thought my knees might buckle.

It was there, exactly like I remembered it, perfectly pre-served behind a glass case sticky with fingerprints. *They really should fire their cleaner*. The small display was in the centre of the circular room beside a mannequin in a long red cloak, stuck on fangs painted scarlet protruding from her plastic lips. I frowned. We were *witches* for Hell's sake, not vampires. The sight of the fake vampire so close to the witch display made my stomach turn. *Not now.* I couldn't think about it, about *him*, now. I needed to focus.

My heart ached as I took in the full display. The walls were lined with damaged pages torn from spell books, some spattered with blood that made my nostrils flare. Witch's blood. Even after years stuck behind their glass frames, I would recognise the scent anywhere. My stomach clenched, grief and anger making my muscles tense. I snapped out of my stupor, glanced down at my watch, and internally berated myself. I'd spent too much time here. I had ten minutes now, if that, before the guard was due in this area of the museum. Five to get what I came for, five to get the fuck out before anyone realised I'd taken it.

I pushed off the wall, heading straight for the glass case and tried desperately to ignore the other *artefacts* displayed meticulously around the room. Stolen family heirlooms, displayed as nothing more than cautionary tales about evil witches, interspersed with information boards boasting of burning my kind at the stake.

If I could burn the whole damn place down I would.

I know the owners of the items would have preferred it. Would probably relish in the cleansing lick of the flame. The humans who had stolen them didn't care about their history, their significance. Then again, most humans didn't seem to care about much except themselves and money. The urge to destroy this pathetic excuse for a history museum in the name of justice heated my blood. But not today. Not now.

By the time I reached my target, my jaw ached from grinding my teeth together to curb the scalding fury in my veins. The grimoire was closed, thankfully, the cover black with silver calligraphy script on the front. The language was old, and judging by the little plaque plastered to the dirty glass, the humans couldn't translate it at all.

Eighteenth Century Witch Spellbook

Collected from the ashes of an unfortunate house fire, this spellbook has been in the hands of the museum for nearly ten years. In that time, no scholar has been able to decipher the title,

3

nor open the book at all. It remains sealed by some potent form of witchcraft. Approach at your own risk.

I rolled my eyes as I read. Hell below, their *scholars* were fucking useless. And it had only been eight and a half years, not ten. Though, they were right about one thing - it couldn't be opened by any of them. They also failed to mention that the *unfortunate* house fire had likely been a premeditated attack or that the magic binding the covers closed posed no threat. I didn't buy the bullshit the human guards spouted in the news reports about it being *coincidence* that the house burned down just days after the witch living in it hexed the guy that looked at her granddaughter wrong.

I reached out, placing my hand flat against the glass. I could feel it, in its cold cage, like a living, breathing thing kept trapped for too long. The ache in my stomach grew stronger, and I bit back the sob in my throat. It was never made to be here, a pretty trophy for humans to display.

As quietly as I could manage, I spoke the *undoing* spell I'd memorised, squeezing my eyes shut to focus.

The second the last syllable left my lips, I pried my eyes open.

Silence, save the dull ringing in my ears. Even the annoying buzz of the light had faded. And then -

Crack.

Fissures spiderwebbed across the glass, until the side my hand rested on was fractured and flimsy.

"Fuck," I swore under my breath, pulling my hand back close to my body and glaring at it.

The seam had indeed come undone - the side able to be pried off if I tried - but the subsequent splintering of the glass had been unintentional. And now, there was no way to remove the pane without breaking it completely and scattering the shards all over the floor. The sound would alert the guards, regardless of the fact that I'd destroyed the alarm on the cabinet the last time I *visited*.

I glanced down at my watch, tasting bile in my throat at the realisation that I had a minute left. Any longer and I wouldn't get out in time. There was no time to figure out, or remember, whatever spell would help now. Mending the glass was impossible with such a short time frame.

There was nothing else for it. If I stayed, I'd be caught. If I ran, at least I had half a chance at getting away.

The sound of the glass shattering pierced the air as I pulled the side away from the case, barely avoiding slicing my hand open on the shards. Almost immediately, a guard shouted from a distance, his yelp of alarm shooting panic through me. Heart kicking into high gear, I reached in, my fingers brushing the soft leather of the book before I gripped it tightly and pulled it free.

Tucking it close to my chest under my cloak, I turned and ran.

Leaving the room of horrors behind, I charged back down the hall I'd come through, taking the turns I'd memorised from the visits I'd taken in preparation for this moment. Distantly, I registered the frantic squeaking of shoes on tile behind me as I left the witch wing and sped towards the delivery entrance I'd used to get in.

I slammed my body against the closed door, cursing every demon in Hell when it didn't budge. Someone had found me, reset the locks, and now I was trapped with a stolen book. Well, reclaimed, considering it wasn't exactly *stealing* if said item was taken from you in the first place.

I gripped the metal handle, shivering from the bite of cold, and began muttering the unlocking spell, my magic rushing to the surface of my skin in answer.

As the last word left my tongue, a shadow appeared behind me, blocking out the little light that had filtered into the alcove.

I shoved my full weight against the door, ducking my head to hide my face and pulling the hood up over my hair as I threw myself into the night beyond.

I choked as someone grabbed the back of my cloak, tugging me back towards the doorway. No, no no *no*. I'd made it so far. I was *so fucking close godsdamnit* -

"Hey!" someone yelled from the right, shock making the guard behind me lose his grip. I stumbled forward, doubled over and gasping as the mystery man continued to talk. I could practically hear a smirk in the stranger's voice when he asked the guard, "I've lost my cat. Do you think you can help me?"

I whirled and took off running before the guard could grab me again, taking advantage of the welcome, if confusing, distraction. I flew past the stranger as the guard cursed after me, catching a glimpse of messy dark hair, full lips curved into a knowing smirk, long lashes, and a flash of teeth. He was tall, at least six foot, and slim, dressed in a black t-shirt and dark jeans with a leather jacket slung over one shoulder.

Any other time, I might've given him more attention. Now, I brushed past him, catching him with my shoulder as I fled, the book warm against my chest.

I didn't take a full breath until I got home.

2

Rory

I groaned as I rolled over, the bright morning sun spilling across the bed. My head was pounding, an insistent drum beat begging me to go back to sleep. I'd stayed up most of the night, setting all three locks on my door and checking the permanent protection spell was in place before I finally crawled into bed. Even beneath the warm duvet, I couldn't sleep, watching the door with my heart battering my chest, waiting for someone to barge in. Logically, I knew I hadn't been followed - my accidental saviour had distracted the guard long enough for me to slip into the darkness - but the fear was still there.

Wincing, I eased out of bed, wiggling my feet to find my slippers tucked beneath the frame. Soft fleece stroked my skin and I stood, stretching my arms above my head and yawning. My whole body felt heavy, my legs aching from running more in one night than I had in the past three years. I wasn't *unfit* per se, but I didn't like to run unless something was chasing me. Clearly, I should practice more.

Peering out of my bedroom, I eyed the front door. The

house was all one level - a little bungalow I'd inherited from my grandmother. Well, I'd inherited the razed land and then rebuilt the entire cottage from memory. Even my childhood bedroom was the same as the original, though I'd modernized the decor and added an en-suite bathroom in the master bedroom. I couldn't bear to change anything else. The locks were still firmly in place on the door, everything as I'd left it. Relief washed over me, calming my senses.

I searched for my phone, finding it on the floor by the bed, and checked the time, cursing myself when I realised I'd somehow both under and overslept. I had approximately half an hour to guzzle coffee and stuff my face with whatever food I had in my fridge. Not to mention making myself look somewhat presentable and less like a criminal who'd been up all night. I sighed, running a hand through my tangled hair.

I moved towards the kitchen, deciding a strong coffee was necessary before I could even contemplate the other tasks, pausing to put pressure on the floorboard I'd lifted last night. It had always been a little loose, even when I was a child, and somewhere around the age of sixteen I figured out I could lift it up almost entirely, a convenient little hiding space concealed beneath my feet. The same wobbly board had originally existed in my childhood room, but it made more sense to spell it into the master when I moved back in. I'd used it to store the usual things I wasn't supposed to have - a water bottle filled with cheap vodka, condoms before I figured out how to ward myself against pregnancy, the first dirty book I ever bought. Now, of course, all those things were out on the shelves, and the hidey hole had a new purpose.

Forty minutes later, I was out the front door, ready and considerably late. Not that it would be a surprise to my manager. I'd worked at the cafe for three years now, and I'd probably been on time twice. But I made the best lavender lattes and lemon muffins, so she'd yet to bother firing me. It probably helped that she was my best friend, too.

I checked the locks for the third time, trying to shove down the anxiety swelling in my throat as I dragged my feet down the little path away from home. The cafe was only a ten minute walk into town, but every step I took away from the book hidden in the floor made my heartbeat rise. What if someone had seen me? What if someone came to find it?

I shook my head, smoothing my hands down my skinny jeans to wipe the sweat away. I inhaled the scent of my floral perfume, allowing the familiar smell to comfort me. It would be fine. It would all be fine. I just had to get through today, and then everything I'd been through to get the bloody book back from the humans would be worth it.

Humanity liked pretending us mythics didn't exist outside of their stories. Elementals, witches, demons, vampires, shifters….all the creatures they wrote horror movies about, the monsters that hid under their beds. There had been a time, centuries ago, that we had lived in peace. But fears had risen, rogue mythics had given us all a bad name, and wars had been waged over deaths and burnings and stakes. Now, only a few of us were scattered around this realm, often forming pockets of community in the human towns and cities, always staying slightly separate from them. The town of Haven was just that - a community of mythics, scorned by humans but still surviving. They sneered from a distance, complained about us and our sister towns on their news channels, but their idle threats never amounted to much. There hadn't been an incident in years, and now they had little reason to make good on their threats. Sometimes, I wondered if they would rather a rogue witch would curse one of them just so they had an excuse to massacre us again. Nausea rose as I thought about the room at the museum last night. It would have made more sense if I'd relocated to Hell when my family passed into the next life, instead of choosing to stay in the human world. But I'd grown up here, gone to school here, worked here my whole life.

I'd seen my family for the last time, here.

I couldn't bring myself to leave. Even if I'd be safer in the Underworld where I would be free to practice magic and immerse myself in the culture that had burned with my ancestors. I'd grown so used to being alone, I wasn't sure I could cope with integrating now.

The *ding* of the shop bell brought me from my thoughts as I stepped into work, the familiar scent of coffee grounds and sugar permeating my senses. Low chatter coloured the air, regulars perched on their stools at the coffee bar chatting to the baristas, a few new faces dotted around the wooden tables. Cloud Nine was a small cafe, specialising in artisan drinks, with a clientele made up almost entirely of mythics. I liked working here - with its bright, airy space filled with plants and deep brown wooden furniture, candles always lit and casting a warm glow over the faces of the customers. The only tells that it wasn't a human cafe were the unusual ingredients we offered - coffee brewed with blood, muffins baked with white bryony flowers to enhance the consumers' beauty, floral tea to - literally - heal the soul. We offered unspelled treats, too, of course, but we catered to the town's tastes.

"Rory!" The cheery feminine voice rang clear through the air, drawing the attention of the few regulars who knew me by name. They nodded their heads at me, knowing fine well I was useless for conversation until at least half an hour into my shift. I needed time to adjust to being awake. Still, a smile pulled at my lips as I met Grace's eyes, her bright blue gaze boring into me. The shifter beckoned me closer, pink glossy lips parted in a wide grin. I obeyed, ducking into the cloakroom to dump my handbag and pull on my apron before joining her behind the bar.

"Morning, Gracie," I greeted in my best attempt at a cheery voice.

"Here." She slid a cup filled to the brim with steaming coffee over to me, and I nearly dropped to my knees in gratitude.

"You're a fucking angel," I told her, humming as I brought the cappuccino to my lips.

"Feline but sure." She winked, her curly red hair spilling across her shoulders as she turned to start on an order. "You look more tired than usual this morning," she said over her shoulder at me as I set about checking what baked goods needed to be restocked.

"Gee, thanks," I shot back teasingly, knowing it was true. "Late night."

She turned from the coffee machine, narrowing her eyes but saying nothing. I knew she'd badger me for details later. Sighing and resigning myself to lying my ass off for the rest of my shift, I escaped to the kitchen to begin measuring out muffin ingredients.

By the time my front door came into sight that evening, exhaustion had burrowed so deep into my bones that I was surprised I was still on my feet.

"Thank fuck," I muttered as I walked up the little path towards the door, shoving a rogue strand of hair out my face, already dreaming of take-out pizza and my bed. I'd fielded questions from Grace all day, and avoided customers by pretending to develop a new muffin recipe in the back. I'd been in no mood to deal with people all day, and that hadn't changed.

I reached the door and immediately choked on a scream.

Reeling back, I plastered myself against the side of the cottage, blood rushing loud in my ears. *Fuck fuck fuck.* The door was open slightly, the locks disengaged and the "welcome" mat that read *Witchy Bitch Lives Here* slightly crooked. It was a gag gift bought by one of the few human friends I had in university, before I dropped out, and I'd never thought I'd need to replace it until now. Who the Hell was in my fucking house?

Clenching my fists, I forced myself to take a deep breath and push off the side of the house. Anger replaced the fear in my blood, hot and furious. It fuelled me as I shoved the door open and ran through the fastest self defence spells in my mind. Failing that, I dug the small pocket knife out of my handbag and held it close to my side.

I stepped inside and saw...nothing.

Everything was the same as I'd left it - the bread left out on the counter from breakfast, yesterday's clothes thrown over the couch, the open plan kitchen and living space in its usual casual state of organised mess. Slowly, I inched towards the white counter top, reaching out and closing my fingers around the handle of a long, sharp kitchen knife. I still couldn't see or hear anything out of the ordinary, but I *knew* I'd locked the damn door this morning, and I wasn't taking any fucking chances.

I shuffled down the hallway to the bedrooms, peering inside the bathroom as I went, finding nothing. It wasn't until I stopped outside my bedroom door that I heard it.

Someone was humming, *singing* under their breath. The voice was low and melodic, and I recognised the tune from the radio. What the actual fuck?

A brand new wave of anger washed over me, burning hot. Pissed as all Hell, I flung the door open, ready to scream at whoever was inside.

But the shout died on my lips when I found my floorboard ripped up and a dark haired stranger sitting on my bed with my book in his lap.

3

Rory

"Oh good, you're home."

I stood, stunned, the knife held out in front of me in my shaking hand. His voice sounded vaguely familiar, but I was in no mind to place it right now. My mouth hung open as he looked up from the book and raised his brow at me, a small smirk on his full lips.

Finally, I found my voice. "Who the fuck are you?" The fire in my words didn't seem to faze him at all. He placed the book down on the mattress and turned so he was facing me, long legs dangling off the edge of the bed.

He wore all black, from his fitted trousers and tight t-shirt to his thick soled boots. A leather jacket was folded meticulously beside him, and his dark hair was short and messy, the top slightly longer than the sides and flopping over his forehead. His skin was brown and annoyingly perfect, his eyes like liquid amber, and he wore a silver signet ring on his right pinkie finger, though I couldn't make out the design.

"Darius," he answered simply as his golden gaze roamed my body, barely catching on the blade I still pointed at him.

I waited for him to expand on that statement but was merely met with silence. "Okay, *Darius*, why the fuck are you in my house?"

I cocked my head to the side, eyeing him up and silently wondered whether it would be easier to stab him or curse him and if I could do either before he reached me. He was lean but held himself with the easy grace of someone far deadlier than they seemed. Frustratingly, he was handsome as fuck and that only made me want to stab him more.

"A *thank you* would be nice," he quipped, the stupid smile never budging from his lips.

"For breaking into my damn house?" Shock joined the anger in my chest.

"For saving your ass last night," he answered smoothly, picking up the grimoire and shaking it a little for emphasis. I moved before I realised what I was doing, snatching it back from him and holding it close to my chest. He let me, relinquishing his grip without a fight and staring at me with blatant curiosity burning in his eyes.

Suddenly, it clicked where I recognised his voice from. "You."

"Me," he said, his smirk growing into a grin as he extended his hand. "Nice to meet you, little thief."

"It's not stealing if it was stolen from me to begin with," I sneered back, ignoring his outstretched hand. "Why are you here?" Curiosity and trepidation coated my words, fury fading slightly at his admittance of help.

"I wanted to see what was worth angering a museum security guard for." He stretched, revealing a sliver of toned stomach that I definitely didn't look at, and then leant back, resting against my pillows with his hands behind his head as if he didn't have a care in the world.

"Get your fucking shoes off my sheets." Right, cause *that* was the problem here. I shook my head, gripping the handle of my kitchen knife harder. "Get out."

He frowned at me. "Grouchy." He kicked off his shoes, the boots landing on the floor near my feet. I stared at them, dumbfounded.

"You have ten seconds to start explaining before I put this knife to good use."

"Come on now, little thief," he cooed, narrowing his eyes at me. "We both know if you were going to stab me, you'd have done it by now. Besides, that little knife isn't going to hurt me. You're smarter than that."

I frowned, then sniffed and fought the growl in my throat. "Demon."

"Incubus."

Same difference. "I have other ways to hurt you," I told him as steadily as I could manage. "Answers. Now." I hadn't seen any demons in the mortal world since I was a teenager. They were manipulative beings, the lot of them, their powers specialising in persuasion and charisma. It made sense now, the anger gradually dissipating behind my ribs. Immediately, I whispered a charm under my breath to protect me from his power as he watched with amusement.

"Fine," he drawled as he rolled his eyes. "Although, for the record, I'd much rather be mysterious."

Maybe I would stab him after all. Just for fun. I wondered what colour demons bled.

"I wanted to see what was worth all the effort," he repeated, shrugging as if we were friends having a casual conversation over coffee. Seeing the death glare I shot him, he continued,

"I followed you. But then you seemed so tired that I thought I'd be nice and let you sleep. So I waited and then you took forever at work and I got bored and so…" He gestured between us dramatically.

I blinked at him.

"Look, I heard you last night when I was walking past the museum. And I'd never pass up the opportunity to piss off a human, plus you smelled good as fuck -" I reared back at that statement, nearly dropping my weapon - "so naturally I wanted to see what was going on. And then there you were - this short little fiery thing clutching some stolen relic like her life depended on it, charging out of sight."

I wasn't entirely sure what the hell to say to any of that. Instead I shook my head, shuddering a little with the shock of it all. "Get out."

"Oh come on, little thief," he smiled, and I hated him for the butterflies that took flight in my stomach at the way his tone dropped suggestively. "Don't I deserve even a little explanation for saving that cute ass of yours?"

No. "I didn't ask you to help me," I reminded him, irritated and turned on and irritated by the fact he was turning me on. *Hell below, I needed to get laid if this was the standard my body had sunk to.* "And I didn't need *saving*. I had it under control."

The look he gave me made it abundantly clear that I wasn't the least bit convincing. I refused to back down under the weight of his stare, straightening my spine and setting my teeth. He didn't need to know about the dark magic curses and spells kept safely in the pages of this grimoire, or why I needed to use them so badly. I doubted he'd understand even if I revealed the gruesome, but fitting, plan I had concocted. I'd witnessed my grandmother use this same book to hex the

17

people who pissed her off for years as a child. She'd promised to teach me properly when I was old enough. But time is a fickle thing, and I took it for granted then. I'd teach myself, make *them* suffer and make her proud in the process. A nice bonus, a cherry on top of the vengeance I was going to wreak on the bastards who'd hurt me. The demon sighed.

"I suppose I should've let the guard arrest you then, huh?" He shook his head with mock severity. "I don't think a pretty thing like you would last long behind bars."

I'd had enough. I surged forward, aiming the knife at his side, swearing at him -

Before I could so much as blink, my knife clattered to the floor and my hand was pinned above my head, back pressed firmly against my wall. The breath left my lungs in a *whoosh*, my heart skipping so many beats it took a minute for it to find its rhythm again. He snatched the book from my arm and tossed it onto the bed, grabbing my free hand when I moved to hit him and pinning it in his grip with the other.

I thrashed, shrieking in his grip, spine slick with panicked sweat. He was so close to me I could feel his breath dust my cheek, his grip on my hands strong and sure but not painful. Heat coiled low in my stomach. I'd never hated myself more.

"Will you listen to me now?"

"Go fuck yourself." I reared my knee up, aiming for his groin, promptly intercepted by his knee pressing between my legs, making me pause and gape.

"You'd like that wouldn't you?" he teased, eyes gleaming as they shamelessly roamed my body. I bared my teeth, furious at the flame that licked my skin under his inspection.

"Let me go."

"Shut up and listen and then I will," he repeated slowly. As much as it chafed at my pride, there was nothing for me to do but obey, bide my time until I could find a way out of this. He was considerably stronger than me - clearly fit - whereas the last time I saw the inside of a gym was that one time I'd fucked the personal trainer that used to frequent the cafe. Darius watched patiently as I forced myself to relax. "Good girl. See, you can behave."

Fuck me. Nope. So much nope. I refused to be affected by his words. Except my body clearly hadn't got the message judging by the growing dampness between my thighs. Ridiculous.

"Here's how it's going to go," he continued, oblivious to my internal chastising. "You're going to tell me what exactly is so important about some old book that you committed a crime to get it. And then I'm going to decide whether or not to help you."

"I don't want your help you fucking dickhead," I screamed, thrashing again, achieving nothing but a sore head when I bashed my skull off the wall. I really needed to stop relying on my magic and take up self defence. "I want you out of my house."

He just smirked at me, and I sneered back.

"Then give me a reason to leave, little thief."

4

Darius

The witch smelled of cinnamon and flowers, and it was driving me fucking insane. Worse, the scent of her arousal was slowly intoxicating me - sweet and dark like molasses. My mouth watered.

The heightened senses that came with being a mythic were both a blessing and a curse.

"Let's start with your name," I suggested, still holding her wrists tightly above her head. The position caused her shirt to rise up slightly, allowing a flash of soft stomach to peek through. I bit back the urge to run my thumb across the exposed flesh. Fire flashed in her eyes, but it banked quickly as she sighed.

"Rory."

Rory. I didn't try to stop the smile curving my lips. "Suits you."

"You don't know me."

"Who's fault is that?" Gods this witch was infuriating. I liked it far too much. Her light brown hair had mostly worked its way free of the elastic, the loose, frizzy ponytail now hanging down her back. I had the awful urge to tug it free completely, thread my fingers through it, and tilt her head back so she could look me in the eye - *shut the fuck up Darius*.

"Fine," she finally said, rolling her big green eyes. "It wasn't theirs to display." Then, under her breath, "it wasn't theirs to take at all."

I narrowed my eyes, glancing away from her to study the book again. I'd tried but hadn't been able to open it. Nearly broke a damn nail wrenching the covers apart to no avail. "Humans do like taking what's not theirs," I mused, turning my attention back to her. "Is it yours?"

"By blood." She'd closed off her expression, though her glare could still cut a lesser man down. The fire in her called to me. It had since last night. It hadn't been a conscious decision to interrupt her criminal ways, but once I'd stumbled upon the scene, it seemed a shame not to get the full story. What I'd told her earlier was true. It was almost cute that she thought those locks could keep me out. It had me questioning why she put them up in the first place.

"It doesn't open," I told her, trying to make conversation so I could study her longer. To glean whether or not to trust her, yes, but also because I couldn't fucking look away if I tried. She was all soft curves and full lips, a mouth made for sin, heavy lashes, and a tattoo in a language I didn't speak trailing up the side of her forearm.

"Not for you."

I raised my brow. "Oh?"

She shrugged, refusing to elaborate. Reluctantly, I dropped my grip on her wrists and stepped back, hoping to all the long dead gods that she couldn't see how the close contact affected me. It had been years since anyone had incited such need in me, especially someone who so obviously despised me.

I snatched the book off the bed, heavy and cold, and held it out to her. Immediately she reached out and grabbed it, holding it tight like a child with their favourite stuffed animal. I smirked.

"Open it."

She scowled, violence written across her face. "No."

I laughed, low and dark. "What's wrong, little thief? Can't do it?"

I knew she took the bait the second she steeled her spine against my words. I didn't notice that the move pushed her chest out. Not at all. She stepped away from the spot on the wall where I'd cornered her and ducked when I tried to stop her reaching for the knife, slipping easily under my outstretched arm and snatching it from the floor. I braced myself, widening my stance to ensure she couldn't topple me, waiting for the blade to be drawn in my direction again.

Instead, she drew it across her palm in a clean cut, deep red blood dripping in thick drops onto the dark cover of what I assumed was a grimoire. I moved to stop her, the sight of her blood seeping from her skin inciting a riot of emotions in me. But she just raised her head, unceremoniously threw the knife to the floor and smirked. I was too busy watching her face, studying the soft curve of her lips, the confident steady fire in her eyes, that I barely noticed when the cover of the book fell open in her hands.

"Blood rite," she said, grinning now. I rolled my eyes at her, finally studying the worn, thin pages of the book. I stepped forward, intent on looking closer, but she leapt back, slamming the damn thing shut again. "There. Proved it. You can leave now." She waved her hand towards the door, a clear invitation to make myself scarce. Unfortunately for her, I had never been very inclined to follow orders. It was why I'd left Hell in the first place.

"I don't think so."

Fury heated her cheeks. She wore every fucking emotion she felt on her face and I loved it. It was slightly inconvenient, this pull I felt towards her. Annoying. I hadn't banked on my late night lost wandering to result in an accidental rescue of a criminal. Although, it did solve the problem of *what the fuck was I supposed to do now?* Fleeing the only home you'd ever known without a plan tended to leave one in a sort of…limbo.

What a fitting distraction she'd turned out to be.

"Get. Out." She gritted her teeth, looking like a cornered dog. Her voice was scratchy and condescending when she added, "I'm sure a big important demon like you has somewhere better to be."

I laughed, surprising both of us. "Nah." I let her squirm under my gaze, inhaling her scent and barely suppressing my groan. "Nowhere better to be than here."

Clearly exasperated, Rory threw her hands up. "Look, dude, I'm fucking exhausted and stressed, and I *really* don't want some random demon in my house right now. Please, just get out."

The utter defeat in her words surprised me, a stark difference from the ball of rage she'd been moments ago. For the first time since she'd come home, a flash of fear shone through the stubbornness in her gaze. I reeled back, confusion and curiosity mixing in my gut. It was understandable, the fear, but why was she only just scared now? Until now, she'd shown no sign of such feelings, at least not outwardly.

"Okay," I said quietly, gaze flicking between her and the

book, "but I'll be back in the morning. Call off work. We have a lot to discuss."

"What?" she seethed, anger nearly vibrating off her. "I'll do no such fucking thing. I have nothing to discuss with you."

There was the fire. "Fine," I smirked, turning to leave as she watched, wide eyed. "As you wish, little thief." With another smirk and a mock salute, I walked straight out her front door without so much as a glance back.

5

Rory

"Rory, babe, wake up!"

I jolted, heart rate spiking, shaking the hand off my shoulder. Slowly, the scents and sounds of the kitchen seeped into my mind, reminding me where I was. "Fuck, sorry."

Grace offered me a sympathetic smile, warm and soft, as she helped me up off the floor. I melted, sinking into her hug and inhaling the smell of coffee that always stuck to her clothes. Owning and working in the coffee shop near daily, it clung to her like a second skin.

"It's fine," she assured me, pulling back and eyeing me. "Ror..."

"I'm fine, Grace," I lied, refusing to meet her gaze. She opened her mouth to object but I just shook my head. "Promise."

I could tell by the set of her jaw that she didn't believe me, but she'd decided not to push it. "In that case, there's someone asking for you."

I frowned, pushing off the wall and moving to peek round

the door of the kitchen to the cafe floor.

"Tall, dark and handsome?" Grace supplied, wiggling her red brows at me. "Smells like he came straight from Hell…" The suggestive lilt to her tone made me laugh. "If it wasn't you he was asking for, I'd be climbing him like a tree."

"Alright, alright, I get it," I laughed, shoving her shoulder playfully. She grinned, flashing her pointed canines. *Who the fuck is asking for me?* I'd shoved the previous day's events from my mind, ignoring Darius' stupid request for me to stay home - so he could break into my fucking house again - but the lack of sleep made me wonder if I should've just obeyed his rude command. Wait -

"Oh fuck no." I emerged from the kitchen, crossing my arms over my chest as I met the gaze of the man who'd asked for me by name. "Nope. Abso-fucking-lutely not. Grace!"

I turned on my heel before he could say anything to me, ignoring the curious glances of the other customers.

"Kick him out," I told my boss, near shaking with rage.

"What? Why?" She looked up from the pan she was frying bacon in, head tilted slightly to one side.

"Long story," I murmured, not wanting to get into it. "But he needs to leave. Please?"

Grace took the pan off the heat and stepped closer to me, reaching out. "What happened?"

"It doesn't matter," I answered lowly. If I told her he'd broken into my home, I'd have to explain *why* he'd broken into my home, and if I did that then I would have to explain all the shattered, sharp pieces of my past I'd worked so hard to hide.

Grace sighed, dropping her hand. "I'm sorry, Ror, I can't just kick out a paying customer for no reason."

My stomach dropped. I couldn't push more, couldn't say more, without her suspicions rising higher than they already were. "I understand."

I turned away before she could see the disappointment in my eyes. It wasn't her fault, but it hurt all the same. Grace was my friend, yes, but the cafe was her baby, and she'd worked hard to make it a safe space for all mythics. Kicking out a random incubus for no apparent reason wouldn't go down well.

I steeled myself, shutting down my emotions as I made my way behind the coffee bar, smiling at the other customers before coming to a stop in front of him.

"Darius."

"Rory." His voice was as low and smooth as I remembered, and I hated him for the effect it had on me. He was wearing a deep navy jumper, though it wasn't particularly cold out, and his hair was as perfectly messy as the last time I'd seen him. His medium brown skin seemed golden under the warm glow of the candles. *Fucking Hell.*

"What brings you here?" I tried to keep my tone even, though the implication was there. *I thought I told you to fuck off.*

"Can't an incubus crave a cup of tea?"

"Not if he doesn't want me to spit in it."

His grin widened, eyes crinkling at the sides. "Oh, little thief, that's not the threat you think it is."

I baulked, taking an involuntary step back.

"I'll have a tea, please."

I blinked at him, anger bubbling to the surface. "What kind," I gritted out, forcing myself to meet his gaze.

He waved his hand at the display behind me. "Your

27

favourite."

I forced myself to breathe past the anger as I snatched a floral tea from the shelf and selected a teacup. It was my least favourite of our selection.

"I thought you were going to take today off," he continued nonchalantly, pretending to study our menu.

I smiled, sickly sweet. "Why would you think that?"

He looked up from the menu, shamelessly letting his eyes roam my body. I refused to acknowledge the heat his gaze spread through me, though by the slow smirk on his face, I was unsuccessful at hiding the effect he had on my body. "Do you not remember our conversation yesterday? I know I'm not *that* forgettable."

Would I be fired if I threw this teacup at his head? "You must be mistaken," I answered as I finished making the tea and inhaled the strong scent of rose and berries. I set the cup and saucer in front of him, perhaps a little harsher than necessary. "Enjoy."

"Actually," he stopped me as I moved to walk away, "I had a few questions."

"I'm working."

"That's fine," he assured me, sipping his tea. "I can always drop by after your shift and talk then."

I clenched my fists at my side, forcing myself to swallow the scream rising in my throat. "You have two minutes."

Slowly, he set his cup down and leaned his elbows on the counter. "Trust me, you'll want more than that."

"Funny," I shot back, dropping my voice low and leaning closer. "I don't think you'll last longer than that."

His laugh was unexpected and warm, turning the heads of the customers next to us. I blushed, and immediately cursed myself for responding at all. "Oh, little witch…" I shivered

28

under the hot weight of his attention. "It's like you're asking me to prove you wrong."

I flushed, breathing heavily. I needed to get out of here, now, before I made any more of a fool out of myself.

"Time's up."

"I have a minute and thirty seconds left," he argued, leaning back and stretching. "Look, I don't know what you've got yourself into, but you're lying to yourself if you think they're not going to try to get that damn book back." He leaned closer again, whispering. "Humans don't like being made fools of. If you're not going to give it back, at least let me help."

"I don't know you," I hissed, "and you don't know me. I can look after myself just fine."

"Sure thing, little thief." He finished his tea and stood. "Guess I'll just go help the other team. I'm sure the investigators would be very interested to know the name and address of the girl who stole a very valuable artefact."

I felt the blood drain from my face as my stomach clenched. He wouldn't. Surely, he wouldn't. Investigators? I hadn't seen anything in the news about the grimoire yet, had no idea they'd already hired people to find me. I'd known, of course, that they wouldn't want the book out in the world. They were terrified of what was inside and I couldn't blame them.

"I don't see how you could be of any help." I tried to stop my voice shaking, but it still wobbled a little. The thought of having the grimoire taken before I could even *use* it was an ache in my chest. Never mind the fact that I knew it belonged with me. My ancestors knew it belonged to me. I didn't want the one piece of family history that I had left wrenched away again.

"Incubus can be very...persuasive," he answered, smile gone

and replaced by determination. "Of course, witches like you have handy spells to stop it from affecting you, but humans aren't so gifted."

My eyes widened. It was illegal to use spells, gifts, powers of any kind on unwilling parties. But then again, he didn't seem like he belonged up here and such laws didn't apply in Hell. No laws did, really. The rulers of the Underworld were more for name and status than actual peacekeeping. Hell, as far as I'd heard, was wild and uninhibited, a place where danger and debauchery were encouraged. Up here, we played by the human's rules.

"It's not like below," I told him. "You can't do that sort of stuff up here."

He rolled his golden eyes. "What are they going to do? Burn me at the stake?"

I flinched, feeling his words like a punch to the gut. His face softened slightly.

"I didn't mean -"

"Are you done?" I snatched the half empty cup from him, turning to take it away. "Tea's on the house. Have a nice day, Darius."

I kept my tone cool and professional. I couldn't allow him to see me break down. Things were already complicated without making a fool of myself at work.

"A tip, then," he replied as he shrugged his shoulders into his tight leather jacket. I heard him slap something down on the counter, but didn't look back until the bell above the door rang, signalling he'd left.

I snatched the paper from the counter, warm and smooth against my palm. Frowning, I ducked into the cloakroom and opened the folded scrap, eyes widening at the words scrawled on the page.

For when you change your mind. Below, a short summoning spell was written out in the old language, signed with his name and "xo". I scoffed, crumpling the note into a ball and shoving it into my pocket, forcing a deep breath into my lungs.

Under no circumstances would I welcome the fucking incubus back into my life.

Someone was watching me.

I could sense it, the eyes on me, but I couldn't see a fucking thing. It was late, nearly midnight, and pitch black outside. I fumbled for the switch for the bedside lamp, trying to keep my breathing even. It knew instinctively it wasn't Darius. No, this wasn't his style. He'd have simply barged into my room like he owned it.

The room plunged into darkness, and I made a show of lying down, curling up under the duvet. The book was stashed in the floor again, this time bundled in blankets and surrounded by random shit to throw any nosey fuckers off the scent. I just needed to keep it hidden long enough that the museum stopped looking, and then I could use it. There was no way I could get all the supplies set up and carry out this plan while people were watching me. As much as I was itching to put it to use the second I got my hands on it, I knew it was reckless. I'd waited six years to do what I needed to do. I could wait a few more weeks.

Something scratched against the window, and I froze, fear whipping through me. What the fuck was I supposed to do? The energy I could feel through the bricks didn't seem human, but I was too scared to cast a detection spell in case whoever it was felt the magic. Exposing myself would only increase their suspicions.

I shifted, rolling slightly, and felt something prod my hip. I hadn't changed into my sleep shirt yet, considering the fact that I never managed to fall asleep before two in the morning anyway. Beneath the blanket, I reached into my pocket, curling my fingers around the note. Fuck it, this was the best solution I could think of. Horribly, I had to admit to myself that Darius might have been right. I couldn't do this alone. Sure, I had the locks and protection spell, but what if they, like the incubus, managed to get past them? I couldn't lose the grimoire, couldn't go back to square fucking one, couldn't risk being found so soon. I was stupid, naive, thought I'd have more time, that I could get this over with and then hide the grimoire until the news became old and stale and the humans stopped looking.

The summoning spell wouldn't alert whoever the fuck was outside my house. The magic was tied to Darius, not me.

My eyes strained in the dark to read the scribbled words, mispronouncing it so badly the first time that I had to try again, whispering the old, melodic language into the empty air before me.

I finished, crushing the paper in my fist again, curled up in a ball beneath the blankets as my heartbeat filled the silence. And then -

"Well, well, well. Couldn't even last a day."

32

6

Ezra

The whole damn house smelled like a bakery.

My wolf growled, but I swallowed the sound, refusing to let the animal instincts currently riding me break our cover. Conan was silent in the grove of trees behind her house, listening to the fucking plants talk or whatever the hell he did. After nearly twenty years, I still didn't understand all his elemental powers. By comparison, having a near feral wolf share my fucking body seemed simple.

All the curtains were drawn, and the one light that had been on had gone dark a few minutes ago. Though if I shifted, I would be able to see perfectly fine, the consequences were certainly not worth it considering we were trying to remain discreet. I'd surveyed the door when we first arrived, but the witch had a million fucking locks installed - gaining access would have to wait until she was at work again. Frustrated, we'd resorted to waiting.

In short, I was bored as fuck.

I backed away slowly, not wanting to stay too long in one place, retreating to the trees to find Conan.

He was in a fucking tree.

"Hell below, Cee," I muttered, head tilted back to make out the dark shape in the branches above.

Seconds later, he was landing lightly in the dirt beside me, barely making a sound. It took everything in me not to jump at the sudden closeness.

"Anything?" His voice was low and gruff, as dark as the night around us.

"No," I answered, shaking my head. "The girl's barely asleep. Can't get close enough tonight."

He sighed, running a hand through his dark hair. "Fine. We'll come back tomorrow."

I groaned, not wanting to draw this out any more than we had to. The museum had hired us a day after their precious grimoire went missing. Claimed it was imperative that it be found. That they'd "acquired" it from a deceased dark witch and felt it was safer for such a thing to be kept contained. It wasn't unusual, getting jobs from humans, but it always set off warning alarms in our heads.

I was nearly certain she had what we were looking for. Conan had researched the fuck out of dark witches, their covens, their grimoires and the death of the original owner. He'd always been good at finding this shit out, but he'd honed the skill to a sharp point over the years. Now, I'd be hard pressed to find anyone better at digging for the truth than him. The museum didn't have a scent profile for the grimoire, given the environment it had been kept in, so this job had largely fallen on Conan thus far. It annoyed me, the waiting. The insistent urge to get out and do something itched along my skin.

Regardless of how certain we were that this witch had the

book, I wasn't about to hand over her name to the fucking guards without making sure. We'd learned years ago that those that hired us couldn't always be trusted to tell the truth, particularly humankind. Ever since, we'd made sure to do our own investigation before blindly handing over those we were sent to find. But still...

"I don't like this," Conan whispered, his shoulder brushing mine. He was taller than me and it nearly knocked me off balance. I shot him a glare even though I knew he couldn't see me.

"Why?" I pinched the bridge of my nose, staving off the headache brewing behind my eyes.

"Why would some random witch from a tiny fucking town want an old spell book from a human museum?"

Conan always thought too hard about everything, especially jobs. He was suspicious of everything and everyone, and I could hardly blame him.

"I don't know," I told him honestly, turning and heading away from the little cottage. "That's what we're here to find out."

"That's not what we were hired to do."

"You know better."

He sighed softly, and I knew he agreed. We were nearly always of the same mind about this shit.

"I thought this place had burned down," Conan mumbled to me, glaring at the cottage like it personally offended him.

I furrowed my brow, making a low noise of confusion. Clearly, it was fucking standing, looking weathered and old. It was even missing a few shingles from its mossy roof.

"When I was researching it," Conan started again, bringing my mind back to our conversation. "I found a news report about it burning down. The woman who owned it burned with it. There was no mention of it being rebuilt."

"It looks old," I thought out loud, ignoring Conan's sigh. "Are you sure you're on about the right place?"

"Hell below, Ez," Cee groaned, clearly tired. "Yes it was the right place. Same forest and patch of land. Obviously, this girl somehow built the fucking thing again."

I frowned. It was cute, I supposed, quaint. Isolated and small, but it did hold a certain sort of charm. But standing staring at it wasn't going to get us any more answers.

Silently, we headed back to the shitty motel we were renting in the next town over. Conan, I knew, could have made the trip in half the time it took us by riding the air currents, but he held back, insisting on running on foot instead so I didn't fall behind. The motel was tiny and smelled of cigarette smoke and dirt. I wrinkled my nose, covering my face with the sleeve of my shirt as we entered our room, quickly locking the door behind us and sticking the back of the chair from the desk under the handle for good measure. I flicked the light on, a sickly yellow glow encompassing the room.

Conan was already flopped on his comically small bed, feet hanging over the edge as he stretched out. I ripped my eyes away and shook my head, the knot at the base of my neck sending a twinge of pain through my skull.

The bathroom attached to the bedroom was even shittier. I cursed under my breath, cringing at the dirt in between the tiles. A tiny bathtub took up one side of the room - far too small for either of us to lie in properly - and the sink was chipped and grimy. The mirror was cracked down the middle and cloudy, so I could only make out half my face, my dark skin coated with sweat from the run back, my deep brown eyes weary and half lidded.

I hadn't even seen thirty yet and already exhaustion had slipped beneath my skin, a near constant ache. At first, the job had given me direction, a reason to keep going, a sense of power over all the shit that had happened to us. Conan and I.

But three years ago, that changed.

And ever since, each time the phone rang, instead of finding that familiar burning determination, the urgent search for justice, all I felt was dread.

I quickly washed my face, brushed my teeth and returned to the bedroom. Conan had stripped, now shirtless and wearing loose fitting grey joggers, the strong muscles in his back rising and falling with each deep breath. He was face down, sprawled like a fucking starfish over the mattress, brow furrowed even in sleep.

I let myself watch for three more breaths before checking the door, changing quickly into whatever comfortable clothes were still clean, and lying in the dark, waiting for sleep.

7

Darius

S he looked so fucking innocent when she slept. Her hair was fanned out around her, her lips parted slightly as she shifted, turning and kicking off the duvet. The silky shorts and tiny tank top she called pyjamas instantly had my blood heating.

"What the fuck are you staring at?" Suddenly, she was upright, glare no less effective despite the crease lines from the duvet on her cheek.

"You," I told her honestly, smirking. I'd watched the door dutifully for a few hours so she could sleep, still delighting in the fact she'd crumbled so fast and summoned me. Her fear, however, had set a slow burning fire inside of me, a need to erase whoever the fuck was outside her house from the face of the earth.

"Well stop," she answered, but her cheeks were pink and she wouldn't meet my eyes. I grinned. "Are they gone?"

The question sobered my mood quickly. "They didn't stay long after you called me," I told her, perching on the edge of her mattress while she scowled at me. She reached for the duvet to cover herself, but I was faster, snatching it from her hand and holding it in place. "Nuh uh, little thief."

"You're a dick," she ground out, rising and offering me a fucking spectacular view of her ass as she bent over to slide her feet into purple fluffy slippers.

"Ah," I answered, rising too and following her through to her kitchen. "But as I recall, I'm a dick you need." I winked.

She turned on her heel, indignation flashing in her eyes as she said sweetly, "I will *never* need your dick."

I laughed, unable to help myself. It only made her scowl deepen. Before she could stop me, I stepped into her space, backing her up against her kitchen counter.

"Is that a dare?"

Shock and anger flicked across her features, only fuelling the amusement bubbling inside of me. She had to tilt her head back to meet my eyes, her messy hair framing her face, those big green eyes narrowed on mine.

Instead of answering, she shoved me away, both hands in the centre of my chest. I let her, stepping back and allowing her space again.

"I'm taking the day off," she announced, clearing her throat and shoving her hair back from her face. She snatched a mug out one of the light wood cupboards, ignoring my exaggerated eye roll and exasperated sigh.

"What a great idea," I drawled, glaring at her as she spooned instant coffee into her cup - purple with a fucking unicorn on the side. When she didn't offer me one, I reached over her and snagged my own mug, a white one with a pattern of little black crows, slamming it down on the counter next to hers. She rolled her eyes at me, but took the hint and filled it, pouring boiling water and milk into them both.

"I wasn't aware demons needed caffeine." She eyed me over the top of her drink as she blew the steam off.

"I wasn't aware witches needed demon protection."

She visibly tensed, looking away from me to eye the forest beyond her window. It was peaceful in the daylight, the trees tall and thick, the leaves just beginning to change with the season. There were no neighbours close enough to see, only the little path that led to the country road into town.

"A bit cliche, no?" I asked, watching her ignore me as she poured herself cereal. "A witch in a cottage in the woods?"

She scoffed, even as she poured a second bowl and handed it over, a scowl setting a line between her brows. "What can I say?" she deadpanned, lifting her spoon to her lips. "Hansel and Gretel was always my favourite fairytale."

We ate in silence after that, though I watched her mouth the entire time. When we were done, she chucked the dishes into the sink and turned to me, arms crossed over her chest. I forced myself to look away from the way it pushed her tits up and brought my gaze up to meet her narrowed eyes.

"Do you have plans today?" she asked, looking up at me.

"No." She frowned, and I could see the questions form in her eyes. I didn't have an explanation for her. "We should probably start by checking the forest."

She sighed but nodded, not taking her eyes off me as she backed away to the bedroom. "Give me five minutes to get dressed." She paused at the doorway, indecision flickering across her face. "Just so you know, I'm perfectly capable of protecting myself. I just…"

"You want to keep your stolen goods safe," I finished for her, gaze softening. I didn't doubt for a fucking second that she was more than capable of defending herself. But the stark fear

40

I'd seen in her last night kept replaying in my mind. It went against everything I'd seen from her so far. It didn't make sense. She had to have known someone would come looking for the book eventually when she stole it. Humans never did well with being told they couldn't have something.

"Yes. That's all."

Liar. Despite the protection spell she had on herself, I could tell that much. She was hiding something. Then again, I'd told her fuck all about myself so it wasn't exactly my place to judge. Still...

"What is it about that grimoire you needed so bad that you'd risk yourself for it?" I pushed, curiosity getting the better of me even as she closed the door. I stood outside, leaning against the wall while I waited for her answer. Her house was cosy and slightly chaotic - random trinkets and coffee cups with the dregs still sitting at the bottom strewn across every flat surface. The living and kitchen space was open plan, and though the cottage itself was old, the interior had clearly been redone, save the stone fireplace set into the left wall. Shades of purple, cool grey and red dominated her house - two grey sofas dotted with purple cushions and a scarlet throw blanket chucked over the arm. The small bag of clothes and necessities I'd been in the middle of procuring for myself when she'd summoned me was abandoned beside the largest one. The kitchen counters were marbled grey, the cupboards pale wood, but her plates and cups and cutlery were all mismatched. Deep brown wooden bookshelves and a desk hugged the walls, weathered books and half used pieces of paper laid out across them.

It had amused me when I first entered, the homey mess, and it fit her perfectly.

41

Not that I knew her. Not that I should want to know her.

But, fuck, I'd never been good at following the rules.

"It's rightful place is with me," she said finally, raising her voice so I could hear. Before I could call her on the clear withholding of information, the door swung open again, and I jumped back. "Let's go." When I did nothing but stare at her, she put her hands on her hips and raised a brow. "You said you wanted to help so...time to help."

But my eyes were glued to the fucking tease of a dress she'd put on - some sort of soft fabric that clung to every curve and knee high socks that threatened to have me drooling.

"I get it, I have a great ass," she said as she crossed to the front door and reached for a pair of ratty trainers. "Put your tongue back in your mouth and get a grip."

I obeyed mindlessly, blinking to clear the filthy thoughts circling my brain. I'd never bothered to take off my boots, but I grabbed my leather jacket from the coat hook and slung it on, frowning when I noticed a chip in the black nail polish I always wore. Absently, I picked at it more as she led the way to the forest, locking each and every lock on her door before we left. Not that they'd stopped me, but I admired her determination.

The scent of fresh morning dew and a cool breeze washed over me, the cold bite of the autumn air focusing my mind. I breathed in slowly, relaxing my muscles and studying our surroundings. It was a clear day, the sky blue and bright, silent except the quiet chirp of birds.

"There," Rory said suddenly, voice low and steady despite the tension in her stance. She pointed toward her bedroom window, scrunching her nose. I followed her lead, inhaling deeply, trying to identify the faint scent that stood out from the woodsy, earthy smells of the forest.

"Fucking mutt," I growled as we got closer, covering my nose with my sleeve. The scent was clearer now, dark and musky and distinctly animalistic.

"Shifter," she clarified, lip pulled back in a sneer. I bent down, running a finger through the disturbed dirt beneath her bedroom window. Whoever it was had cleared their tracks but the earth here was turned, as though they'd swiped their shoes over it before leaving.

"Do you know any canine shifters?"

She shook her head, her throat working as she swallowed thickly. Her eyes were glued to the disturbed ground, hands clenched into fists at her side. Unconsciously, I lifted my hand to comfort her, catching myself before I touched her and dropping my arm back to my side. Fuck, this witch was shredding my self control, and I'd known her for all of a day.

"The only shifter I know is Grace, and this definitely isn't her."

I recognised the name as the woman I'd first seen in the coffee shop - red-headed and sweet and distinctly feline. "Then I think we both know what this is."

Rory stiffened and slowly raised her head to meet my eyes. I rolled my shoulders, holding her gaze. "Already?"

"Guess that little stunt of yours pissed them off."

"Fuck." She looked around, anger rolling off her in waves, but there was nothing else here to point us in any sort of direction. "Fuck!"

I watched her through narrowed eyes as she tried to keep herself together, jaw tense and fists clenched so tightly her knuckles were white.

"Not to piss you off even more," I ventured, leaning against

43

the side of the house and crossing my arms over my chest. "But you must have expected this."

She paused, turning to face me. "Obviously," she spat, running a hand through her hair and visibly deflating. "I just thought I'd have more time. I just need a little more time —"

"For what?"

"To hide it."

"You didn't have a safe place lined up before this shit?"

"Fuck off, Darius."

I was on her in a second, backing her up against the brick of the cottage, caging her in with my arms. I gave myself a second to relish in the closeness, the spicy scent of her sending a thrill through me.

"Tell me now, Rory," I warned her, voice low. "If you want help, I need to know. Why did you take that grimoire? And don't give me the whole 'blood rite' bullshit. You're a terrible fucking liar. I know there's more than that."

She stared up at me, exposing her neck in a way that made me want to wrap my hand around it.

"A secret for a secret."

"What?" I asked, caught off guard.

"How do I put this in a way you understand?" Sarcasm dripped off her words. I wanted to taste it on her lips. "I'll show you mine if you show me yours."

"Little liar," I murmured, leaning down until we were sharing breaths. "Be careful what you wish for."

Satisfaction flooded me when her breath hitched and her lips parted on a ragged exhale. She recovered quickly, though, to my disappointment, collecting herself and straightening her spine.

"I need a spell in it."

I waited for her to keep talking, but she pressed her lips together and raised a brow. "What spell?"

"Your turn," she answered, steadfast and unmoved by my exasperated sigh. I leaned away, pushing off the wall to distance myself. No matter how fucking hot she was or how much I wanted to find out how she tasted, she was driving me fucking insane.

"Fine. What do you want to know?"

"Why are you helping me?" I went to answer, but she held up her hand. "The truth. You can't possibly just randomly have the free time to help a stranger who fucked up stealing something."

Well, then. Brutal honesty it was. "I have nowhere else to go."

"Why?"

"Game's over."

Not that either of us really knew anything more now. But I didn't want to explain, didn't want to dive back into the place I'd only just clawed my way out of.

So instead I turned on my heel and made myself walk away.

8

Rory

The fucking demon was eating me out of house and home. We'd barely spoken since we came back inside but he apparently had no problem raiding my kitchen cupboards. Currently he was eating tea biscuits out of the packet, pausing after the first bite to stare at them.

"You're supposed to dip them in tea."

I watched him far too closely as he turned on the kettle and once again dug through my cupboards for tea and honey. I was curled up under a blanket on the sofa, desperately trying to think of a solution to the giant fucking problem spying on me in the middle of the night. I hated having to call on this near stranger for help but fear had a tight grip on my throat that I wasn't sure I could shake on my own. And, while I was damn good at casting, I was incredibly rusty at hand to hand combat. I'd tried to take self defence classes a few years ago, but the second the instructor put his hands on me to demonstrate the move, I freaked, screaming and clawing until he let me go.

I was politely asked never to return after that.

Tea and biscuits in hand, Darius sauntered over to me, kicking off his boots before flopping down on the sofa across from me, miraculously not spilling a drop of his drink in the process.

"I assume you spelled the current hiding spot," he said casually as he dipped a biscuit.

I scoffed, rolling my eyes. "Yes."

"Good." He hummed in appreciation before waving the packet at me in offer. I shook my head. I wasn't hungry after our discovery. I was sick to my stomach, constantly shifting to look out the windows, books discarded next to me as I tried to look for another home protection spell.

"So, this spell…"

"I don't want to talk about it." I *couldn't* talk about it. He already knew far too much. He opened his mouth, likely to argue with me, but the sudden loud pounding on the door stopped him in his tracks.

In a second, he was on his feet, eyes darkening from their usual gold to the smoky colour of dying embers. Fear snaked around my chest, squeezing until I was breathless. I stood on shaky legs, but remained still when Darius held up a hand and shook his head sharply. Understanding, I tucked myself close to the wall near the door, so that I could hear whatever was about to happen while remaining unseen. I didn't have time to mask my scent, but there was no point. The whole house had the same smell, not to mention Darius' which was, much to my annoyance, beginning to linger in the air.

Putting a finger to his lips, Darius moved towards the door, standing tall and pasting an impressively bored look on his face.

He swiftly unlocked the door and swung it open.

47

Instead of greeting whoever stood on the other side, he just crossed his arms over his chest and stared at them. After a few uncomfortable seconds, the person on the other side cleared their throat.

"Good morning."

"It was," Darius drawled, top lip curled into a sneer.

"Right, well," a second, gruffer voice joined in, and I froze. "I don't suppose you know where the homeowner is?"

I inhaled deeply while Darius raised a dark brow in disdain, my heart attempting to climb out my bloody throat when the deep, wild mix of scents hit my senses. One, distinctly shifter, matched what we'd found outside, though now it was much stronger, my body standing to attention subconsciously. The second was woodsy, like the smell of earth after rain, or smoke after a candle's blown out. I couldn't place who it came from, I'd never smelled anything like it before. Regardless, my stupid fucking body wanted more. I wished their scents were repulsive, but instead I had to stop myself breathing them in again, a soft ache curling low in my belly.

For fuck's sake. First the demon, now my two bloody stalkers. *Great choices, Rory.*

"She's predisposed."

"We heard you talking," the first voice argued. "We'd like to speak with her."

Immediately, anger cooled the desire rising inside me. The low demand in his voice had my hackles raising. Shifters, by nature, were brash and bold and hated being told *no*. I'd seen Grace kick customers out on more than one occasion because they'd said something she didn't like. Apparently, this man was no different.

"It's lovely to meet you too," Darius smirked, sarcasm coating the air. "Whatever happened to niceties? Introductions?"

A heavy sigh, followed by the shifting of feet. It was driving me insane not being able to see what was happening. As it was, all I had a view of was Darius' side profile and as unfairly handsome as he was, the fact he was fighting this battle for me rubbed me the wrong way.

"Ezra," the first voice said, a deep brown hand extended in offer to Darius. The demon just looked at it, disgust smeared across his face. It took every ounce of control I had not to laugh. As much as I disliked my new house guest, he *was* proving himself useful. And, dammit, he was nice to look at.

Finally, Darius raised his eyes to, presumably, look at the other man. The stranger cleared his throat but didn't bother with an attempted handshake like his colleague.

"Conan."

"Well, now that's over," Darius moved on swiftly, leaning an arm against the doorway and cocking a hip in a lazy motion. "I can address you by your names when I tell you to fuck off."

"I'm afraid we can't-"

"Conan, Ezra, it was a displeasure to meet you. Now kindly get the fuck off the property with your tail between your legs like the dogs you are."

The sound of their protest was cut off by the abrupt slamming of the door in their face. Darius dusted his hands before turning to me, bright eyes honed on mine.

Anger, anxiety, and curiosity mixed in my gut, making me nauseous.

"Who were they?"

"My guess is that they're here for the book," Darius sighed. "They didn't have any identifiers on them but they definitely aren't standard museum guards. Private investigators, maybe."

I swore under my breath, forcing my body not to shake. "What now?"

Darius shrugged. "Ball's in your court, little thief."

"They won't leave, will they?"

"Not likely," he said, looking through the peephole and grimacing. "They're still here. And judging by the way the dog was skulking around your house last night, they're not going to be discouraged by much."

"I don't want to hide like a coward," I said with a fire that surprised even me. "The fucking grimoire doesn't belong to that shitty museum. It's *mine.*"

"If it's yours, how did they get it?"

"I'm not the only fucking thief, Darius," I spat, near shaking with rage now. How fucking dare they come here and try to intimidate me for reclaiming my family's history? Not that they knew *why* I was so hell-bent on reclaiming it now but that was besides the point. Undoubtedly, it wouldn't help my case. "I was not raised to shy away from men."

Darius moved to stop me, hand glancing my elbow, but I was faster, reaching the door and yanking it open.

Two shocked faces met me head on, a fist raised to knock the door I'd pre-emptively opened dropping back to his side.

"Do you know what witches do to unwanted visitors?" I hissed, taking them in. The shifter was tall and well built, a tight t-shirt clinging to biceps the size of my fucking head. Dark brown eyes met mine, narrowed, and his full lips curled in a near snarl. His hair was short, tight curls cut close to his scalp, and his dark skin shimmered slightly with sweat. "Did you not read the fairytales?" I *tsked,* moving my gaze to the man standing beside him.

His scent still confused me. He, too, was taller than me, but thinner than his friend. Still, the air of danger around him set me back slightly. While the shifter's danger was obvious, he could probably crush me with his fist, this man unnerved me. His hair was dark and long, hanging nearly to his shoulders, his eyes bright blue and skin paler than mine.

"We know the fairytales," he said, looking bored as he took me in. I was nearly offended before I remembered he was now my mortal enemy. "Unfortunately for you, we aren't lost children."

I choked on my laugh, having half a mind to curse them both on the spot.

"I thought you were *indisposed*," the shifter, Ezra, said dully, eyeing Darius behind me.

"Yes, well," I answered, crossing my arms over my chest. "My guard dog informed me that you wouldn't take a hint and fuck off. So you better make up for wasting my time." I waved a hand, as if unbothered by all this, while my stomach tangled itself in knots.

"We have a matter of great importance to discuss," Ezra continued tersely as if he hadn't heard me. "Can we come inside?"

"No. You can talk perfectly well out here."

"As you wish. We're here to discuss a missing object. I don't suppose you know anything about that?"

"You're going to have to be more specific," I said, shrugging. "Lots of things go missing every day."

His laugh was short and humourless. "Of course. A book. From Thornebank's Museum."

"Never been."

"It's a lovely little museum, next town over," he said with a smirk. "You should visit sometime. I hear they have an excellent witch exhibit."

A scalding spear of anger shot through me. I felt my magic flare to life with the emotion, begging for me to recite a spell or curse and set it free. To punish this stranger for insinuating that any of our history belonged in glass for the amusement of humans.

"You should check out their zoo," I suggested, forcing sickly sweetness into my tone. "I hear they have an excellent wolf enclosure."

Satisfaction melted like sugar on my tongue at the flash of fury in Ezra's eyes.

"Now, if that's all-"

"Where the fuck did he go?" Darius' voice rumbled behind me, and I started, brow furrowing before I realised what he meant.

Conan had fucking vanished.

9

Conan

Her bedroom was a fucking mess. Clothes were strewn over the floor, half finished cups of coffee sat on top of a stack of books on the night stand, makeup and hair tools in disarray on the vanity. It made me itch. The scent of cinnamon and flowery perfume permeated the space and I scrunched my nose.

The floorboards squeaked when I walked over them and I rolled my eyes. It really was too fucking easy sometimes. Especially when you knew what to look for. I'd been doing this so fucking long it felt like child's play now. Boring. Couldn't she at least give us a *little* challenge?

"There you are..." I whispered, feeling a small draft against my ankle. I bent down, careful to keep my movements hushed with a cushion of air, and ran my fingers across the floor beside me. While it wasn't my strongest element, it helped more than the others in investigations like this. Made it easier not to leave fingerprints, too.

A slight resistance met my fingertips and my brows furrowed as I searched for what she'd spelled. Most of the time, I'd learned, witches needed to spell a certain object, or write the casting in chalk on the object, for the magic to take. There, a tiny, barely visible line of chalk under her bed. I snorted, flicking my wrist and scorching the spell from the floorboards.

Now that the spell was broken, the floorboard came away without much resistance as I pried it up, my hand outstretched in front of me to direct the current of air suspending the wooden board. Beneath was a small hole in the floor, stuffed with blankets and other junk. I sorted through it quickly, allowing the floorboard to fall softly to the ground so I could better channel the air into rifling through the mess.

It took all of ten seconds to uncover it. A thick, leather bound book with old inscriptions on the cover. It screamed dark magic and I immediately recoiled, stumbling back a little and clattering the loose floorboard. Fuck.

Despite my aversion to the thing, I snatched the book from the hole and stood, bracing myself for the imminent arrival of the fucking demon I could hear charging towards the room. Sighing, I held the book at arms length and stood, facing the door.

"What the fuck are you doing?"

Instead of the rude demon fucker, it was the girl. Well, woman. She was short, with long, messy brown hair and green eyes currently zeroed in on the book in my grip. Fury was written in the tension in her jaw, and she crossed her arms over her chest.

"My job," I answered shortly, ready to be done with this whole shit show. Clearly, she was guilty. I was holding proof. The sooner we turned her in and moved on the better. I no longer had the energy to care why she had it, or read into why this whole fucking thing felt *wrong*. We were hired to find the book. We'd done it.

Time to go.

Not that I knew *where* we'd go. Wherever the next job took us, I supposed.

"I don't give two shits about your pathetic fucking job," she argued, raising her chin. "If you want to play puppy and heel to the humans, be my fucking guest. I was raised better than that. Give me my property back and leave. Now."

I had to give it to her - had I been anyone else, it might've worked on me. But I felt nothing except mild annoyance. I doubted Satan himself could get a rise out of me now.

"No."

"*No?*"

"No. N-o," I spelled it out for her, a familiar weariness stretching out and filling my mind.

"Don't fucking touch her," the man behind her snapped at Ezra, who was currently trying to push past her.

"Scared I'm going to hurt your little girlfriend?" Ez teased, though his tone was laced with darkness. I refused to look at him. I couldn't.

"Not my-"

"Shut the fuck up, all of you!" the woman snapped, fists clenching at her sides. There was a fire in her eyes I hadn't seen until now, and a small, half dead part of me raised its head in interest. "I've had *enough* of men barging into my fucking home and thinking I owe them anything. That book-" she raised a steady hand, long pointed black nail pointing directly at me - "is mine. Nobody will take it from me again."

Ezra blinked, clearly shocked, but a rumble of laughter built inside me. Fucking hell, what was happening to me? The low noise only made her anger rise, and her lips began moving again, though I couldn't hear what she was saying.

Too late, I realised. *Latin*. The language of curses. Of Hell and witches and burning women on pyres. The language of magic.

The book hit the floor seconds before I did.

I wasn't laughing any more.

10

Rory

I hadn't made a conscious decision to keep Darius awake. Hadn't really registered it at all until the two dickheads were on the floor and he was still standing, something suspiciously like lust in his eyes when he turned to look at me. Although, I suppose he had his uses, given the fact that I was currently holding a mug of elderflower tea he'd wordlessly handed me, sweetened with honey.

What happened to hating his guts?

"They are going to wake up, right?" he was asking, though he didn't sound particularly concerned. He was laid out across my sofa with his legs propped up on the arm like we'd been friends for decades. At least he hadn't put his shoes on my furniture again.

"Probably," I said, just to see the amusement play across his face. Fuck, did he have to be so nice to look at? "Give them half an hour. They're big enough to shrug it off by then."

"Want me to tie them up?"

"Are you in the practice of tying people up?" I answered, ignoring the little kick my heart got out of the question. I only wanted to know the answer for practical purposes. Obviously.

He stretched, his shirt riding up on his stomach slightly, revealing a distinct *v* at his hips. I looked away quickly, taking a drink to distract from the flush on my face.

"It's been a while, but I'm sure I remember how." He winked and stood, looking around my home. "Rope?"

"Uhh…" I wasn't entirely sure the silk ties in my bedside cabinet would do the job. "There should be some in the shed out back." He nodded and moved towards the front door, but I called after him, cringing. "Don't mind the heart in the jar!"

"The *what?*"

"The heart."

He cocked his head to the side, looking me up and down. "Rory, why do you have a heart in a jar?"

"It's from the last demon who messed with me," I lied, running my tongue over my teeth to savour the honey taste. He smirked and advanced on me, bracing one hand on the cushion behind my head. I inhaled sharply, crossing my legs.

"Little thief… " he whispered, eyes bright with mischief. His nickname for me sent a shiver over my skin. "Is it wrong that I don't think I'd mind being hurt by you? Not when you'd look fucking exquisite with blood on your hands."

Faster than I could answer, he pushed off, distancing himself from me so quickly I reeled at the loss of contact. He was out the door before my tongue had caught up with my brain, leaving me panting and shocked in his wake. I forced my heart to resume its normal pace, and tried to convince my body that I was *not* going to let that man into my pants, no matter how wet they were right now.

I shook my head, trying to make myself focus again. We'd left Ezra and Conan where they'd dropped - neither Darius nor I wanted to try to drag them somewhere else. The spell I'd used hadn't been enough to hurt them, just make them shut up long enough for me to think. Besides, if I wanted to hurt them, I'd have had to prepare the components for a curse and I had bigger plans for the heart.

Sighing, I grabbed the grimoire and hoisted it onto my lap, putting my tea down on the coffee table. I snatched up the letter opener laid beside it, the one shaped like a tiny dagger, and pressed it to the tip of my finger. Dropping it on the sofa beside me, I squeezed the small cut with my free hand, making blood well, and traced the scarlet liquid across the inscription on the front of the spell book.

It opened soundlessly. One second it was sealed shut, the next the cover fell open easily as soon as I tried. Something warm and reassuring calmed me at the sight, even as I stuck my finger in my mouth to stave the bleeding.

The pages were thin and aged, but the ink hadn't faded and every spell was still intact. Some spanned ten pages, others only took up half of one, but I skipped straight to the back, where the one I needed was.

In my mind, I could see my grandmother sitting across from the fire, illuminated by the flames, this book open in her lap as she stared into the sparks, a faraway look in her eyes. Occasionally, she'd let me run my small hands over the words of a spell as she recited it, or help her arrange the animal bones and herbs it called for.

And then they'd come.

Someone cleared their throat behind me and I jumped, startled from my thoughts. I craned my neck to see Darius, an amused smirk on his face and a bundle of rope in his arms.

"How are dumb and dumber?"

"Haven't moved an inch."

"Good." He peered over my shoulder. "Uhh....little thief, this wouldn't have anything to do with the fucking creepy ass heart would it?"

I laughed, a short, harsh sound. "What, like it's not a staple in every household?"

"Not in Hell."

I paused, narrowing my brows as he came round to face me. "You've been to Hell?"

"Lived there my whole life," he said, as though it was obvious. I just stared at him, a thousand questions clogging my throat. But the only one that made its way to my tongue was -

"Why did you leave?"

His expression shuttered and he shook his head. "I'll go deal with our problem," he said instead, shaking the rope and averting his eyes. I nodded dumbly, a sour taste in my mouth.

It was hypocritical to be mad about the secrets. Especially since he was helping me commit yet another crime without a full explanation. But some stupid part of me was hurt by the omission.

I returned my attention to the page while listening to Darius swear about *how heavy can this lanky fuck be?* Unlike other mythics, witches' magic only surfaced when harnessed through a spell. I'd memorised dozens - simple healing spells, recipes for stress relief and energy, sleeping spells like the one I'd used on the men currently being bound. But longer spells, curses and death magic, the darker arts, were harder to remember. Especially without fucking up and causing serious, irreparable damage.

Grimoires weren't always dark. Some, like those of green witches, were full of intricate healing spells, or seemingly endless lists of ingredients to use in potions. Green witches were once our sister race, working in tune with the dark covens, balancing us out. I'd seen them as a child, when I was friends with the other witchlings in town. But dark witches were different. This spell book had been in my family for generations, since before the humans had risen up and rebelled, burning my ancestors at the stake and causing a mass retreat of mythics back to Hell, where they could be safe. Most of us didn't want to hurt humans. Didn't care enough to.

But one witch, one vampire, one wolf and the unspoken but carefully constructed cohabitation agreement collapsed. The three mythics had become sick of behaving, of coexisting, believing that they deserved more power. Between the three of them, they'd killed hundreds. The balance tilted, age old prejudices rose quickly to the surface and once again, we were divided. Humanity attacked back, murdering whatever mythic they could get their hands on with their burning pyres and stakes and sharpened swords. In the aftermath, both mythics and humanity suffered and, while we were permitted to stay here, in our own towns, packs, nests or coven, the majority of us had returned to our homeland, Hell. Humanity never gave up their grudge against us, not really, and even now a lone mythic in a human city was almost asking for violence. The green covens had hated us since, blaming the dark witches for the fall of us all. They were goody two shoes who couldn't hack the necessary violence, if you asked me. In comparison, dark witches had only grown more brutal.

I lost count of how many people my mother and grand-mother helped bury by the time I came of age and grown into my magic. Lost count of how many vials of grave dirt I collected and arranged on my grandmother's mantle. She liked to keep track, to know how many favours she'd done the world. They made sure I was never there for the deaths, though, believing it was bad luck to see the life leave another's eyes before my magic had strengthened me.

It had taken me a while to begin to follow in their footsteps. They'd been killed, the grimoire had been taken and I had grown accepting. Graduated school. Made friends. Had relationships, though none that lasted. Got a job I liked. I had never felt the bloodlust like they did, heard the call of the dark witches that had birthed our line.

Until him.

Until I realised what it meant to be powerless. Until I vowed to never feel that way again. So I'd learned, studied, memorised every line I could, gathered herbs and stocked the pantry. But *revenge* had slipped through my fingers, a ghost in the dark, never quite tangible enough for me to grip on to.

Now, it was in front of me and I burned with desire for it. It was heady, the need for vengeance, and the subsequent hatred of those trying to keep it from me. I'd remembered a few of the ingredients I'd seen my grandmother use growing up, but more than half of them were lost to me, and I'd never heard her speak the words clearly enough to commit any of them to memory.

"Hey, Rory?" Darius called, a slightly worried tone to his voice that had me slamming the book shut and rising from my seat. "Dumb's moving."

I reached him and immediately grinned. They were both bound - wrists and ankles tied with sturdy, neat knots.

"Impressive," I noted, biting my lip. Conan was shifting, a low groan escaping his lips. I toed him, eliciting a louder complaint from him. "Wakey wakey," I taunted.

"You have a plan right?" Darius asked, a teasing lilt to his words.

"The plan went straight out the fucking window the second you broke into my house, demon," I reminded him, refusing to look his way.

"What the fuck…" Conan grumbled, eyes flickering open. Immediately, he tried to sit up, but with his hands tied behind his back he flailed, unable to find his balance that fast. I snorted, enjoying the upper hand Darius' knots had given me.

"You've been put in time-out until you learn to behave," I told him, bending slightly to meet his eyes. "Oh, and until you learn not to fuck with witches in the woods."

11

Ezra

Someone was slamming my head against the ground, I was sure of it. There was no other logical explanation for the nauseating pounding in my skull, the ache that radiated through my body.

"What, don't you like being tied up?"

Who the fuck was that? I didn't recognise the voice, female and teasing, as it broke through the haze in my brain. I needed to wake up, to move, to open my eyelids despite the fact that they felt weighed down.

"Perhaps I just don't like being knocked out."

Oh fuck. Conan.

I snapped upright, immediately regretting the movement when my whole body ached in reaction. My arms were pulled behind my back, my shoulders straining as I struggled to move them. Something thick and scratchy was holding my wrists together, so tight my fingers were cold, my ankles too, now that I realised…

"Fucking demon," I growled when my eyes found his, curved at the corners with a shit eating grin on his face. "Untie me."

"Nuh uh," the woman said, turning her gaze from Conan to me. I remembered her now, as I began to register my surroundings and noticed we were laid in the doorway between her bedroom and the hall. "Not until I say so."

"I believe that's your cue to shut up and listen," the demon said gleefully. I began to protest, but a sharp elbow in the side from Conan stopped me.

"Now I'm going to assume that neither of you meatheads know how to take *no* for an answer," she began, walking away to grab a stool from its place at the kitchen counter. It squealed across the floor as she dragged it and I felt Conan cringe beside me. She stopped it in front of us and hoisted herself onto the leather cushion, crossing her legs and looking down at us through her lashes. Irritation had me grinding my teeth together. The clear power trip she was riding shouldn't have piqued my interest, but fuck it.

I was listening.

"So here are your options." She took a deep breath, uncross-ing her legs and leaning forward to stare down at us. God she was stunning. If she hadn't been our fucking mark I'd have had her against a wall by now, screaming my name. "Option one - you leave here without your memories. It might take me a while to find the right spell but I'm sure you won't mind waiting it out in the basement." Conan snarled next to me, but all I could do was grin. She was insane. "Option two - you help like this asshole," she gestured to demon dude beside her. "And I don't fuck with your brains."

"*Help you?*" Conan burst out, straining against his ties.

"Yes," she answered primly.

"We don't even know you," I reminded her, though her good girl act was making for excellent entertainment.

"*You* came looking for me," she shot back, rolling her eyes. "Shouldn't you have done better research?"

"We tracked the book by scent," I lied, sighing. The less she knew, the better. For now, at least. "All we knew was that you were female and a witch." Conan grunted his agreement, maintaining his glare.

"Rory Evelyn Ciarda," she introduced, a too-sweet smile on her full lips. I wanted to kiss it off her face. "I wish I could say it's a pleasure to meet you but, well…"

I laughed, shaking my head. "I can make it a pleasure."

She raised her brows at me and stood from her chair, crossing to us and kneeling down in front of me. She reached out, one dark, pointed nail catching me under the chin and tilting my head to look at her. "Oh, puppy," she said, voice low and velvety. "You wouldn't know what to do with a witch like me."

She stood abruptly, her nail scratching my skin as she snatched her hand away, sneering at me before returning to the demon's side. I stared at her, hard and slightly insulted. The second I got out of this fucking rope, I'd prove her wrong.

"Alright," the resident demon stepped forward, shooting her a glare. "Make your choice boys."

Conan looked at me out of the corner of his eye, shaking his head slightly. But I was already talking. "You know, we were hired to *find* the book," I said casually, watching as Conan finally freed his hands from the rope. "Not to deliver the thief to them. We're always *very* careful with the wording of our contracts."

Conan stretched his arms out in front of him, rotating his wrists and rolling his eyes when the demon darted in front of Rory.

"Relax," he said, sounding as bored as ever. "They were starting to chafe."

Amusement sparked across Rory's face, quickly dissolving into the fury I was becoming used to.

"Here's what we'll do," I said, shifting to let Conan untie my wrists. His hands were warm as he gripped my arm to keep me still, and seconds later I was rubbing at the rope burn on my skin and grinning up at the witch. "We won't report what we found to the guards...yet. But we can't leave."

"Yes you fucking-"

I held up a hand to stop her in her tracks before reaching down and freeing my ankles. "Like you said, we don't know you. We don't know why you wanted a dark magic grimoire. We don't know what the fuck you plan on doing with it." To my right, Conan stood and shot daggers at me with his eyes, fists clenched at his side. He could be pissed off at me all he wanted, but I didn't fucking see him coming up with any better alternatives. "So we'll need to stay."

"You're not fucking staying."

Conan sighed, his calm cracking. "Look, princess." Disdain dripped from his words as he looked both her and the demon up and down. "We don't want to stick around here either. In fact, I'd happily throw you to the fucking humans to pick apart if it means I can get this shit show done with. Luckily for you, my partner has stronger morals." She flinched, then tried to hide it behind the fire burning in her eyes. "The way I see it, you don't have much choice."

"Fuck you," she spat, near shaking with rage.

"Soon, hellhound," I grinned back, raising a brow at her. The nickname suited her. I wanted to know if her bite was as bad as her bark."You better show us the guest room first."

12

Darius

"You can't be fucking serious."

The shifter stared back at me, head cocked and a stupid fucking smirk on his face. Hell below, I wanted to punch the confidence out of him.

"You can't argue, Darius," Rory said quietly behind me, a storm brewing in her words. I tensed. "You're no fucking better."

Ouch. "I'm trying to help you, Rory. They're trying to take you down!"

"You broke into my home, they broke into my home," her voice was dangerously low. "You refuse to leave, they refuse to leave. And here I fucking am, stuck between three men who think they know what's best. News flash, dickheads, none of this has anything to do with any of you! Just leave and lie to the snivelling piece of shit that hired you. They're far guiltier than I am!"

She turned on her heel, taking a detour to snatch the book from the sofa and walked straight out the door. Ezra watched her go with a hungry gleam in his eyes, no doubt taking her outburst as a challenge. Conan, on the other hand, stared at his friend, something that looked suspiciously like hurt lingering in the tight clench of his jaw.

"Thanks for that," I told them, rolling my eyes and stomping to the kitchen, peering through the window above the sink. She'd disappeared from sight, though, and all I was met with was a view of the overgrown path leading to the country road into town. I spun back around, glaring at the shifter. "You serious about staying?"

I sure as Hell wasn't leaving if they weren't. No chance I was letting them be alone with her, regardless of the hurt that soured my stomach in the aftermath of her words. Sure, I had literally nothing else to do now, but that didn't mean helping her wasn't important to me.

"As a heart attack," Ezra answered, flopping into the stool. It squeaked under his weight, and I grimaced. Conan hadn't moved an inch. I moved closer and waved my hand in front of his face, worried he was having some sort of episode.

His hand was around my wrist faster than I could track. Swearing, I tried to yank it back, but he held fast, stony blue eyes dark and unfeeling. "What the fuck, dude?"

"Who are you to her?" he asked, voice deep and mildly threatening. I sneered.

"Mildly higher up on the friendship ladder than you two," I said honestly, shaking my arm to try to regain feeling in my hand when he finally, reluctantly, released me. "An accomplice."

"Great," Ezra said in a way that made me think he thought the exact opposite.

"You can't be serious about working for them." It was odd, the thought of them willingly taking jobs like this from humans. Though mythics and humans weren't entirely at odds any more, the divide caused by their violence would forever stain our relationship. Not to mention the relics they insisted on keeping under lock and key. It didn't surprise me at all that Rory had got fed up and taken matters into her own hands. What did surprise me, however, was two of our own kind siding with them.

"We agreed to find the book," Ezra said carefully, glancing at Conan as if unsure how much to say. "Nothing more. We're always cautious when working with their kind. We don't mean any harm."

"Sure," I drawled, studying them. Ezra, clearly, was a fucking powerhouse - more muscles than I could count, his strength clear. But it was Conan I was wary of. He gave me the distinct impression that I should never turn my back to him. "That's why you were creeping around her window last night."

Ezra's eyes flashed animal for a split second.

"I could smell wet dog a mile away," I elaborated, relishing in the anger radiating from him.

"I wasn't aware anyone but her was home last night," Ezra said, his voice tense.

"She called me," I told them, smirking. "After she sensed *you*."

"A guard demon," Conan cut in, a tiny hint of amusement in his tone. "Cute."

I clenched my fists, forcing my body not to move. "She's not going to be happy if you're still here when she gets back."

"Sounded like she wasn't too happy with you either," Ezra pointed out.

"I'm the least of her worries."

"We're just doing our job," Conan growled.

"And what exactly is your job title? Professional stalkers?"

"Private investigators," Ezra responded through gritted teeth.

"Ah," I nodded, making a show of acting impressed. "So what does that involve? Peering through telescopes into people's bedrooms? Setting up camp in a car across the street to track their comings and goings? Oh, obviously hanging around their house in the middle of the night, right?"

"We help people," Ezra insisted.

"Sure. Help steal back family history from mythics."

"Do you even know what that grimoire is?" Conan huffed a humourless laugh, stalking towards me until we were nearly chest to chest. I met his eyes unflinchingly, finding his filled with unspoken threat.

"Enlighten me."

"It's old, dark magic," he hissed, shaking his head. "Stuff that would make even demons like you have nightmares. What in Hell's name would she need that for, huh?"

"Maybe to curse the next man who breaks into her house," I snapped back.

"Looks like we're all fucked then," Ezra offered, shrugging. I groaned.

"You can't assume she's guilty, just because she wanted it back," I told Conan. "It's a piece of her family. Dark witch or not, she deserves to feel connected to her roots."

I didn't stop to think about why I was so angry on her behalf, so determined to keep her out of these men's grip. She intrigued me, impressed me, interested me in a way I couldn't shake. The second I'd felt the pull of her summoning me, I'd answered, eager to spend time with her again. My little criminal.

No. Not mine. She could never be mine.

"Fine." Ezra's hand was on Conan's chest, pushing him back away from me. Conan resisted for a second before allowing it, glancing down at his friend's hand with an unreadable expression. "She has two weeks. Our contract needs to be fulfilled by then, one way or the other."

"You won't hurt her, understood?"

"Not if she's innocent."

Well, that was all I could really hope for. "Well then," I sighed, resigned to the inevitable storm we had coming our way the second Rory returned. "Who wants tea?"

13

Rory

"Ror, what's going on?" Grace leaned over the counter, wiping coffee grounds away with her sleeve. Her red brows were pinched together in worry as she watched me down my cup of tea - the calming blend I'd mixed on my last shift that helped when my skin began to feel too tight for my body or panic took up camp in my lungs. "I thought you were sick."

"Not sick," I muttered, setting my teacup down only to have her refill it just as quickly. She knew me as well as I did. It was one of the reasons I adored her. "Just couldn't make it into work this morning. But then I had to get out of the house and I didn't know where else to go and..."

"Hey, chill," she said softly, placing a warm hand on my arm. The lunch rush had subsided now, given that it was nearing three o'clock in the afternoon, so the cafe was quiet. "Are you okay? Are you safe?"

"No, and I think so? I'm honestly not sure."

"Shit, babe, tell me what's happened."

"Uh, that's the thing," I admitted, running a hand through

my hair and staring at the murky green tea. "I can't."

Her concern deepened, lips turning down slightly in a frown. "What? Why?"

"I don't want to drag you down with me," I said, swirling the liquid until it sloshed over the edges onto the saucer.

"As if you could ever drag me anywhere," she joked half heartedly. I tried to offer a smile, but it came out more like a grimace.

"It's fine," I lied, sighing. "I just needed out of the house." *And away from the fucking harem of men invading it.*

"Why? You love your house," Grace asked, suspicion seeping into her tone as she grabbed a damp cloth and began wiping down the coffee machine.

"I had an unexpected visitor."

Her eyebrows hit her hairline. "Ooh, who? Tall, dark, handsome? It would be so good for you to meet someone, especially after -"

"No," I shook my head, cutting her off. It was sweet, the way she cared about me, but I didn't want to talk about *him* now. I wasn't sure I could handle those memories in the midst of the mess my life was quickly becoming. Especially since he was the reason I was in it in the first place. "Nothing like that."

"Oh." She looked so disappointed, I softened.

"I'm fine, I promise," I told her, smiling. "I just needed to see my best friend." She grinned back, but the flash of feline in her eyes made it clear she knew I was hiding something. She was made of patience when it came to me, though, one of the reasons we were friends. I didn't give up information easily, and she didn't make me. Just sat and waited for me to be ready.

I wasn't sure I could ever talk to her about this, though.

74

What I'd done. What I was planning. Grace was soft all over - a sugar cookie personality. Sweet and friendly and impossible not to like. I didn't want to bring her into my darkness.

Still, her presence, and the smell of coffee and pastries and quiet chatter of the few patrons dotted around the tables, soothed me.

"How did your date go?" I changed the subject easily, trying to steer the topic away from me. Beneath the counter, I toed the tote bag holding the book closer to the boards. The straps hung around my ankle so nobody could snatch it away. I sure as hell wasn't leaving it with them, but I had nowhere to hide it now. So, with me it would go.

Grace sighed, and I narrowed my eyes at her.

"Need me to kill her?" I offered, only sort of joking. If she asked, I would happily remove someone's head from their body for her.

"No," she laughed, setting down the cloth and rubbing hand sanitiser into her hands. "Just…meh. There was no *spark*, you know?"

I didn't know, but that was fine. Grace was a hopeless romantic. She deserved the love story she so craved - a love letters and passionate kisses in the rain and a whole airport chase scene before the end credits type of love. I, on the other hand, had given up on 'sparks' entirely.

What about Darius? A small voice in my mind echoed. I stomped it out abruptly, angry at whatever part of me decided that was an okay thought to have. He was attractive and I was sex deprived. That was all. Simple biology, nothing more.

Maybe I needed a fling.

"Want to go out tomorrow?" I asked her, surprising myself with my enthusiasm. She jolted, as shocked as I was by my willingness to go to a club.

"But you don't like…people," she said carefully, eyeing me.

"No, but I like you," I reminded her, rolling my eyes. "And you deserve some fun. Plus, I think I'm growing cobwebs."

She laughed, the sound light and bright and the cure for the darkness surrounding me. She was right, I wasn't one for crowds and loud music, but if there was alcohol and dancing, I was willing to compromise. Besides, I'd need as many excuses to escape from my house as possible now.

"Hell yes!" Grace agreed, squealing. "I just got the cutest dress…"

We chatted until customers filtered in again for coffees and cakes and Grace was too busy to deal with my sulking ass. I blew her a kiss and grabbed my bag before leaving, trying to prepare myself for whatever scene I'd find when I returned home. I was pissed as all Hell that they'd managed to turn my sanctuary into a place that I dreaded going back to. Fuck that and fuck them and fuck all of this.

The day was still clear, but a crisp wind whipped my hair around my face. I winced against the chill, wrapping my arms tightly around my waist. I should've grabbed a coat before I left but I hadn't had any thoughts in my head other than the suffocating need for space. The path was lined with tall trees and bushes that, come spring and summer, would bloom with berries. Something rustled through the undergrowth on the opposite side of the path, and I stilled, narrowing my eyes at the shaking leaves. I waited, watching, but whatever it was had left. Some small animal, no doubt. I sniffed the air but caught nothing except the cool, fresh scent of grass and leaves.

My feet took me home on autopilot, and the cottage came into view before me. It looked no different than normal

- overgrown ivy covering one side and my slightly askew doormat still announcing who lived there. I took a deep breath before I worked up the nerve to enter, knowing better than to hope that I'd find it empty.

I still found myself disappointed when I walked in and instantly hit with the heavy mixture of male scents.

"Fucking great," I muttered under my breath as I kicked my shoes off and fought the urge to sink to the floor and scream. Instead, I steeled myself and padded into the living room, where Darius and Ezra were stretched out over both sofas, the TV playing old reruns on low volume.

"Oh, good, you're home," Darius smirked up at me, wiggling his brows.

"Oh good, you're all still here," I responded, exhaustion twisting my tone. "Where's dumber?"

"Showering," Ezra answered, not even bothering to look my way.

"What?"

"The bath at the motel isn't big enough for one fucking leg," Ezra continued, shrugging. "And since we're staying with you for the next two weeks, we thought we'd take advantage of the amenities.

"You are absolutely fucking not staying here for *two weeks*," I protested, anger burning hot in my blood.

"I suppose we could all go and explain to Thornebank Museum where exactly their precious book has gone."

The threat sent a chill through me. I shook my head, backing away, even while Darius called my name. A high pitched ringing started in my ears, a headache brewing at my temples.

I slammed the bedroom door shut behind me, internally chastising myself for never getting a lock installed on this door, too. Instead, I dragged the chair from my vanity over and propped it beneath the door handle.

I threw the book down onto my bed and stared at it, grief burning a hole in my chest. Was it worth all this? Could I have carried on without it, pretending none of my past had happened? Was I going to let the three idiots making themselves right at home stop me?

No. I couldn't. I wouldn't.

I'd survived the past six years. I could wait another two weeks.

14

Conan

"Where is she?" I knew I'd heard her come in, and a door slam somewhere, but all I could see when I entered the living room was Ezra and Darius stretched out over the couch, the demon flicking through a book with a shirtless man on the cover. I raised a brow but said nothing, waiting for Ez to reply. He sighed and sat up straight, shrugging.

"She's pissed," he said, rubbing a hand over his face.

"Obviously." I thought that was clear. But this whole thing was Ezra's idea - he'd made this fucking bed for all of us and now we had to lie in it.

"She's in her room," Darius piped up, glancing up from the page. I nodded, looking between them.

"Excellent." Far from it, but at least I wouldn't have to fake niceties with her. I'd seen the way Ezra looked at her, the desire and hunger in his eyes. Anger flashed hot in my blood, and I looked away from him, unable to stand it.

"Pizza?" the demon asked casually as he set the book down on his stomach. I furrowed my brow, even as Ez began nodding.

"Pepperoni for me," he answered, apparently unbothered by whatever the fuck was happening here.

"So what?" I asked, annoyance heavy in my words. "We're all just best friends now?"

Darius shrugged. "Figured we'd make the best of the situation, you know?"

"No, I don't know," I shot back, grinding my teeth. "This is *business*, Ezra."

"You want us to be miserable for two weeks?" he asked, staring at me with confusion in his deep brown eyes. I tensed. "It's just pizza, Cee."

"You weren't complaining about business when you were taking advantage of her shower," Darius pointed out, smirking.

Well, no, but I at least felt slightly more alive again after it. The shitty motel we'd crashed at had barely had clean water, never mind space for either of us to bathe properly. Although, I'd had to put my dirty clothes back on since we hadn't brought our bags with us. I itched at the feeling of them on my skin.

"I'm going to get our shit," I told them, running a hand through my damp hair. The journey would give me time to breathe, to sort out my head before I returned.

"You got a car?" Darius asked, cocking his head.

"Don't need one."

"I thought you were staying in the museum town..."

"Thornebank?" Ezra filled in, nodding. "But there's no point in hiring a car. Too easy to track, too much information to give out to fill in all the forms."

"So you walk everywhere?" Darius looked like he couldn't imagine anything worse. I snorted.

"Some of us don't mind exercise."

"Some of us would rather travel in comfort."

I rolled my eyes. "Trust me, we're fast enough without human vehicles."

"Sure," he answered sarcastically, waving me off. "Better test that theory or all the pizza will be gone by the time you get back."

I flipped him off over my shoulder and left, relishing the wash of cool air that swept over me as I stepped out the front door. I heard Ez call my name but ignored it, tilting my head up to the darkening sky.

I forced a deep breath into my lungs, willing my muscles to relax. I was so wound up with anger that my body ached. I tipped my head to the side, cracking my neck and relishing the quick burst of release it sent down my spine.

Ez and I had disagreed over plenty of things in the past. What to order for dinner. Whether or not to get shit faced drunk the night before a job. Whether to spring for a more expensive hotel or save the money. But this particular disagreement stung.

He was perhaps the only person I could recall that I didn't want to argue with. I was self aware enough to know that I rubbed people the wrong way, and I didn't give a fuck if they liked me. Ez, though, was different. Had been since we were eight and playing tag in the playground.

He'd helped me, never caring if I turned up to school dirty and with my stomach growling. He always brought me extra snacks, even leant me his clothes when I got older although they were always too short and wide. I'd been alone since the grand old age of ten, when my mother decided eloping with her new boyfriend was more important than her son, but with him I felt like…like maybe I wasn't someone who only existed to be abandoned. When his father was murdered, five years later, and our careers as investigators began, I saw an opportunity to help him the way he'd helped me. I buried his father's killer, summoned the earth up to swallow his ashes, and we'd run from our aching pasts with nothing but each other.

He was the only thing in my life I'd never questioned. And yet, apparently, I wasn't that for him.

I couldn't talk to him right now, not until I'd sorted through the heaviness in my chest.

15

Ezra

She didn't come out of her room the rest of the night. Darius and I barely spoke, considering he was glued to the book he'd picked off her shelf, letting out bursts of laughter every now and then. Pizza was ordered, then delivered, then left outside Rory's door after she refused to open it.

It was clear none of us were welcome here, but that wasn't anything we weren't used to. But the house was warm and, though it was messy, it was clean, so nothing else really mattered. Still, I was on edge until Conan returned, constantly watching the door for him. I wasn't sure when it happened, but somewhere over the years I'd sort of…forgotten…how to function without him. We'd been friends since we were two grieving school kids, and with each year and the eventual blood soaking our hands, we'd become inseparable.

"Step up from the sofa," Conan observed as he strolled in through the guest room door, mild approval lifting the corners of his lips. I'd found the room being used as a sort of all purpose storage space, but there were two single beds in between the copious amounts of *stuff* and bedding in the hall closet. It was decorated like a kid's room - sticky glow in the dark stars glued to the ceiling in haphazard patterns, a bag of old plastic toys in one corner, a little crescent moon night light still plugged into one of the outlets.

"Darius didn't complain." In fact, he'd volunteered to sleep on the sofa. It made more sense and, besides, I think he wanted to act as a sort of barrier between us and Rory. I had no idea what their relationship really was, but he was clearly protective of the witch.

Conan huffed as he sat on the edge of his mattress, chucking our bags into the space I'd cleared between the two beds. I thanked him, snatching up my bag and digging out a pair of loose grey sweatpants. The house was hot, thanks to the fire, and though I much preferred to sleep naked, that didn't seem like the best idea.

"No questions from the motel?" I checked, pulling my shirt over my head and stuffing it into my bag.

"No," Conan sighed, propping himself up on his elbow as he lay down. "Nothing else from the museum either."

"Good." I nodded, stripping down. Conan turned away immediately, and I laughed, confused. "Suddenly scared of me?" He'd seen me naked numerous times. I had no idea why he was looking away now.

"It's called being polite," he answered, but his voice was stiff. I frowned, stepping into my sweatpants quickly and sat back on the bed. He turned over again, brows pinched together.

"We need to see what's in that fucking book," I sighed, changing the subject back to neutral ground. I didn't like the uncomfortable tension hanging between us, the easy atmosphere we'd grown accustomed to pulled taut.

"Nothing good," he grumbled, shifting in bed and flopping his head back on the pillow, staring at the little plastic stars. "Besides, there's a bigger problem."

"What do you mean?" A cold sense of unease slipped through my veins and I shivered. If Conan thought something was wrong, something was dangerously wrong. While analytical and untrusting, he was nearly never rattled.

"Someone's watching us."

I shot upright, panic rattling in my chest. *"What?"*

"Well, us or one of them," he clarified, sighing. "That's why it took me so fucking long to get back."

"Cee, for the love of Hell, just fucking tell me." I needed all the information, now, so we could decide what to do. Regardless of the fact I didn't really know either of the two others in the house, I didn't want them hurt. Or, at least, not until we figured out what they wanted.

He sighed again, the sound heavy. "I thought I felt someone when I set off, but I was so fucking concentrated on controlling the air current, I didn't pay enough attention." Guilt was evident in his voice, and I fought the urge to lean over and reassure him. "They'd have seen me leave though."

"Fuck." I shook my head, shoulders falling. "You flew?"

He nodded. I wasn't surprised. It was the fastest way for him to travel and normally he could summon a rain shower to clear the streets, or manipulate the air enough to render himself nearly invisible as he rode an air current to wherever he was going. I was envious as fuck of his elemental powers, but not of the fact it made him stick out like a sore thumb.

"It just takes so much of my power..." he trailed off, shaking his head. Conan was strong as fuck, but out of all the elements, earth was his strongest. The others always took much more from him. No wonder he looked fucking exhausted. "I should've just stayed, investigated it. I was far enough away from the cottage that they shouldn't have been able to track but...I stupidly assumed that it was just someone walking in the woods, exploring or some shit..."

"Spit it out," I urged, a slow determination creeping into the set of my jaw. My wolf snarled in my mind, demanding to be let out to hunt.

"They were gone when I returned, but their scent remained," he said finally, watching me out the corner of his eye. "Ash and smoke."

"Hell," I confirmed as Conan nodded. "No idea what species of mythic?"

He shook his head. "They'd done well to cover their tracks. Apparently better than you did," he joked, and I scowled.

"I thought you were gonna blow my scent away!"

"Not my fault your wolf fucking stinks," he teased, laughing and breaking the nervous energy in the room. I threw my pillow at him, but laughter pulled the corners of my mouth up.

"Fuck you," I snorted as he chucked it back at me. His face shuttered, and I blinked at him, confused as fuck. "Conan, what the Hell is going on with you?"

"Nothing." He answered too fast, avoiding my eyes once again.

"Don't insult me like that."

"I'll go out in the morning and see if there's any more signs of them," he said, dismissing my concern entirely. Annoyance bubbled to the surface and I ground my teeth together.

"I'll come with you," I offered. Clearly, my wolf needed the run.

"Wouldn't rather stay here with the witch you've been fucking with your eyes all day?" he asked, tone too harsh for it to be a joke. I froze, furrowing my brow, icy cold hurt washing over me.

"Where the fuck did that come from?"

"Don't try to deny it, Ez."

"She's hot, what about it?"

He pinched the bridge of his nose, the tattoos on his bicep rippling with the movement. "Never mind."

"No, not 'never mind'," I chastised, needing to figure out what the hell was going on with him. "Does it matter if I want to fuck her? Can you blame me?"

"You can't fuck suspects, Ezra!" he growled at me. "She could be planning something horrendous with that grimoire and all you can think about is sticking your dick in her!"

"That is not-"

"You don't think we can all see it? Hell below, Ez, do you not have any fucking morals left?" He paused in his lecture, breathing heavily. "Do not have sex with her."

"I think you're mistaken, Conan," I said back, that iciness creeping into my voice. Beneath the confusion and hurt, I was angry. Angry that he was angry, and angry that I didn't understand *why*. "You don't get to decide who I fuck."

I turned off the bedside lamp with far more force than necessary, the light wobbling on its stand, and rolled over. I wasn't fighting over this. It was ridiculous. *He* was ridiculous.

I fucking hated being told no.

16

Rory

I stayed in my room like a fucking coward until the rumbling in my stomach became too loud to ignore. Reluctantly, I tugged the chair away from the door, pausing when three pairs of eyes immediately locked on me. I was still in my pyjamas - a baggy t-shirt I'd stolen from Grace years ago and a pair of silky shorts.

"Look who decided to grace us with her presence," Ezra said sarcastically, blatantly looking me up and down with heat in his eyes. I fought the urge to shiver, mentally chastising my stupid fucking body. Tonight, I decided, I'd find some hot stranger to get rid of this fucking urge. Or else living with these three assholes was going to be torture.

I ignored him and stalked to the kitchen, finding a hot cup of coffee already sitting on the counter. Frowning I looked around, only to find Darius smirking at me.

"I'm going out," I said, ignoring the drink and the lump it caused in my throat.

"What? Where?" Conan immediately jumped up, glaring at me. I sneered back, crossing my arms over my chest.

I glanced at the clock. It was noon, so I had hours before I was due to meet Grace, but I had absolutely fuck all desire to stay here any longer. Their presence was making my skin itch. Worse, I knew they could make my life a living nightmare with a click of their finger. I groaned.

"With my friend," I answered, rolling my eyes.

"You are not going out."

"You are not my fucking master," I spat, picking up the cup just to have something to do with my hands so I didn't wrap them around his throat. I didn't miss the flash of darkness in his eyes and the flexing of his fingers as he took in my words.

"Woah, woah, little thief," Darius cut in, hands up in surrender. "What if I go with you? Then dumb and dumber won't throw a fucking fit about you planning the end of the world or whatever it is you're doing."

"I'm not-" I cut myself off, shaking my head. They didn't need to know what I was planning. I just needed to find a way to get them off my back without digging myself an even bigger hole.

"*I'll* go with her," Ezra said definitively, much to the annoyance of everyone else in the room. "We still don't know what the fuck is going on with you two," he continued, gesturing between the demon and I. "And Conan would rather cut his dick off than go to a bar."

I grimaced, biting my tongue so I didn't accidentally-on-purpose make him shut up.

"No one is coming with me," I protested, fire building in my chest as my magic rose with my emotions. Before I could continue my argument, Ezra was in front of me, one hand on either side of my waist, gripping the counter so hard his knuckles lightened. His face was so close to mine I could feel his breath on my skin, see the soft ring of silver around the deep brown in his eyes, marking him as a shifter. My heartbeat skyrocketed, and I pressed my thighs together in hopes that none of them would sense the shift in my body. What the fuck was wrong with me?

"If you think any of us are letting you walk out that door alone, you're delusional," he said, voice low and smooth. I could do nothing but stare wide eyed at him while my mind desperately tried to catch up. "I come with you or you don't go at all. And that fucking book stays here."

Finally, rational thought kicked back in and I pressed my palms flat against his chest, shoving with all my might. I tried desperately not to register the feel of his muscles beneath my touch. He didn't move an inch. Frustration burned red hot in my veins.

"Move," I ground out.

"Agree," he countered, one brow raised and a smirk curling his full lips. I wanted to smack it off his face. Or give his mouth something better to do. *No. Bad Rory.*

"You stay the fuck away from me," I told him. The last thing I wanted to do was explain to Grace why the fuck there was a giant, stupidly attractive shifter following me around like my personal bodyguard.

"Right," he drawled, shaking his head a little. "'Cause that's what we both want. Distance." He said it so lowly that I thought I misheard him. Shock rendered me still.

"That is what I want," I lied as heat pooled between my legs. Having him so close, so cocky and self assured, was wreaking fucking havoc in my body.

He *tsked*, clicking his tongue off his teeth and exposing his sharpened canines. Heat rushed through me. "Such a pretty little liar."

This time, when I shoved him, he moved, stepping back and turning to the other two grumpy assholes who'd watched the whole exchange. I flushed.

"You'll need to stay and watch the book," Ezra told Conan calmly, as though he hadn't just all but told me he wanted to fuck me. "And the demon."

Darius protested, grumbling something under his breath about not being a child. I ignored them all, abandoning my coffee and snatching a muffin I'd taken from work the day before from the counter. Pushing through Darius' complaints, I stormed off in the direction of the bathroom, needing to wash the scent of Ezra off of me and deal with the ache between my thighs.

I threw the brown bag with my breakfast in it onto the bed beside the grimoire and rummaged for a change of clothes, grabbing the towel from the hooks off the back of my door. I ducked into my bathroom, eternally grateful that I'd added an en-suite to the master bedroom when I rebuilt the house.

I stripped quickly, turning the water on high and hot. The second I stepped in, my skin turned pink and steam began to fill the room. I concentrated on lathering lavender and vanilla shampoo into my hair - I needed all the calming properties I could get - and ignoring the heat still simmering low in my stomach. Fuck Ezra and the way he fucking smelled and his fucking smirk and his stupid fucking words.

Fuck the fact that he was right.

I didn't want distance. I wanted to know how those canines felt on my skin, if he'd be strong or gentle with me, if he'd be as feral in the bedroom as I expected he would. I'd never been with a shifter before.

Fuck it all to Hell, I wanted him. Well, no. I wanted his body. I also wanted to slap him and scream at him and to tell him to get out of my house and never look for me again.

But I couldn't do any of that.

Before I realised what I was doing, my hand slid down my stomach, my fingers dipping between my legs, finding my clit. A small gasp flew past my lips as the first bolt of pleasure shot through me, and I leaned against the tile, the cold press of it against my back only focusing my senses. As my fingers dropped lower, pressing inside my soaked entrance, I imagined it was him. His voice, low and breathy in my ear telling me how much he wanted me. His fingers hitting just the right spot inside me to make me cover my mouth to stifle the moan. His mouth hot and insistent on mine, taking exactly what he wanted from me. Tension coiled inside me, my orgasm closing in fast. I cursed him, even as I bit my lip to keep quiet. I was nearly sure that, with the rush of water from the shower and my efforts to make no noise, they wouldn't hear me, but knowing my fucking luck one of them would be stationed outside the bathroom door. Although, I wasn't exactly opposed to the idea.

A wicked thought flitted through my mind, my heart skipping a beat in my chest as I slowed my rhythm to try and focus my head. They'd fucked with me enough - literally *breaking in to my house*, not to mention threatening to ruin everything I'd fucking worked for. And Darius, well...I wasn't sure what he wanted, exactly. But I didn't trust him, any of them. It was time for a little revenge.

I'd seen the way Darius looked at me, and Ezra had all but confirmed he wanted me. Conan just outright hated me, so this would likely make him want to murder me, but I was past

92

caring. This was my house. My rules. I refused to sit and cower for the next two weeks.

I freed my lip from my teeth and breathed deeply, slipping one hand back down my body again as the other rose to play with my nipple. The pleasure had me gasping and my legs threatening to give out. I was already close, considering the tease in the kitchen and the fact I'd basically edged myself a second ago, and this time when I moaned for myself, I didn't bother being quiet.

I wanted them to hear.

I wound myself tighter and tighter, until I was gasping for breath, picturing his hands in place of mine. When I came, it was with a cry, muffled only by the running water. Pleasure shot through me, weakening my knees and causing me to half collapse against the tiles. My breath came in short, ragged gasps as the fog of lust in my mind cleared, leaving only the crisp sound of the shower and the realisation of what I'd done.

There was no way at least one of them hadn't heard me.

But even as I stood to finish washing myself, legs still a little wobbly, I couldn't find it in myself to regret it.

17

Ezra

"Holy shit," Darius murmured. We'd all paused at once, meeting each other's gaze with the same glassy shock shining in our eyes.

"She didn't…" Conan trailed off, the most stunned I'd ever seen him. A hilarious combination of confusion, all out shock and anger.

"She definitely fucking did," I told him, blinking away the heady lust glazing my mind. Fucking hell. Even over the shower and through the fucking walls, we'd all heard her. Although, with my shifter hearing, I'd undoubtedly heard her the clearest. That fucking moan had me hard instantly, and every instinct in my body screamed for me to go to her. I was about to do just that when the demon spoke up.

"Sneaky little thief," he said, chuckling and running a hand through his hair. Conan frowned, crossing his arms and glaring at nobody in particular.

"What?" he asked, voice gruff.

"It's war," Darius said, as though it was obvious. "Revenge."

I blinked at him. "She's punishing us?"

He nodded. "I'd bet she was loud on purpose. No way that was an accident."

I laughed, shaking my head. I didn't really give a fuck *why* she'd done it, only that she'd done it at all. I couldn't fucking help but picture what she'd looked like - water dripping down her skin, mouth parted, eyes closed, hand between her thighs -

"This is insane," Conan muttered, turning and heading to the guest room. "She's fucking insane. You can't expect us to stay here." He wasn't looking at me, but I knew he was talking to me.

"You're joking," I answered in disbelief. "We can't leave. We've been over this. Hearing her orgasm is the last fucking thing that's going to drive me away."

The look Conan gave me over his shoulder chilled the fire in my blood. I froze, watching him go with a slack jaw and furrowed brow. It had been anger, white hot, and poorly disguised hurt written all over his features.

"Grumpy," Darius teased, raising a brow as Conan slammed the door behind him.

Music began blaring from the direction of Rory's bedroom, a pop-y upbeat song that I didn't doubt I'd be hearing more of at the club tonight.

"I assume you're not leaving, either," I asked him, changing the subject away from Conan and Rory and the fact my dick was still hard.

"I'm the only one here on her side."

I sighed. "It's not about *sides*, demon," I told him. "It's about right and wrong."

He tutted, a sly grin crinkling the corner of his eyes. "And you think there's such a clear distinction? I would've thought in your line of work, you'd know better by now."

I frowned at him, tilting my head to the side. "If I thought it was black and white, I'd have taken her straight back to Thornebank the second we found that fucking book."

It was the truth. But Conan and I had learned the hard way not to take our client's word as gospel. We had too much blood on our hands, and only some of it was intentional. We certainly weren't saints, not considering all we'd done and enjoyed doing, but we didn't send people to captors without getting to the bottom of the story. Although, there wasn't much I could see her doing with a dark magic book that resulted in us, as Darius had put it, *siding with her.* Psychological warfare or not.

"Bare fucking minimum," Darius murmured under his breath. My hackles raised, the wolf pacing around my fucking head suddenly at attention. A low growl echoed in my chest.

"What would you know about it anyway, demon?" I asked, advancing on him. To his credit, despite the flash of wolf I knew was showing in my eyes as the animal climbed closer to the surface, he didn't flinch. "Isn't it paradise down in Hell for our kind? Easy access to whatever your heart desires?"

He laughed, the sound humourless. "Ever been?"

"To Hell?" He nodded. "Once or twice."

The realm wasn't what humans made it out to be. It was hot, sure, but only in certain places. Hell was where the first mythics had risen from, millennia ago. Humans, seeing them for the first time and the magic they could wield, proclaimed them gods. Worshipped them for years, until more mythics joined them and the shiny, new appeal we had wore off. But we had never been any closer to godliness than they were. While humanity had been formed from the soil and air, mythics had been born of the fire and floods of the underworld. It was wilder, more feral than Earth, but below, mythics could live freely, without fear of persecution or burning. There were few humans that chose to travel between the realms - it was harder for them, anyway - but they weren't barred, just like mythics could still make their home above. Conan and I had yet to find a home anywhere we travelled. We didn't need one as long as we had each other. We were one another's home.

"Perhaps it's not the place I speak of," Darius countered, sadness softening his golden eyes. "But the people."

He stepped away quickly, flopping down in the armchair across from the fire he'd lit earlier and snatching another book from the coffee table. Rory had hundreds of them around the house - most either spellbooks of some form or another, though I'd not seen any other dark magic books aside from the stolen one, or romance novels. It was the latter the demon was interested in. I had no interest in either, not that I could think straight with my wolf itching to run. It had been a while since I'd shifted just for the freedom of it. I hadn't stopped long enough to think of anything but work in a long time and, though technically we were still on the job, I had no idea what to do with myself now.

"I'm going to check the forest," I told Darius. He held up a hand that indicated he'd heard me as I pulled my shirt over my head and dumped it on the side of the couch.

"Whoa, what-" he began asking, eyes widening.

"Relax," I reassured him. "Just don't want to ruin a perfectly good outfit."

Soon, I was down to nothing but my underwear. I tugged that off, too, before sauntering out the front door and darting off to the right into the treeline. I needed to be far enough away from her fucking scent when I shifted or else my wolf would likely barrel into her room just to see what smelled so fucking good.

Thankfully, the earthy scents of the forest blocked hers out quickly enough, and I allowed the wolf control, feeling the stretch and pop of my joints as my body hunched, my hands hitting the dirt just before they transformed into paws as I fell to the ground.

It still hurt, the shifting. Never as much as the first time, though. No, that had felt like being ripped apart, every bone shattering then reforming, blood boiling then cooling, jaw snapping and growing. Now, it was a mild inconvenience, painful for the few seconds it took, then fading fast. I'd had thirteen years to get used to it. The first shift occurred during a shifter's teen years, anywhere from the age of thirteen to eighteen. I'd been fifteen and it had been terrible fucking timing.

The wolf took over, happy as all Hell to be out, sniffing the air and inspecting his new surroundings. We were, at once, both separate and inseparable. Two halves of one soul. Two voices in one head. Two creatures sharing one body. But one could not exist without the other. Shifters that went feral, whose animals took over entirely, lost the part of them that made them…aware. Their mind became so fractured by the split that they never recovered. They were dangerous, nearly impossible to save.

Thankfully, my wolf and I tended to be in agreement. And, right now, who we both *really* wanted was singing, very badly but very loudly, along to her playlist back in the cottage. I urged us forward, away from temptation, in search of the stranger Conan had sensed watching us yesterday.

"You're trying to fucking kill me," I announced when she walked out of her room. She'd emerged briefly earlier, wrapped in a fluffy towel, to yell that if *you must come with me like an overbearing guard dog* we'd be leaving at nine to meet up with her friend. It was twenty past the hour now, but Hell below did she make the wait worth it.

Her dress was skintight, deep dark red, and short enough to reveal the large floral crow tattoo on her upper left thigh. The inexplicable urge to trace the lines with my tongue hit me with the force of a truck, nearly knocking me off my feet. Her brown hair was curled and pinned away from her face. Bright red lips matched the shade of her dress, and black eyeliner swept across her upper lid in a point. Strappy black heels topped off the outfit, making her taller but not tall enough to meet my eyes without having to tilt her head back.

"Never seen a woman's body before?" Rory shot back, pouting her red lips exaggeratedly. She snatched a little black bag from the coat hooks by the door and slipped her phone inside, examining the contents and nodding.

"Why, want to give me a tour?" I hadn't brought up what we'd heard earlier, but the knowledge of it hung heavy in the air between us. I was dressed simply in a fitted black shirt and jeans with my usual black boots and pocket knife hidden in my sock.

"Book's on the bed," she called out to Darius and Conan, though the latter had yet to emerge. He was pissed, and I knew I had to get to the bottom of whatever the fuck was going on with him soon, but right now I needed to focus on the task at hand. Not tearing the clothes of the witch before we made it out the door.

Darius was leaning against the kitchen counter, blatantly staring at Rory's tits. "Keep a good eye on her," he told me as she turned and opened the door, not even stopping to look back before she walked out. I nodded at him and followed without hesitation.

The trip to the bar was short, thanks to the car Rory's friend had called, though fraught with awkward questions and clear shock.

"You didn't tell me you were bringing...him!"

Grace had begun badgering Rory for information about me the second we'd settled in for the ride, apparently not caring that I could hear every word. Rory had deflected as much as she could, trying her best to ignore my presence altogether, claiming we were just *sort of friends*. Grace was clearly unconvinced, and kept glancing between us with suspicion in her eyes. My wolf instantly recognised her as a shifter, though her scent indicated feline of some sort. Panther, maybe? Or perhaps lynx...

I kept quiet, namely due to the daggers Rory was shooting my way, but also through the careful training I'd drilled into myself. Never give too much away. Grace obviously didn't know that her best friend was a wanted criminal, and I got the impression that small talk might end up with my balls nailed to the fucking taxi door.

We arrived early enough that the line was short, and entry painless. The club was dark but spacious, a large dance floor framed by small booths, half already full. Shining metal stairs rose to the left, leading up to the platform where the DJ was set up. The girls immediately peeled off towards the bar, giggling to each other while they ordered drinks. I took up a seat away from them, at the end of the bar, so we were separated by a few other customers sipping their drinks and chatting quietly, not quite tipsy enough to be up dancing.

I ordered lemonade, needing to keep a clear head, and attempted to get comfortable on the bar stool. I kept my distance while the crowd grew, and the music got louder, and Rory and Grace ended up on the dance floor. I left the bar, pushing to my feet and watching from the edge of the now crowded space, unwilling to let the witch out of my sight. I couldn't have torn my eyes from her if I tried.

She was dancing, moving her body as though the music was in her very blood, swaying her hips in a way that made my fists clench. Her dress had risen up to the point of indecency, not that she seemed to care, the curve of her ass just visible below the hem. Her head was tilted back as her mouth moved with the lyrics, her hands around her friend, a smile on her lips. They were both tipsy, but neither of them drunk.

The song changed to something slightly slower, the music dark and seductive. One moment she was dancing with Grace, the next she was in the arms of a man I'd never seen before, her eyes wide with surprise even as she continued to dance. The sight of her pressed against him had anger coursing through me, hot and heavy. I was shoving my way through dancing bodies before I could think better of it, fucking furious that she'd let someone else touch her after the shit she'd pulled earlier.

The man saw me before she did and moved fast, ducking into the safety of the crowd and leaving Rory confused. Grace was dancing with another girl, her hands on her waist and lips pressed to her ear, so she didn't stop me when I pulled Rory close to me and dragged her away. She protested as I pulled her off the dance floor and into the alcove behind the stairs, where the music was slightly muffled and there was no crowd.

"Get off me!" she yelled, wriggling away from me. I growled, wrapping a hand around her waist and backing her against the wall quickly, caging her in with my body. Beads of sweat gleamed on her forehead from dancing, her chest rising and falling fast from exertion. She crossed her arms over her chest and set her jaw, glaring daggers at me.

"Who the fuck was that?" I ground out, flexing my fingers on the wall against the urge to find the guy and knock his teeth out.

"I don't know," Rory answered like it was obvious. "Some hot guy I wanted to dance with. It's a club, Ezra. People dance together."

"You want a guy to dance with? You dance with me."

She snorted. "You looked like dancing might kill you."

I frowned. I didn't dance, she was right, but that was far from the point. "He clearly wanted more than to dance with you."

"So? Maybe I did too." She tilted her chin and raised a brow in challenge.

"You're a filthy fucking liar," I told her, backing her up further so we were nearly pressed together. "He's not who you want to fuck." She didn't answer me, but her breathing picked up, and she didn't fight me when I leaned down until my mouth was inches from hers. "He's not the one you put on a fucking show for. He's not the one you want making you scream." I shifted, moving my hands off the wall, sliding them

102

down her waist to her hips and fighting the urge to groan at the feel of her. I breathed in the spicy scent of her, her arousal clear, and smirked. My control was thinning, dangerously close to snapping.

"I hate you."

"Sure, hellhound," I replied coolly, voice low to hide the desperation in my body. I flexed my hands at her hips, desperate to tear the satiny dress away and find out for myself if her skin was as soft as it looked. I lowered my lips to her ear, so my mouth skimmed the sensitive skin below it when I whispered, "say it again."

"I hate you." It was fractured this time, more a plea than anything. I grinned against her neck, flicking my tongue against her pulse and relishing the way she shivered in response. *Fuck.* I was going to drop dead if I didn't get her naked in the next five minutes.

"That's it, baby," I responded, dipping my hand to the hem of her short dress. "Tell me how much you despise me. How much you want to hurt me. Keep convincing yourself. Maybe by the time I'm done with you, you'll believe it."

She gasped as I fisted her skirt and pushed it up her waist, leaving her exposed. We were tucked away, and I was blocking anyone's view of her regardless, but the whole fucking bar could've been watching and I wouldn't have stopped.

"This is a terrible fucking idea," she said through gritted teeth as I trailed my hand over her thighs, running my thumb over the outline of her tattoo.

"Do you care?" I asked as I ran my hand higher, tucking my finger into the tease of black lace barely passing as panties. I waited, unmoving, for her to respond, listening to her try to catch her breath. As much as I wanted to ruin her, right here

103

while the thumping music hid her moans, I wouldn't if she protested.

"All of my best ideas are bad," she answered before crashing her mouth to mine. I froze for a second, shocked. Her tongue traced the seam of my lips and I opened, shoving her back against the wall and tasting her fully. The sweet spark of the cocktail she'd been drinking was on her lips, and she kissed me like she was as fucking desperate for this as I was. I dug two fingers under her underwear and tugged, yanking fast so they snapped. She moaned against my mouth, reaching up to fist her hand in my shirt. I repeated the motion on the other side, snatching the now useless piece of lace from her body and shoving it into my pocket, not missing how wet the fabric was as I did.

"Fucking Hell, Rory," I muttered as I pulled back to look at her, dress bunched up and pussy exposed. She was sin incarnate. She opened her mouth to answer, staring at me like she was in shock, but before she could, I grabbed her ass and lifted her, moving closer to hold her against the wall, opening her legs for me. She blinked, letting her head fall back against the brick, licking her lips in anticipation.

I grinned, my dick pressing uncomfortably against my zipper. I didn't care. I needed to touch her, feel her come around my fingers, on my tongue, before I buried myself inside her. Patience shredded, I released her ass with one hand and dragged my finger through the centre of her. Her breath caught in her throat and I groaned.

"So fucking wet, hellhound." She only nodded, eyes a little wild as I studied her. "I should tease you for the fucking stunt you pulled."

"No-"

"But I won't," I clarified, indulging in the sheer relief in her hooded eyes. "Not now. I need to see if you look just like I imagined you do when you come."

Before she could so much as process my words, I speared two fingers inside her drenched pussy. She shuddered, a choked moan that sounded suspiciously like my name spilling from her lips. I withdrew my hand slowly, watching her reaction when I began fucking her with my fingers in earnest, brutal, unforgiving thrusts that made it fucking clear who's cock she'd be coming around later. She whimpered, trying to grind against me though it was nearly impossible at her angle.

"Such a needy little slut." I felt her appreciation even as she fought to scowl at me. I crooked my fingers, finding the spot that made her moan, eyes fluttering shut. She shuddered around me as I kept the pace, coating my thumb with her arousal before circling her clit, needing to watch her come apart.

"Fuck, Ezra," she moaned, gasping. "Hell below, fuck, please-"

I gave her what I knew she was asking for, sliding my thumb over her clit as I lowered my head, kissing her pulse, feeling it flutter beneath the swipe of my tongue. When I repeated the motion with the points of my canines, she shattered, crying out and clenching around my fingers.

I pulled back, watching her orgasm drag her under, her eyes shut, mouth open, the moan pouring from her mouth threatening to push me over the edge. Fuck, she was gorgeous. I'd never needed anything as badly as I needed her right then.

Before she'd recovered, I withdrew from her heat, ignoring her small noise of complaint, and freed my cock from my jeans. Her eyes flew open when she registered the sound of the zip.

"Are you on birth control?" I asked, raising a brow at her.

She nodded, smirking slightly. "I'm a witch, Ezra. Magic does it for me."

"Come here," I demanded, losing my patience. Mythics didn't have to worry about human problems like STIs. Perks of magic and all.

To my surprise, she didn't argue, but leant forward as much as she was able, threaded her hand through my hair and tugged my mouth to hers.

"Hurry up and fuck me before someone finds us."

18

Rory

I was sure this was a bad idea, but I couldn't remember why. I clung to Ezra, fixated on him. It was so fucking dark, especially with his giant frame blocking the lights of the club behind us. His eyes glowed silver in the dim light, the animal in him allowing far better night vision than any other species of mythic.

"Relax, hellhound," he practically purred in my ear. I was still shaking slightly from the aftershocks of the first orgasm, but I needed more. Needed him.

He guided his cock to my entrance, coating himself in my release as I shivered. I tilted my hips, trying to get him to hurry the fuck up, grinding against him the best I could. He laughed, the sound dark and seductive.

I opened my mouth to yell at him, but before I could get so much as a sound past my lips, he slammed into me, burying himself deep in one thrust. The breath left my lungs at once as I cried out at the stretch. *Fuck* he felt good.

"Ezra-" I tried to wriggle away, the intrusion too much too soon. My mind was spinning, body writhing with pleasure and shock. I had no time to adjust to him as he held us flush together for a second before pulling out nearly entirely and slamming back into me, hard enough that my head hit the wall. "Fuck." My voice was breathless and nearly unintelligible. I was spinning, pleasure burning in my veins, legs wrapped around his back as I urged him closer.

"Hell below, Rory," he growled, holding my hips to keep me still as he fucked me with ruthless strokes. He was bigger than I'd anticipated, and I moaned, unable to stay quiet. "You feel fucking incredible."

I tried to answer but he dug his fingers into the skin on my hips, the pain blossoming under his touch only pushing me closer to the edge. I whimpered, shifting to meet his thrusts. He let me this time, encouraging me with his hands, gaze fixated on the place where we were joined.

His name flew past my lips in a rush as he adjusted the angle so he was hitting a spot inside me that set me on fire.

"Touch yourself," Ezra said, voice strained slightly as he kept his pace. It took me a second to process his request, my mind foggy with lust. A second too long, apparently, as his patience snapped and he grabbed my hand, driving it between us. "Make yourself come all over my cock."

The demand in his voice was impossible to disobey. I couldn't have even if I wanted to. I was burning up, intoxicated by the feel of him, the low curses he muttered under his breath. I slid my finger over my swollen clit under his command and he growled, the sound low in his chest and purely primal. A choked cry escaped my mouth as my pussy fluttered around him while I wound myself tighter, the combination of him and my own hand driving me to the edge faster than I could control.

"Come," he demanded, his thrusts losing their rhythm. "Let me feel you, Rory."

A small part of me wanted to disobey him, just to see what he'd do, but I was too far gone, lost in the tidal wave of pleasure as it crested. I swore, back arching off the wall as I was swept under, body going limp in his grip as he followed me.

"*Fuck,*" he ground out, thrusting into me hard and dropping his head to my neck, breath hot against my skin.

We stayed like that, both panting and desperately trying to catch our breath, him still inside me, my arms and legs wrapped around him. I wasn't sure I could stand if he put me down. He'd fucking *broken* me in the best possible way.

Not that he could know that.

Faster than was wise, I unwrapped myself from him, forcing him to pull away. I tugged my skirt down, trying really fucking hard to ignore the wetness dripping down my thighs. He'd destroyed my panties so I'd have to go without, but it didn't matter. I was sure my hair was a mess but the lights were low and by now people would be drunk enough that it wouldn't matter.

My legs shook a little, and I clamped my thighs together to hide it. My body felt like it was floating as I pieced myself back together, trying to find it in myself to regret what we'd just done.

But, Hell below, it had felt good.

"Don't you dare," he hissed, narrowing his eyes at me as he fastened his jeans back up and straightened his shirt. To my annoyance, he looked casual as fuck, as though he hadn't just given me the best sex I'd had in years. I gritted my teeth.

"What?"

"Don't stand there and tell me it was a mistake."

"It's the truth," I said, trying to shove past him, needing out of here before this got any worse. He blocked me, hand strong on my waist. I struggled in his grip, but he was twice my fucking size and didn't budge. He tugged me to him, my back to his chest, and banded his arm around my waist. I tried to hide the effect his touch had on me, but the scent of sex was still heavy and heady between us.

"Did it feel like a mistake when you were strangling my fucking dick as you came?"

I inhaled sharply, tensing so I didn't shudder. "Don't flatter yourself."

"I don't need to," he replied calmly. I could hear the smirk in his voice. "You did that for me."

"Let me go."

"Not until you admit that that was good as fuck." He caught my ear lobe between his teeth, and I hissed, squirming. "Or do I need to break you down until you can do nothing but tell the fucking truth?"

Yes. "No."

"Ror?" A light, female voice cut through the tension like a knife and we both jumped, Ezra releasing me so fast I rocked on my feet. Seconds later, Grace came into view, eyes round and worried. "Oh there you are-" Her nostrils flared as she scented us, and then her pink glossy lips fell open in shock. "RORY!"

I cringed, jumping away from Ezra and running to her. "Shut up," I hissed, ignoring her giggling. I grabbed her arm, leaving Ezra behind us and pulling her away to hide in the bathrooms where he couldn't follow.

"We're just friends," she mocked from outside as I locked the cubicle door behind me.

110

"Shut up, Grace," I whined, suddenly exhausted. I cleaned myself up, but the smell of him on my skin wouldn't budge. I leant against the cool wall, letting my eyes drop closed. "It was a big fucking mistake."

"Was it worth it?" I could hear the teasing in her tone, pictured her wiggling her eyebrows at me. I snorted. "Come onnnn, Ror, tell me!"

I could never hide anything from her, not when she sounded so damn happy for me. "I can barely fucking walk straight."

Her squeal kickstarted my heart, sparking some life back into me. I opened the stall door to see her grinning wildly.

"Alright, enough," I told her, thoroughly pissed off at myself despite the amusement radiating from my friend. "What happened with that girl you were dancing with?"

She took the bait, sighing. "Nothing."

"Aw Gracie," I said, tugging her close and wrapping my arms around her. "You just need to jump back into it. Don't let the breakup ruin sex for you." My tone was teasing, but she knew I wasn't joking. The last girl she'd dated broke her heart, and she still hesitated to move on nine months later.

"You smell like wolf!" she complained, shoving me away and rolling her eyes. I scowled at her, sniffing my dress. I did. His dark, musky scent mixed with mine in a way that made my stomach flip.

For fuck's sake.

"Shut up!" I bumped her with my shoulder, trying to force lightness into my tone. It evidently didn't work as her face softened. "I need a drink."

She nodded eagerly, taking my hand and pulling me out the bathroom, making a beeline for the bar.

"Tequila?"

I nodded, grateful that she'd given up her line of questioning. "Tequila."

19

Rory

My head was pounding. Everything fucking hurt. I rolled over, groaning, and threw my arm over my eyes when a shaft of sunlight broke through the gap in the curtains. I'd got back late, drunk out my mind and leaning on Grace as she walked me up the path to the door. Ezra had to find his own way home after we left without him and was waiting at the door for me.

Thankfully the boundary I'd set up around my room before I left was still in place so he couldn't follow me into the bedroom, instead bouncing off the invisible wall while I cackled hysterically at him.

It was still funny now, though my head spun when I laughed. Fuck, I needed coffee. Lots of it.

Reluctantly, I dragged myself to my feet, giving my room a cursory glance to check the grimoire was still on the vanity where I'd left it in view of Conan and Darius last night. They'd both been asleep when we returned, though I was sure I'd heard Darius throw something at Ezra for waking him up.

I smudged the chalk on the floorboards with my slippers,

dissolving the spell in place. I felt the magic dissipate around me like mist.

The living space was mercifully empty as I left the safety of my room, though I could hear the shower running in the main bathroom so I probably didn't have long before someone invaded the space. Hurriedly, I heaped two teaspoons of instant coffee into a cup and filled the kettle before rummaging through the cupboard where I kept my spell ingredients for a peppermint leaf to chew to stave off the nausea.

I was stirring milk into my drink as the shower switched off. I jumped, dropping the spoon on the counter with a clatter and narrowly avoiding spilling boiling hot coffee all over myself.

The door to the bathroom swung open, and Darius stepped out, towel low on his waist, skin still spattered with water droplets.

I gaped at him, unable to tear my eyes away despite the fact that I definitely fucking should have. His dark hair was wet and tousled, his body lean and fucking mouthwatering. He wasn't muscular, but the way he held himself with permanent easy confidence told me he was far more dangerous than he seemed. Tattoos spanned his upper left shoulder and across the side of his chest. From my distance, and through my hungover haze, I could make out a skull and something written in the same language as his summoning spell. Not that I could make out *what* it said, but still.

"Morning," he greeted far too casually. My brain finally turned itself on and I picked my jaw up off the floor.

"Uh, right," I mumbled back, staring into my cup like it would give me the answer to get out of this fucking shit show. "Morning."

He sauntered closer, apparently unbothered by his nakedness.

Oh, Hell below, he was fucking naked. He'd chucked the towel over the back of a chair. Heat flooded my cheeks.

"Have a good night last night?" His voice was light and teasing, a smirk on his face and eyes sparkling like he knew the world's best secret.

I blinked at him, confused. "It was fun…"

He bit his bottom lip as he looked me up and down. "What's on your neck?"

I frowned, my hand flying to the place he was staring at. "What-"

Oh fuck. Oh *fuck!*

"You smell like sex," he said lowly, stepping closer. "You smell like *shifter and sex.*"

"I have no idea what you're on about," I lied, pushing my way past him.

"Oh, little thief," he called after me. "If you're going to lie, at least do it to my face."

I halted my escape, spinning to lock eyes with him. Anger, at both him and myself, had me gripping the cup in my hand so tight my knuckles went white. "You must be confused."

"You're so fucking cute when you're in denial," he licked his bottom lip, sinking his teeth into it. "Tell me, little witch. Did he make you moan as sweetly as you did yesterday?"

It was too early for this. I hadn't had time to wake up let alone deal with my resident demon. Especially not while he was wet and naked.

"I'm sure you'd love to know," I answered tightly, rolling my eyes.

"I really fucking would," he answered, voice dropping as he

closed the distance between us. "I'm insulted."

I frowned, taking a sip from my too hot drink to steady myself. "Why?"

"If you needed someone to fuck so badly, you should've come to me."

I nearly spat out my drink. "Why would I ever do that?"

"Because I'm not the one trying to get you locked up," he answered smoothly, shaking his head so his hair fell over his forehead. "And all you did by screwing the shifter was piss Conan the fuck off."

My stomach turned. "What?"

Darius eyed me, shoulders dropping like he pitied me. "You should've fucking seen his face earlier."

How had I fucked my life up this badly in the space of five fucking days? "Well, he'll survive," I said with more vigour than I felt. "Why he's so concerned with where Ezra sticks his dick is beyond me. Besides, it's not happening again so it doesn't matter now."

"You're right, it's not happening again," Darius echoed, grabbing his towel and wrapping it around his waist again. My gaze dropped to the motion on instinct and he grinned. "Because next time he'll have to sit and watch you scream my name instead."

I nearly dropped my mug, heat shooting through me at the dark promise. "None of you are getting anywhere near me."

"So fucking cute," he murmured before straightening and turning away like nothing had happened.

I darted back to the bedroom, feeling imprisoned in my own damn house.

If any of us were going to survive the next two weeks, there needed to be rules.

They were all in for a fucking wake up call.

20

Conan

"I can't fucking believe you."

"This, *again*, Cee?"

"Don't fucking call me that!" I was anger incarnate, fury coursing through me. The second I'd fucking realised what had happened last night, I'd felt sick.

"Hell below, Conan, would you calm down?" Ezra threw his hands up, shaking his head. He was halfway dressed, searching his bag for a clean shirt. I wanted to grab him and shake him until it knocked his fucking brain back into place.

"What were you thinking?" I spat. My skin was on fucking fire. I was burning. My powers always flared when I was pissed.

"That she's hot and I wanted to fuck her," he said simply, finding a dark grey t shirt and tugging it over his head. "That's all I was thinking. It's not the end of the fucking world."

"She's a fucking target," I reminded him, fists clenched and heart hammering so fast my chest ached. I was sure that was why my chest ached. "We don't fuck the targets! She's a criminal."

"So are we!"

"That's different-"

"How?" He spun to stare at me, meeting my eyes with defiance, unflinching in the face of my wrath. "Do you remember how much blood we have on our hands? Are you sorry for it? Cause I'm not. We agreed to stay until we got answers. Me fucking her doesn't change that."

"You can't be that naive," I scoffed, fighting the urge to connect my fist with his face. He wasn't listening. Did he even know what he'd done? He'd fucking ruined everything -

"Fuck off, Conan. Just fuck off. I don't need to sit here and take this again. I get it. You're pissed."

His eyes flashed wolf then he turned, slamming the door behind him and leaving me with my fury in the shitty guest room of a wanted criminal's house.

This was fucking insane.

I followed him, ready to drag him back into the room by the scruff of his fucking neck and beat some sense into him. Why her? Couldn't he have found literally anyone else? That thought didn't make me feel any better.

I needed to hit something, hurt something, make something bleed. Anything to ease the fire.

Before I could reach him, I was caught in the trap of the last fucking person I wanted to see.

"Sit down."

I snapped my eyes to hers, a new wave of anger drowning me when I saw the mark on her neck. Canines. *Ezra fucking bit her.* Shifter's bit to claim - if done deeply and with the right intention, the bite bonded them, creating an invisible, permanent link between the two. It allowed both parties to feel the others' emotions, communicate somewhat and

119

generally be…connected. While I knew that's not what had happened this time, the implication still sent a chill through me.

I didn't think I'd ever seen his mark on someone before. I'd seen plenty of his one night stands come and go from whatever shitty hotel we were staying at that night, but none with his mark on them.

I felt like I was going insane. Like I might actually fucking burst into flames if I had to be around them for another minute.

It wasn't anger that was killing me.

It was the fucking jealousy, the hunger that had been slowly tearing me apart for years. The ache that was growing so wide it nearly devoured me whole.

"Sit the fuck down, Conan," she demanded again, nodding to the sofa where the other two were already waiting like well trained dogs.

"No."

"Cee, just-"

"I'll stand." I didn't follow orders. I gave them. I saw Darius roll his eyes out the corner of my vision and tensed, trying to keep the flames under control as they ripped their way through my blood. I kept my face in a cold mask, refusing to let any of them see the destruction beneath.

"Fine," Rory conceded, throwing her hands up. She stood at the junction between the living room and kitchen, hands on her hips. Mercifully, she'd showered so I didn't have to smell him on her. He still carried the sweet, spiced scent of her on his skin. I couldn't fucking look at him. "There needs to be some ground rules around here. I don't fucking want any of you assholes here any longer, but you've all made it clear I don't have a choice. So -"

She was cut off by a loud *bang*, followed by the front door wobbling on its hinges.

"GET DOWN!" Ezra shouted. All three of them ducked, Rory hitting the floor as Darius grabbed her, tucking her down behind the sofa and out of sight.

I stood, watching the door rattle. The fire in my blood cooled, a familiar cold calm washing over me. I grinned, tilting my head as I approached the door. I could barely make out the whispered protests Ezra and Darius were shooting at me over the dull ringing in my ears.

Before I reached the door, I adjusted the light around me, manipulating the air until it shimmered and rendered me invisible. I registered a shocked shout from Darius and a soft gasp that must have been Rory, but I was focused on whoever the fuck I could sense on the other side of the door.

It flew open with a gust of strong wind. It was always easy when I was like this, my magic so riled up, so on edge it was like a living being coiled in my veins, demanding to be put to use. I'd crash later, I knew, but the empty ache would be better than the hurt currently hollowing out my chest.

There was no one there.

I paused, inhaling, but barely catching the faintest notes of charcoal on the breeze. It was the door that had my attention. Vivid red blood was splashed across the front of it, fresh by the bright scent of copper invading my senses. I wrinkled my nose, furrowing my brow as I realised what the fuck I was looking at.

A note, written in blood.

You'll burn, too.

What. The. Fuck. The writing was jagged and dripping -

words formed by someone dragging their fingers through the thick mess of blood, rapidly losing their definition. Careful to keep my steps light, I exited the house, ensuring the culprit really had left before the others appeared.

There was nothing but the cold bite of the autumn breeze and soft chirp of birds.

21

Darius

"What the fuck."

We all stood in a row, staring at the mess smeared on Rory's door. The blood had begun to congeal, the threat barely readable now, and the air was tinged with the smell of metal. My little thief just stood there, spine straight and body tense, as she watched red seep into her doormat.

"I really liked that," she said a little sadly, toeing the *Witchy Bitch* welcome mat with her bare foot. Collectively, we gaped at her. "Oh well."

She shrugged - *shrugged* - and walked inside, leaving the three of us staring after her in shock. She reappeared quickly, a clear glass jar in hand, and held the container up to the door, collecting the blood as it seeped down from the wood.

"Little thief," I started, clearing my throat and trying not to sound as confused as I was. "Care to explain what the fucking Hell just happened?"

She sighed. "Give me a minute. I may as well make use of

this. It's sheep's blood."

"How do you know what kind of blood it is?" Ezra asked, sleeve over his nose to block the smell.

"Don't you?" I asked him. I'd have thought, out of all of us, wolf boy would've been able to tell the difference in animal blood.

"Well, yes, but I want to know how she does," he answered like it was obvious, voice muffled by the fabric of his shirt.

Conan had reappeared again, though I was still reeling over seeing him disappear in the first place. He said nothing as he stood, emotionless, on the threshold of the cottage. Rory paid him no mind despite the weight of his eyes on her as she screwed the metal top onto her jar, now nearly full with scarlet liquid.

Satisfied, she turned back to us. "Let's discuss this inside."

I never thought I'd see the day she purposefully invited us into her house. Ezra looked between her and the mess.

"What about the door?"

"I'll cast a cleaning spell on it." She waved his concern away with the sleeve of her oversized jumper, the threads at the edge stained slightly red now, and closed the door behind us.

The jar clattered as she placed it on the counter and sat down on her bar stool, crossing her arms over her chest. Her hair was in two braids today, and despite the bloody state of everything, all I could think about was wrapping them around my fist.

"Explain." It was the first Conan had spoken in this whole ordeal.

Rory rolled her eyes. "It's nothing to worry about."

I gaped at her. "Did we witness the same event?"

"Trust me," she laughed. "That was child's play."

"What is that supposed to mean?" Ezra cut in, a sharp edge of protectiveness in his words. I didn't miss the way it made her eyes widen. Interesting.

"That I'm a big girl who knows how to take care of her own problems."

"Humour us," I encouraged, lounging against the wall.

"Someone doesn't like the fact that they didn't get what they want," she said vaguely, pressing her lips together so they thinned.

"Expand, hellhound." It was a demand, and I blinked at the new nickname he'd given her. Jealousy spiked hot in my blood. For fuck's sake. I was in no place to deal with that emotion.

"He didn't get to ruin me," she said lowly. Instantly, I pushed off the wall, sensing the hurt edge in her voice. "And occasionally he reminds me of what an insolent child he is. Throwing tantrums to taunt me. He thinks I've given up on my claims to revenge."

"But you haven't," I finished for her, unable to stop the impulse to go to her. The puzzle pieces were finally falling into place. "That's why you need the grimoire."

Her sigh was heavy, but her voice was strong when she spoke. "I can't have it tracked back to me. The only way to ensure that it can't be is through one of the spells in that book. I've been through every other option in my mind, but all of them end up with me in chains. I won't be punished for his crimes."

"What exactly is *it?*" Ezra asked her, voice barely above a whisper.

"Murder." She looked up from the jar of blood and met each of our gazes, landing on Conan last. "I'm going to kill him. And make it hurt."

22

Conan

Murder.

That's what all this was for. There was more to it, undoubtedly, but she was fucking unreadable as she sat there, head high, hand curled around that fucking jar.

Nobody spoke as her words settled in.

It wasn't like we were strangers to the idea. I'd seen the life drain out of countless eyes. Most of the time, I enjoyed it. But whatever she'd done to anger the person who'd thrown blood at her door remained to be seen. But if they wanted her gone that badly...

I broke the silence first, needing to know. "Why didn't they just come in and kill you if they want you dead so badly?"

She rubbed her temples. "He can't come in. None of his kind can. I spelled the house four years ago after he smashed my windows and left a corpse staged on my sofa. If he tries to enter now, it'll burn him. Took me fucking ages to find the right spell book for it, and even then I passed out after, it drained me so badly."

"He did *what?*"

She shrugged, like this was just another fucking day. Hell below, maybe Ezra had been right. There was so much more to this than we first expected.

I fucking hated it when he was right.

"Left a dead body splayed across my couch," she answered. "Had to buy new furniture and everything."

"Hellhound," Ezra cut in, the nickname stealing my breath for a minute. "Who is he?"

The reluctance on her face was clear. She wanted to tell this story about as much as I wanted to hear Ezra call her that fucking name again.

"An ex," she began slowly, scratching the palm of her hand absently. "We started dating when I was eighteen. I was feral at that point. I dropped out of college after my grandmother was murdered - always drunk, fucking strangers, anything that would make me *feel*. I was hollow after all the loss. And then, he found me." She took a deep breath, as if steeling herself, and Darius backed away to turn on the kettle and grab a tin of tea out the cupboard, not once taking his eyes off her. "He was supposed to make me feel better but all he did was fuck me up worse. Got me involved in shit I had no desire for. But I did it, for him."

"What did he do to you?" Ezra's voice was dangerous.

"It doesn't matter," she said quickly, holding up her hand. "All that matters is, I'll get my revenge. On all of his little fucked up group. I'll make them wish they'd never even heard my name."

"Drink," Darius instructed, placing the mug down beside her. It smelled of peppermint and lavender, and was a murky sort of green. I scrunched my nose, but she accepted gratefully.

"I'm not a victim and I don't need your help. I'd have done it years ago if it wouldn't have landed me in a jail cell rotting until the end of my days. Stupid human laws. But that's the beauty of the darkest of magic." She smiled over the rim of the mug, eyes gleaming. "If you do it right, nobody will ever know it was you at all."

"So you stole the book to commit mass murder?" Darius clarified, not sounding the least bit bothered by this information.

"Only six people," she argued. "Just the leaders."

"Leaders of what, exactly?"

"The cult."

I flinched and Ezra's jaw dropped open. Darius just laughed.

"This is not worth the money," I muttered. Darius shot a glare at me that I ignored. When we'd taken this fucking job, we'd agreed to find a damn book. And now, we were knee deep in some sort of cult revenge plan.

"Let me clear this up," Darius said, leaning close to her so their shoulders touched. "You went off the rails, started dating a psycho cult leader who fucked you up and now you want to murder him and his friends?"

"Yup," she said happily, swinging her legs on the chair. "Occasionally he sends one of his brothers," she held up her fingers in air quotes around *brother,* "to put the fear of Hell into me. But I'm not the same girl I was when I met him. I'm not scared any more."

"This is a common occurrence?" Ezra growled, looking between her and the fucking jar.

"This is the seventh incident in the last five years," she answered with a shrug. "I was beginning to think he'd given up. No such luck." She tutted, drinking her tea and watching us all process what she'd just told us. "Figured you were going to have to find out sooner or later. See, I'm not some crazy lady planning to take over the world with ancient evil or whatever. Just a little home-made justice."

"This doesn't mean anything," I told her, still flicking through all the information in my head. "For all we know, you're lying. You haven't told us any names, or even the fucking species of these so called maniacs."

"Vamps," she shot back. "Convincing scared girls that blood rituals will *cleanse* them. For the worst recruits, it took more than one to rebirth us."

Confusion muddled my mind, and I watched the emotion mirrored in Ezra and Darius' features. I made the connection first, anger sparking through me.

"Fuck," I hissed under my breath as Ezra and Darius let out similar sounds of protest.

"They didn't-"

"He told me it would make me feel better," she answered, something dark and sad in her eyes. I looked away when it tugged at something in my chest. "But there's only so many times a girl can handle being drained of blood and fucked raw before she realises it's not salvation. It's abuse."

"Hellhound…" Ezra reached for her, but she stood and shook her head.

"If we're quite done here, I'd like to clean the shit off my door."

"Wait, little thief," Darius called as she started to walk away, reaching out and grabbing her arm. "I'm sorry."

She shook her head. "Why? You didn't know."

"Thank you for telling us," Ezra echoed, though his gaze was murderous. "We'll find him-"

"You'll do nothing," she snapped, turning to him, still in Darius' arms. "This is *my* kill, you understand? I don't need you."

Ezra exhaled through gritted teeth, but nodded once in admission. I didn't blame him. I wanted to rip the bastards limb from fucking limb and bathe in their blood. I'd show them *salvation*.

"You owe me one," she addressed us as a group, chin high and arms crossed over her chest as she stepped away from the demon. "The way I see it, you all know far too much about me and I know fuck all about you."

"You want a fucking share circle?" Darius laughed, shaking his head. She frowned, eyebrows drawing together.

"No, Darius," she drawled, tongue flicking out to wet her bottom lip. "I want a fair exchange."

"What are you thinking, little thief?" His gaze was dark as he looked at her, a slow smirk on his lips.

"I showed you my darkness," she continued, placing a hand on his chest and dragging a nail down his torso. "Now you show me yours."

His eyes widened, and Ezra growled. Something sharp hit my chest, and I inhaled through the pain.

"I'll deal with the fucking door," I told them, needing to get away from all this. From him. From her.

I want to know what the fuck was going on between them. Or why the whole fucking thing was ruining me. We'd been here for three days, and already we were falling apart.

That witch needed a fucking lesson.

An image of her tied up and gagged, ass red with the imprint of my hand, flashed through my mind. Maybe then she'd learn her place.

130

I shook myself, slamming the bloody front door behind me and spraying my arm with the cooling liquid. I couldn't fucking think about that, about showing her, showing him, how to behave. No matter how much the thought had my cock hardening in my jeans.

I wouldn't go there. I couldn't.

Not with either of them.

23

Rory

Conan stormed out, carrying a cloud of anger with him. Ezra watched him leave, a curious combination of annoyance and hurt in his eyes.

"One player down," I said, sighing dramatically. It didn't really matter. I doubt he'd have played even if he was in the room. Explaining my past to them had ripped open the ache in my chest I'd tried so hard to seal back up - just a fracture, just enough to have hurt and shame begin to seep into my bones. Not again. Never again would I allow shame to become a part of me.

I wasn't eighteen any more. I wasn't naive or chasing anything, *anything*, that would make me feel alive. I wasn't a victim.

I was a fucking reckoning.

Except, the three men in my house had delayed the schedule and now I was pissed. More than ever, after the stunt he and his group of sick fucks had pulled, I wanted to watch them bleed.

I needed to get Darius, Ezra and Conan on my side. And

who said I couldn't have a little fun doing so?

"What do you think we're playing?" Ezra asked, frowning at Darius. Clearly, he'd much rather we were alone. I wasn't convinced either of us had moved past hating the other, but it made the desire in my blood burn hotter. I didn't want gentle, loving sex. No, I wanted brutal, rough fucking. Something to remind me that my body was mine, that I'd survived. That I'd never stopped being strong.

I was pretty damn sure all three of these men could deliver.

Not that I'd fuck Conan. The hatred between us was alive and well. The mere sight of me seemed to piss him off and the feeling was fucking mutual.

"For every question you answer, I'll take off a piece of clothing," I promised, raising a brow and watching the shock ripple over their faces. Ezra looked like he couldn't decide whether to be outraged or intrigued. Darius, as I expected, looked fucking ravenous.

I clenched my thighs as heat pooled between them. I'd only intended to do this to tease answers out of them, because they were both stubborn assholes who'd yet to tell me anything, but maybe this was a bad idea. The attraction I had to them, both of them, might kill me before this was over.

"Why the fuck is he still in the room?" Ezra asked, voice so low it was nearly a growl. A spike of pleasure shot through me at the possessiveness in his tone. He might not like me, but that didn't mean he wanted to share me with anyone else.

Unfortunately for him, I didn't give a fuck what he wanted.

"Because he's player number one," I said like it was obvious, reaching up to push a strand of hair out my eye. I'd dressed simply today, in loose dark jeans and a tight, low cut green jumper with flared sleeves and little daisies stitched into it. If

I'd planned this better, I'd have put more layers on.

Too late now.

"Are you fucking serious?"

"Deadly," I answered, biting my bottom lip as I looked up at him. "Did you think you were special because I fucked you? Poor little pup doesn't know how to share?" I knew I was pushing him, but I wanted him on the edge, wanted him angry, not watching what he was saying.

I was slammed up against his chest before I could so much as finish the thought. He fisted my hair, yanking my head back and forcing me to meet his gaze.

"Let me make one thing very clear, hellhound," he said, tightening his grip until my scalp stung. "You are mine until I say otherwise. Your pussy is *mine.*"

Fuck me, this man was going to kill me. Either from lust or annoyance, there was hardly a shortage of either. "My pussy is mine, actually," I responded as casually as possible. "And just for that, you won't be fucking it tonight."

I shoved away from him, thoroughly enjoying the anger in his eyes when he glared after me. "Darius?"

"You want to play, little thief?" he asked, arms crossed as he leant against the wall, eyes dark from watching my exchange with Ezra. "Let's play."

I wasted no time, taking Ezra's silence as reluctant agreement.

I targeted Darius first. "Why did you leave Hell?"

He froze, the heat in his gaze frosting over slightly. "Bad ending to a bad relationship."

I narrowed my eyes, then rolled them when he raised a brow at me. "I answered, little thief."

Reluctantly, I turned to the shifter who was still glaring

daggers at me.

"How did you and Conan become friends?"

He, too, froze at my question. If I was doing this, I was going to make them work for it. I was serious about demanding answers.

"We met when we were children," he said slowly, sparing a glance for the door Conan had left from. "Became closer as teenagers." When he sensed that I wasn't going to take that as an answer, he blew out a short breath and shook his head. "We solved our first case together. Made our first kill together. That's the kind of shit that bonds you for life."

I nodded, licking my lips at the darkness in his gaze. The thought of them both, bloody hands and satisfied grins, had me slightly breathless. I was the last fucking person who could judge them for it, though I was curious as fuck as to who they'd killed.

"Strip, hellhound."

I met his eyes as I tugged on the hem of my shirt, turning to look at Darius as I lifted it over my head and let it drop to the floor. The purple bra I wore left nothing to the imagination - more sheer lace than support. Satisfaction and power warmed me when they both released twin breaths, eyes burning into me.

"Hell," Darius breathed, clenching his jaw and fists as if fighting not to touch me. Good.

I leant back on the counter, the position emphasising my chest, and grinned at the effect it had on Ezra.

"Do you really have nowhere else to go? Seems like a badly thought out plan, Dare," I addressed the demon. He raised his eyes to mine, a challenge in the golden depths.

"I didn't have a plan at all," he admitted, running his thumb over his bottom lip as he surveyed me. His voice was all smoke and sin. "I just ran."

A chill shivered down my spine as I nodded. He eyed my mouth as he added, "I'd never been above before. Never saw the point. It's not all that different, really. But no, until I found you, I had nowhere to go."

I lowered my gaze so my heart would stop its stupid flopping. *Get a fucking grip, Rory.* This was about getting answers, not feelings. And, maybe, dick.

Priorities, and all that.

"So you broke into a random girl's house?" I asked, trying to lighten the mood again. Darius *tsked*, shaking his head.

"One question, little thief." He nodded to Ezra. "Wolfie's turn."

Ezra glared at him. His stance was stiff, his eyes hard and determined.

"How many people have you killed?"

I wanted to know, to have at least something to hold over their heads if they fucked me over.

"Nine," he answered without hesitation. *Okay...*

Obeying the rules, I reached for my jeans. "Just tell me this, Ezra," I said as I unbuttoned them slowly, refusing to look up at him but knowing he was watching. "Did they all deserve it?"

He was silent as I began to pull the denim off, the weight of his gaze lingering on the tattoo on my upper thigh. I didn't think he would answer at all as my trousers joined my shirt, revealing my matching purple thong.

"No." His voice surprised me, so low it was a mere whisper, dark and rough. "Not all of them."

24

Rory

I had the inexplicable urge to reach for him, to comfort him, soothe the ragged ache I could hear in his confession. I should have shied away, been disgusted, felt anything other than the soft sympathy currently curling around my ribcage.

I didn't fucking know this man, and I shouldn't want to. But the guilt in his dark eyes made me want to reach out and comfort him.

Instead, I fixed my face into a mask of calm coldness, as if nothing about any of this was affecting me. I pulled my gaze away from Ezra's to turn to the demon looking at me like he wanted to eat me whole.

"I hope you know what game you're playing here, little thief," he murmured, setting me alight with desire at the barely controlled want in his voice. Shit, I'd underestimated how hot this would be. Me, nearly stripped bare, them both still fully clothed.

"Why did your relationship *go bad?*" I pressed, trailing a hand up my body to tease along the edge of the cup of my bra, dragging his golden gaze with it. He didn't bother hiding his desire.

"Because I didn't want to be with a narcissist," he answered coolly, looking up from my breasts through his lashes. "But the marriage was already arranged. Alliances made."

I cocked my head. "Your parents arranged it?" I guessed, noting the edge to his voice.

"My father did. My mother would've hated the idea," he answered matter of factly. Then he shrugged, his pupils wide as he stared at me. "I'd much rather be here."

Heat shot through me, settling between my legs. Fucking hell, I'd ruin my panties before I took them off.

"What the fuck is going on with you and Conan?" I asked Ezra. He'd lost the sadness in his eyes in favour of annoyance and heat.

"What do you mean?" His voice was gruff and confused. I laughed.

"He's pissy as fuck," I said, thinking it was obvious. "Obviously something happened. And it's making all our lives more difficult, so it's better if you just 'fess up."

"I didn't do anything," he insisted, frowning. "He's just a grumpy bastard."

I shook my head. While I could concede that he was indeed what Ezra described, this was deeper.

"Is he pissed you're staying here?"

"Probably," Ezra said, moving closer to me until I could feel his warmth. I swallowed thickly, the closeness driving my body insane. "But I'm not."

Darius closed in from behind, his fingers skating up my sides. I gasped, trying to downplay my reaction even as I shivered under his touch. I tilted my head back to find them staring at each other over my head, a silent conversation passing between them. Finally, Ezra grunted and nodded, returning his attention to me and grabbing my chin to force my eyes to his.

"You cheated, hellhound," he said, voice dark with promise. My heartbeat rocketed, pounding against my ribcage.

"What?"

"You thought we wouldn't notice?" Darius cut in, breath hot on my skin as he bent to ghost his lips over my bare shoulder. His fingers reached my bra, expertly unclasping it and urging the straps down my arms.

"I didn't cheat," I insisted as I was stripped nearly fully. His hands reached around, cupping my tits and pulling me back against him. I clenched my teeth to stop from moaning at his touch, but couldn't force my body to wriggle away from his grasp. Truth was, as much as I knew I should hate him, I wanted this.

I thought Ezra would walk away, leave Darius to do whatever the fuck he was about to do with me, but he stepped closer again, eyes darkening as his pupils dilated.

"We answered all your questions," he said, reaching out to run his hand down my stomach. I inhaled sharply as he reached my underwear, hooking his finger into the strap at my hip. "But you owe us these. You asked one too many, and didn't hold up your end of the deal."

Fuck. He was right, but I protested anyway. "Did not!"

It was a childish retort, and he laughed, easing the soaked fabric of my panties down my thighs, exposing me fully to them. Oh gods…

"Fuck," Darius cursed behind me, pinching my nipple between his thumb and forefinger. I yelped, squirming as pleasure shot straight to my clit. Fucking Hell, this was a terrible, terrible-

"She's fucking soaked," Ezra murmured, dropping the purple fabric in his hand onto the pile beside me. Darius groaned. "Show him, baby."

"What?" I gasped, though it came out breathless. Darius tightened his grip on my waist, rolling my nipple between his fingers again in a way that made my head spin.

"Spread those pretty thighs," Ezra demanded, gripping one thigh in a bruising grip. Slowly, I obeyed, knees shaking a little. Darius was practically holding me up as I leant against him, pressing my ass closer against his hard cock. "Good girl."

Fuck. I felt myself get wetter at his praise. His hand slid higher, and he slipped one finger through the centre of me, coating himself with the evidence of my desire. He held his hand up, showing Darius proof.

I was going to combust. This was slow, delicious torture. Ezra alone had been hot as Hell last night. Both of them, now?

It was almost too much.

"Fuck, little witch," Darius cursed again as he watched Ezra. I pressed against him further, grinding my ass on him until he groaned. "You have no idea the things I want to do to you."

I wanted it. I wanted it all. Both of them. Ezra grinned at the eagerness in my eyes.

"Get her on the sofa," he told Darius, shooting me another scalding hot look. I barely had time to wonder at their plan before I was scooped into Darius' arms and carried over to my couch, laid down gently on my back.

I tried to catch my breath, but I couldn't. The air was thick with desire and it was intoxicating as fuck. "Dare-" I said, reaching for the demon as he stood and surveyed my naked body. "Come here."

He narrowed his eyes at me, running his thumb over his bottom lip as his gaze settled on my pussy. I spread my legs for him teasingly, relishing in the way it made him groan. Still, he didn't move. "I think you've got it all backwards," he answered, smirking. "You're not in control any more, Rory."

Ezra came back into my line of sight, a grin spread across his face and the silver in his eyes slightly more pronounced.

The shifter's mouth was on mine before I could question anything, demanding. I kissed him greedily, grateful for the small amount of release it gave my pent up body. Ezra leaned over me, catching my lip between his teeth and fisting my hair in his hand. I moaned against him, trying to get closer, to ease this ache in any way possible.

"Poor little witch," Darius' voice cut through my lust fogged brain. I blinked as Ezra moved away from me, bringing the demon into view. "So empty."

I whined, not caring how needy I sounded. "Then fill me up, you asshole."

He laughed. "Careful."

"Or what?" I spat the words, my whole body on edge. If they'd wound me up just to leave me wet and needy, I was going to fucking kill them. Before I knew it, Darius' hand was around my throat, his body over mine, his eyes hard and mouth set in a harsh line. My pulse beat wildly under his palm as he squeezed, my body hot and sensitive under his touch.

"Or I'll make it hurt."

I fought to find the words to answer. "Maybe I want it to hurt."

He swore, flexing his fingers against my neck, before reaching between us and shoving two fingers inside me. I

141

cried out, though not in pain, already trying to grind against his hand.

"Gods, Rory," he said through gritted teeth, "so fucking wet."

"I'll feel better around your dick," I said, knowing I was pushing him, but so desperate to see what he'd do.

"I think you need something to keep your mouth busy," he answered darkly, and my eyes widened. He nodded over my shoulder, and I heard the unmistakable noise of jeans unfastening. I'd nearly forgotten Ezra was there. I sat up and immediately, Darius yanked me to the edge of the cushions.

Darius slid down my body so he knelt on the floor between my legs, forcing them further apart. His fingers moved lazily inside me, sparking pleasure in my blood, teasing me without ever getting me close to where I desperately needed to be.

"Open your mouth," he demanded, looking up from his hand to see if I obeyed him. I swallowed hard, wetting my lips before doing as he asked.

As soon as I did, Ezra was there, cock in his fist as he stroked it lazily. The sight heightened my need, and I clenched my fists at my side. He was long and thick, the tip already wet with precum. He was still dressed aside from the jeans and boxers he'd shoved down just enough to release his dick. There was something about me being the only one bare that drove me wild, the power they held over me enough to make me feel drunk. It should've scared me, but somehow I felt utterly secure in the knowledge that in this moment, neither of them would harm me.

"That's it, baby," he encouraged as he stepped closer, standing slightly to my right so I could reach him without Darius moving. "Wrap that mouth around me."

I did, eagerly, taking him as deep as I could and moaning

142

at the taste of him. He yanked me up slightly by my hair, adjusting the angle so he hit the back of my throat. I pulled back a little to drag my tongue across the underside of him before sucking softly on the head. He groaned, watching me, before losing patience and shoving my head down, his cock choking me. I took it though, swallowing around the invasion, loving the way he moaned at the feel of me.

I was so lost in him that I jumped when Darius' tongue met my clit. He gripped my hips and forced me to stay still as he repeated the motion, the warm flat of his tongue teasing me in torturous circles. I moaned around Ezra's dick, and his hand tightened in my hair. I faltered, pulling back to breathe.

Darius stopped, raising his head. "You stop, I stop, little witch."

My eyes widened. The last fucking thing I wanted was for him to stop when what he was doing felt so fucking good.

"You can have your orgasm when you take his cum down your throat."

Fuck. A fresh rush of arousal drowned me, and Darius grinned his approval as he dragged his finger through the wetness pooling under his gaze. I tried to press myself into his touch, aching for him to make me come as hard as I was sure he could. But he only narrowed his eyes at me. I got the message.

I turned back to Ezra and wrapped my mouth around him once more, dragging my tongue over the head of his dick and moaning when Darius returned to his task, sucking gently on my clit. He teased me as I teased Ezra, never giving me as much as I wanted.

I took Ezra deeper, bobbing my head on his length. He swore under his breath, his free hand joining the other in my hair. He took control, fucking my mouth with quick, brutal strokes. There was nothing I could do but take it, opening wider for him as he bumped the back of my throat. Saliva dripped down my chin, and I choked slightly, but he only increased his pace, winding my pleasure higher with his.

I moaned, eyes fluttering shut, when Darius dipped his tongue inside me, fucking me with it as Ezra fucked my mouth. I was burning, tension wound so tight inside me that it hurt, desperately needing release. I hollowed my cheeks around Ezra's cock, sucking him harder as his breathing became ragged and his thrusts less rhythmic. He was close, and I wanted him undone, his cum coating my tongue. My eyes pricked with tears as he shoved me down his length, the hot spurts of his release painting my throat as he groaned. He held me there, releasing me only when he was done. I swallowed, but as he withdrew, cum dripped from the corners of my mouth.

"What a mess," he said, voice low and ragged as he tried to catch his breath. I could only gasp, breathing deeply, tongue darting out to collect what I'd missed. He tilted my chin back, running his thumb over my bottom lip, gathering up the mess. He parted my lips, making me taste him on his thumb, and I sucked eagerly. "Good girl. So fucking good."

I gasped at his praise, then moaned as Darius returned his attention to my clit, slipping his fingers inside me. I was so wet now that I could feel it on my thighs. This time, he didn't tease. He ate me with single minded determination, his talented tongue demanding pleasure from me as he hooked his fingers inside me, thrusting deep and hard. My head fell back against the arm of the sofa, a choked cry escaping my swollen lips.

"Come for him, hellhound," Ezra said, sitting beside me and urging me to look at him. "Come all over his fucking tongue." As he spoke, Darius dragged his teeth over my clit, the bite of pain combined with the burning pleasure of his fingers shoved me over the edge. I came hard, back bowing off the sofa, eyes tight shut, pleasure drowning me in wave after wave.

Darius licked me slowly as I came down from my high, groaning against me. "Gods, little thief," he murmured, kissing the inside of my thigh. "I could get drunk on your taste."

If I'd had any energy left, I'd have urged him to do just that. But I was limp and gasping, unable to so much as keep my head up.

The door opened with a squeal, and we all froze. I was naked, legs still spread, the demon still crouched between them, Ezra cosied up to me, his cock still out and jeans shoved down.

The scent of lust was as heavy in the air as the shocked silence that surrounded us as Conan's voice cut through my post orgasm haze.

"What the fuck is happening?"

25

Ezra

"Put your fucking dick away."

I was fucked. Royally fucking fucked. Conan's glare was impossible to look away from, even as he was seething at me. I was already ahead of him, tucking myself back away. I wasn't sure whatever conversation we were about to have was going to be improved by my being half dressed.

Rory was still naked on the couch, face flushed and lips swollen, looking like sin. I'd planned to give her one of my shirts to wear after we were done with her. If I had to share her, I wanted her carrying my scent. My wolf needed it, needed the primal reassurance that whoever scented her would know she was ours. I hadn't had a second to give it to her, though, and Conan glanced at her, made a disgusted noise and then grabbed my arm, dragging me away from the scene.

The door slammed behind us as he dragged me outside, shoving me down the steps and advancing on me, breaths coming fast and heavy.

"What the *fuck* is wrong with you, Ezra?" He was burning

with rage, heat radiating off him even at my distance. Fuck this was worse than I thought. He rarely ever lost control of his powers like this.

"Conan, calm down," I urged, putting my hands up in mock surrender.

"Calm?" he practically growled, top lip pulled back in a sneer. "Fuck you, Ezra. Fuck this."

"What's that supposed to mean?"

"You're in there having a fucking threesome while I clean up blood?" I winced, but he continued without mercy. "You're sticking your dick in a girl we might turn over to the guards in a week. A girl literally planning to murder people. This is a *job*, Ezra!"

Anger flashed through me, and I strode up to him, shoving him back, ignoring the heat that singed my palms, even through his shirt. "We are not turning her in. We both know that."

"Do we?" His words were cruel and harsh.

"Yes!" I yelled, coming alive with frustration. How he could be so fucking unfeeling after what Rory had told us, I didn't understand. Once, he'd been free with his emotions, shy but caring. As we got older, started working, he closed himself off, though he was always different around me. But after everything happened with Yasmin, he shut down completely.

"I hope her cunt's worth it," he hissed, looking down at me with sheer loathing in his blue eyes. My heart twisted painfully in my chest.

"Don't fucking talk about her like that," I argued, feeling myself begin to fall apart. We didn't fight. Ever. Rory had been right. What the fuck was happening to us?

"You think I don't see how you fucking look at her?" he

shouted back, pointing at the house. "Like she hung the fucking sun in the sky. Tell me what the fuck that's about."

"So what, Conan? Am I not allowed to like someone?"

"No!" Then, quickly, "not her."

"Why? Because you've decided she's the villain? She's the *victim*, Cee," I tried to reason with him, desperate to fix this. I couldn't lose him. I'd lost everything else. He was supposed to stay. He was supposed to be permanent.

"Don't call me that."

Gods, this *hurt*. "Conan, come on, this is stupid! You've never cared who I fucked before!"

"Maybe I did!" His answer shocked me, and I frowned, floundering. "But this, *her*…this is low, even for you Ezra. We don't mix work and play." He spat the words like they were poison.

"Well maybe I'm sick of working!" My answer surprised both of us, but it was true. I was tired. "We have nothing else! No home, no family, nothing but work! We have money, Conan. What are we doing this for?"

"For him," he hissed under his breath, shaking his head. "For your fucking father, Ezra. To help people who can't do this! To give them answers, to make things right-"

"Don't bring my father into this," I snapped. I was too fragile for that now. It had been thirteen years, and the man responsible for his death was resting in pieces, but the loss was an ever open wound in me. "He wouldn't have wanted this for us."

"Well we can't always get what we want." There was something sharp in his statement, but I couldn't figure out what.

"What are we arguing for?" I asked, drained, confused,

fucking *scared* of what was happening with him. "'Cause I fucked someone?" He started to speak, but I cut him off. "Don't bullshit me, Conan. What the fuck is going on with you?"

He stared at me for a long moment, his chest rising and falling with quick breaths, still burning, his blue eyes bright, his jaw tense.

"I can't do this," he said, so quietly I almost missed it.

"Can't do what?"

"I'm done."

"Done?" I echoed, fear curdling my stomach. He couldn't leave. He wouldn't.

Right?

"You stay and get your dick wet," he spat, turning away from me and staring out at the forest. "I'll finish this job but I'm not staying here. I'm done, Ezra. This is the last one. Then this," he gestured between us, "is over. Since you're so fucking tired of it. I'll do us both a favour."

"You're not serious-" I called after him as he walked away. "CONAN!"

But he didn't so much as look over his shoulder at me.

"CONAN!" I screamed, feeling my control pull apart at the seams. I wanted to run after him, to grab him and make him see sense. But I was fucking frozen, watching my best friend walk away from me, from *us,* and disappear between the trees.

26

Ezra

"Don't you have a phone?" Rory was asking as I paced, shaking. She was dressed again, in her own damn clothes and the sight nearly tipped my wolf over the fucking edge.

"Burners," I told her through clenched teeth. "We change them every time. Too easy to track otherwise."

She frowned. "How do people get hold of you, then?"

"Magic," I said, voice blunt and dull. "Word of mouth. We answer ads sometimes, too. Online. Check websites looking for hired uh…help."

"Sure, *help*," she repeated slowly, blinking up at me. I couldn't decide if I wanted to scream at her or fuck her, punish her for breaking Conan and I apart. Except, it wasn't her fault, not really. I wasn't even sure it was mine.

Nothing fucking made sense. It never did when he wasn't around.

"Where the fuck is Darius?" I mumbled, staring at the front door. I'd stayed outside after Conan left, waiting for him to change his mind and come back. But he hadn't. At some point,

I found myself inside, numb and hollowed out, explaining what had happened in short, clipped bursts to Darius and Rory.

"He'll be back soon," she soothed, standing and running her hand down my arm. "It'll be fine, Ez. He'll come back."

"Don't call me that," I snapped, the ache inside me growing. She jumped back like I'd electrocuted her, expression shuttering. Guilt slammed into me, but I didn't reach for her. I didn't have it in me to comfort her right now.

Conan and I had never fucking fought like this. Not as children, not as grumpy teenagers. Not even after Yasmin.

What changed?

"If Darius doesn't find him, I can send him a message as long as we have something of his," she said softly, glancing at the closed door to the guest room. I nodded. I could shift and track him down myself but I was terrified of letting my wolf out right now. The animal was anxious, half fucking feral, taking all my strength to keep him contained.

I wasn't sure what he'd do if I let him out. Wasn't sure if he'd let me take back control.

And that was a risk I couldn't take. Not even for Conan.

"Maybe we should just let him go?" she asked slowly, shrugging. "He'll come back when he cools off."

Anger cut through the emptiness. "You don't know him. He never fucking does this. Something's *wrong*."

She frowned. "What did you fight about?"

I sighed, running a hand down my face. My wolf snapped at me inside my head, a low growl emanating from my chest. I swore, resuming my pacing just to have something to do. "He didn't want me fucking you."

She inhaled sharply. "I don't see why that's any of his

business."

I scoffed. "He didn't want it interfering with the job," I said, then shook my head. "He *didn't like the way I looked at you.* Whatever the fuck that means. I don't know, Rory. Maybe it's just you."

She didn't even respond to the dig, regardless of how low it was. Instead, her eyes widened and her mouth dropped open.

"Oh." She blinked at me, biting her bottom lip and scratching her arm absently. *"Oh."*

"What?" I snapped, needing to know what the fuck she thought she'd figured out.

The door slammed open before she could respond. It was clean now, thanks to Conan. The thought made my chest ache.

Darius stood in the doorway, lit by the afternoon sun, a grave expression on his face. His golden brown skin was covered in a thin sheen of sweat, and there was something on his hands -

I inhaled, the animal clawing at his cage inside my brain battering the fucking locks when I realised what it was.

Blood.

Conan's blood.

I had Darius' shirt in my grip before I even realised I was moving, slamming him against the wall so hard the door shook.

"What the fuck happened, demon?" I growled, barely retaining any form of control.

Darius, to his credit, didn't react, only holding his stained hand away from me. "He's gone, Ezra." He waited until I was finished shaking him to continue. "But the blood was fresh. Not much of it, either."

Rory appeared by my side, strapping something to her thigh. "Let him go, Ezra."

I obeyed mindlessly, tearing out the door as soon as the demon was on his feet again, shifting as I ran towards the trees.

There was no controlling the wolf now. Not when the only fucking person who'd mattered to us in ten years was in danger.

I would burn both fucking realms to ash to find him.

27

Conan

I t smelled like copper and rot.

The ground beneath me was soft and damp, and I was propped against something hard and rough - a tree trunk judging by the way the bark scraped my skin through my shirt. It was cold, a bitter breeze blowing my hair off my forehead and making what I assumed was undergrowth rustle.

I fought to open my eyes but was met with nothing but absolute darkness. My lashes scraped against something rough and scratchy, tied tight around my eyes. My hands, too, were tied together with some sort of binding, so tight I couldn't so much as twist my wrists. I tried to shift my feet, but they were bound.

I was getting really fucking sick of being knocked out and tied up.

A splitting pain shot through my skull, probably an effect of the blow I'd taken earlier, considering I couldn't sense anyone around me. I had no idea how much time had passed while I was unconscious, and the loss of control made me itch. My magic strained as I tipped my head back against the tree, reaching out with slow, sluggish tendrils of power to feel for any signs of life in the ground. There was nothing, not even a whisper, just an eerie emptiness about this place and the plant life that made my senses sharpen.

I wound my magic back in, finding nothing that would help me.

The anger I'd felt towards Ezra dissipated, leaving only a determined numbness in its place. I couldn't afford the messy emotions I'd been hurling around earlier to intervene now. No, I needed to be the cold hearted killer, the side of me that was all most people ever saw. Except him. A pang of guilt shot through the hollowness as I thought of him, and I tried to force it down. I'd been hurt earlier, a mess of raw emotion that became too big for me to control. I wanted to make him see it, see *me.* Instead, all I'd done was make him feel the hurt, too.

Fuck, I was a dick.

As soon as I figured out where I was, and made the place run red with the guts of whoever had shoved me here, I'd fix it. I'd fix us. The truth was clear to me now, alone and cold in the middle of fuck knows where.

I could run as far as I wanted, but nowhere would be worth anything without him.

The thought of actually saying any of this to him made me want to keep fucking running. But I wasn't a coward. We were already broken. Even if he never wanted to see me again after I told him, I could hardly get any fucking lower than I was now. I'd left. Fuck knew if he'd even want to see me when I made it back.

Clearly, whoever had taken me didn't know what I was. They wouldn't have bound me with anything other than iron if they did. Which meant that it wasn't the person from the woods. They'd know, if they'd seen me, what I could do. My current suspicion was that it had been one of Rory's tormentors, scouting to see if she'd left any avenues open for them. I'd tear them apart, too, if she didn't fucking kill them soon.

Shit, Ezra had been right. I was fucking sitting here planning the murder of men I'd never met. I couldn't be pissed at her for planning to torture the men who'd tortured her for so long.

I still didn't know how to feel about her. Whether the anger was a symptom of the feral fucking lust that I felt when I thought about punishing her for fucking Ez, or whether I just didn't know how to feel *need* for someone without the accompanying burning sensation of rage. I *was* pissed as fuck that she had him before I did. Not that it was her fault, but still. I'd felt nothing for anyone but him in years and seeing them together was like a dagger in my chest. I didn't understand what had happened between the three of them, Darius, Ezra, and Rory. Ezra didn't even share *food* well, never mind lovers. Darius seemed the kind of man to get off on that kind of shit, but Ez? His role confused me, even as it made an idea form in my mind. One that I definitely couldn't fucking entertain.

Gods, I was a mess in more ways than one.

My head pounded as I forced a steady breath into my lungs. There'd be time to sort through this shit later, after I got the fuck out of here. I strained to hear, but there was no sound - only the heavy sort of silence that seemed to swallow the very air from the area.

But I couldn't sense anyone there. No scent or sound of my captor.

I didn't even get a fucking glance at them before they'd smacked me hard over the head in the woods, the cold kiss of what felt suspiciously like a heavy metal bat meeting my skull with such force I'd nearly vomited.

And the next thing I knew, I was here.

I'd let my guard down so far after all the shit with Ezra that I couldn't even blame anyone but myself. But I'd bathe my frustrations in blood before I took them back to the cottage and ruined everything even more.

I waited for a few more breaths, ensuring nobody had entered, before calling the fire to the surface. The smell of burning rope filled the air, combining with the horrible metallic smell still lingering and making me scrunch my nose.

The second my hands were free, I wrenched the fabric off my eyes and squinted. It was dark but hair thin strands of silvery light fought their way through the thick branches above me, giving me just enough brightness to see if I focused hard.

I reached for the rope around my ankles, heating my hands to burn it away as I inspected the clearing. I was placed on the edge of a circle of trees, the top of their branches bent together to create a ceiling of orange and brown leaves, like a little room in the middle of the woods.

I was alone, although there was a small pile of *something* set in the middle of the circle. I tore the rope away from my legs and rose to my feet slowly, my bones aching with the movement. Gods, the fucker had hit *hard*. My instincts screamed at me to hide myself, but I was drained as it was, and I couldn't afford to waste resources making myself invisible if I wanted to find my way back to Ezra. Exhaustion was a cold hand on the back of my neck, weighing me down as I crept towards the centre. It was too fucking quiet and I held my breath, a familiar feeling of dread making the hairs on the back of my neck stand on end.

Why the fuck was there no one else here? And where the fuck was I? What the fuck -

"Shit," I muttered lowly, frowning as I stared down at the mess in front of me.

The bouquet of red and white roses was neatly arranged, the petals spattered with dark, crimson liquid.

In the centre of the flowers, laid out like an offering, was a still bleeding heart.

28

Rory

We'd been looking for two hours.

My legs felt leaden from running, and sweat was dripping down my back. I slowed, cursing under my ragged breath, and Darius paused at my side. Ezra had fucked off miles ago, his huge paws leaving tracks in the damp soil that we'd followed since. The wolf he'd become was massive - with deep grey fur and teeth the size of my fucking palm. A ridiculous part of me wanted to run my hands through his fur and see if it was as soft as it looked, to tame his wolf from the wild thing he'd become.

But the only person that could do that now was Conan. And as much as I hated the bastard, it didn't mean I wanted to see him dead. At least, not before I killed him for being such an asshole.

"Shit," Darius cursed, running a hand through his dark, messy hair. "This is a mess."

I nodded my agreement, searching the trees for any sign of the wolf. He'd caught a scent neither Darius or I could pick up, and now both of us were lost in the middle of the forest trying to ignore the awkward, unspoken thing hanging between us.

What the fuck did one say to a near stranger who'd just eaten her out while another guy came down her throat?

Thanks?

"No shit," I answered, forcing my mind back on task. It was clear to me, now, what Conan's fucking problem was. Once we'd established he wasn't actually dead, I'd confront him about it. Although I'd need to lock the front door first so he couldn't fucking run away again.

I hadn't had him pegged as a coward. I found a part of myself disappointed in him. Which was ridiculous. I didn't give a fuck about him.

I was a terrible liar. I hated him, with a fire that threatened to burn me, but *fuck* did he have to look so damn good? Apparently two men at once wasn't enough for me.

"Greedy fucking bitch," I swore at myself, suddenly disgusted with what I'd done. What the hell had I been thinking? I should be focused on making sure I had all the shit I needed for the spell, finally ridding the world, and myself, of the horrible fucking cunts that had tortured me and countless other girls for Hell knew how long.

Instead, I was out searching for an asshole in a forest.

"What the fuck did you just say?" Darius was painfully still, eyes narrowed at me. I turned to him, gritting my teeth. Every time I looked at him, my body remembered what he'd done. How he'd made me come so hard I'd seen stars.

"Nothing."

Before he could question me again, I grabbed the dagger out of the holster I'd strapped to my thigh - the dark leather older than I was - and unwound the scrap tied to the hilt. With the blade, I drew a thin line across my palm, barely noticing the sting of pain, and squeezed it onto the strip I'd torn from Conan's shirt.

"What are you doing?" Darius probed, standing so close to me our shoulders brushed. The innocent contact sent a thrill to me and I wanted to punch him for it. I shouldn't be reacting to him like that, to anyone like that.

I didn't get attached. That was the rule.

"Finding him myself," I answered, squeezing the cloth in my bloodied hand and strapping the dagger back in its sheath. Quietly, I recited the words to the tracking spell I'd memorised in a rush, careful not to trip over any of the words and cause a fucking disaster.

"Why did you need to cut yourself for that?" Darius asked, a hint of anger in his tone. I steeled myself, annoyed at him for interrupting me. I finished my incantation, then turned to him, shoving the bloody strip of t-shirt into my pocket.

"Dark magic always requires a sacrifice," I answered, a bite to my tone that made him flinch. "Bigger the spell, bigger the sacrifice."

"Hence the heart in your shed?" he guessed, tone flat. I only smirked in response as magic washed over me, sending a rush through my bloodstream. I always felt more alive like this.

A soft, insistent tug yanked me forward, like a hand around my wrist. I took off, Darius close by, not even sounding out of breath, the bastard. We ran through the trees, dodging branches and fallen logs, Darius grunting under his breath when he tripped and narrowly avoided falling into the thick trunk of a tree.

The tug stopped abruptly as we approached a wall of closely connected trees, their branches entwined like lovers.

It was beautiful, in an unsettling, alarming way.

161

Darius crashed into me, grabbing my waist to steady me. I inhaled sharply, the sudden contact sending sparks of electricity along my skin despite the fact I could scent blood in the air when I breathed in, mixed with the heady scent of the demon holding me.

I pulled away quickly, noticing a gap in the trunks.

"Rory..." Darius called after me, trepidation in his voice. I ignored him, dread bubbling up in my stomach as I approached the tear in the boundary, clear claw marks dug deep into the trunks.

"Ezra," I murmured, stomach twisting as I ducked inside, instinct urging me to turn around again. "Ezra!"

The wolf was crouched in the middle of the clearing, a deep growl emanating from his chest. Conan stood beside him, the animal so tall his head was level with the man's chest, whose pale skin was so light he looked like a ghost. It was dark inside the dome, tiny shafts of moonlight filtering through the gaps in the dying leaves.

Both men were staring at something glistening on the ground before them. I approached slowly, giving both of them space, sensing the tense, heated air between them. When I got close enough to see what it was, I gasped, backing away quickly. Darius caught me, tucking him close to him. This time I didn't object, leaning into his warmth and letting him steady me.

"Red and white roses," he murmured under his breath, pushing me behind him slightly as he knelt beside the bloody flowers. "Oh fuck."

The heart at the centre of them was fresh, the blood only just beginning to congeal in the cold night air. I grimaced, though the sight wasn't exactly new to me. It was the careful,

162

almost loving way the display had been arranged that chilled me.

"Darius." I grabbed his arm, but he didn't turn away from the organ. "What does that mean?"

Conan didn't say a word, but his gaze was entirely trained on Ezra now, as the wolf bared his teeth at the bouquet.

"We need to leave," he answered, his voice tense and strained. "Now. We need to get the fuck out of here."

My heart kicked up a gear as a chill swept over my skin at the sheer urgency in his voice as he rose, grabbing me and pulling me away. I resisted, looking back at the display, confusion and horror rolling over me in thick waves.

"Conan, Ezra," he shouted, urgency enveloping us. "Move!"

Conan's gaze snapped up, narrowing on Darius. The wolf didn't budge, the low growl filling the air again.

"Ezra!" I tried, moving towards him. Darius snatched me back, his grip a vice around me. The wolf didn't move an inch.

"Conan," Darius tried, his grip on me tightening. My breath was shaky, his panic clouding the air. I had no fucking idea what was going on, but I didn't like any of it. The familiar low buzz of fear began echoing in my head. "We have to go." He slowed his speech this time, trying to break through. Conan looked exhausted, crusted blood matting the hair on the back of his head. For the first time since I'd met him, he wasn't a force of will, a violent promise wrapped in a beautiful, deadly package.

He was just a man.

Slowly, Conan raised his hand, sinking it into the fur at the wolf's neck. The animal turned, finally, his lip still pulled back to expose his long canines. I watched, unable to tear myself away, as he ran his hand down his back in long, soothing strokes. He murmured something under his breath that we were too far away to hear, but it made Ezra's ears prick up and his hackles drop.

Finally, he nodded, raising his eyes to us again and approaching with long, measured strides. Conan spared me a weighted look, his gaze dark and a little sad, but he walked past me before I could figure out what it meant.

Darius breathed a heavy sigh of relief, pushing me in front of him and ushering us out. Ezra followed closely, brushing my leg as he bounded past in chase of Conan.

"Dare," I tried again, hissing to him as I sprinted beside him to keep up with his pace. His legs were far longer than mine, and though I knew he must be as tired as I was, he moved like he was being chased. *"Dare."*

"What?" he snapped and I reeled back, confused.

"What do the roses mean?" I pushed again, needing to know what the Hell we were running away from.

For a minute, there was nothing but the sound of our breaths and the steady thump of Ezra's paws. Conan was leaning against him now, the animal strong beneath his grip.

Finally, Darius relented, a pained expression crossing his golden features.

"Death."

29

Ezra

The wolf wouldn't let go.

Conan was lying in bed, his face grey and eyes heavy. He didn't seem to be hurt, aside from the head injury, and he wouldn't move his eyes from me. I wrestled the animal for control, but he was determined, curled up on the floor beside his bed, needing to reassure himself that Conan was okay.

He'd gone fucking rogue the second he'd scented his blood. I didn't try to stop him. I was faster in this form, stronger, my senses heightened. The wolf didn't understand why Conan had left, or why I was upset with him, begging me to nuzzle up to him and breathe in the comforting scent of him. Except, he still smelled like blood, and it was driving both my wolf and me insane.

"Ez," Conan's voice cut through my thoughts. "Come back."

The wolf let out a low growl of displeasure at being told to retreat. I doubted he'd let me back out until Conan smelled okay again, with no scent of fear or blood lingering on him. Conan sighed, running his hand over his face.

"Come on, I need to talk to him," he coaxed the wolf, eyes pleading. Gone was the man who'd screamed at me earlier, who'd told me he was done. My heart ached, a low whine escaping the wolf's jaws as he felt it, too.

"Okay, fine," he relented, sitting up and wincing at the movement. "I know you're listening, Ezra. I'm sorry."

He'd said it in the clearing, whispering it to me like it was reverent. *I'm so sorry*. Conan didn't apologise to anyone, for anything, and I didn't know why he was doing it now.

"I'm not leaving," he continued, looking as though the words were causing him pain. His voice dropped when he spoke again, his eyes lowering to bore into mine. The wolf sat up, sensing the shift in the mood. I waited, straining at the reins, feeling the wolf soften slightly. "I'm never leaving."

Fuck. My heart shuddered in my chest. There was an aching vulnerability in his voice that I'd never heard before, and it was tearing me apart. I didn't know what he was saying, only that it hurt in the best way.

"I can't have this conversation with your wolf," he sighed, shaking his head even as his lips quirked up slightly. He reached out, scratching the animal between the ears. The wolf relaxed, our body growing less tense and worried under Conan's touch. My wolf sniffed the air pointedly, the best communication possible without vocal chords, and Conan huffed a laugh. "The blood, huh?" A low noise of affirmation echoed from my wolf's chest and Conan rose, snatching a towel off his bed and exiting the room. Without hesitation, the wolf padded after him, unwilling to leave his side.

Conan glanced down as we reached the bathroom, frowning but not stopping the animal as he barged inside after him. The wolf was beyond listening to me, and I sat back, hoping it wouldn't be long before the blood was down the drain and the animal retreated.

Conan turned away, hanging his towel on the back of the door and reaching into the walk in shower to flip the water on. Steam immediately began filling the room, the sound of rushing water bouncing off tiles filling the air. Conan stripped quickly, and I was suddenly very glad to be hidden by the body of the wolf.

He disappeared behind the glass door, so only the outline of him was visible, blurred slightly by the steam on the glass.

In minutes, the blood was swept down the drain, replaced by the soft scent of soap and clean skin.

My animal retreated fast, and I snapped back into my body, groaning at the quick shift that made my bones ache.

Suddenly, I was hyper aware that I was naked on the floor of the bathroom while Conan showered. We'd seen each other naked before, but this was different. This felt intimate.

My heartbeat was loud in my ears, my heart ricocheting off my ribcage. *Why the fuck am I nervous to talk to my best friend?*

"Conan?" I ventured, grabbing his towel off the door to cover myself with. Somehow, that made it more awkward, like I was acknowledging this unspoken thing in the air. "Uh, I'll leave you to shower. Sorry."

I reached the door, hand on the cold metal handle, when his voice met my ears.

"Stay."

I froze, breaths hard and fast. *What?*

"Don't you need to shower?"

What the fuck was happening. And why the fuck wasn't I saying no?

"Uh, yeah, I guess," I answered, voice thick as I tried to keep

167

it steady. I *did* need to shower - my skin was sticky with sweat and dirt - but he couldn't be implying what I thought he was…

"So stay," he said again, and I turned around, finding him peering round the glass pane to meet my eyes. His own were dark, his lashes wet with water, hair sticking to his forehead. It did something to my heart that I was not prepared to process.

"You want me to shower…" I asked slowly, desperately hoping I wasn't misreading this situation. "With you?"

"Is that a problem?"

Fuck fuck fuck. "No?" It came out as a question but the thought of it set me skin alight. Slowly, I dropped the towel, replacing it on the door and ensuring it was locked. I waited until he was under the heavy stream of water again before I turned, begging my body not to embarrass me. Conan had always been attractive. No, that was wrong. He'd always been devastating. I'd have to be blind not to notice. But I'd never stepped over that line, never crossed the invisible boundary that kept our friendship intact.

Slowly, I stepped onto the tile, holding my breath as I took him in. I kept my gaze trained on his face, body tense as I watched him tilt his head back to rinse his hair out.

"Conan, what is this?" The question escaped my mouth before I'd even thought about it. But I needed to know. My emotions had been fucked around enough today.

He ran his hands through his hair, slicking it back from his face and opening his eyes. Slowly, purposefully, he dragged his gaze over every inch of me, my skin tingling under his inspection. His breathing sped up, hands flexing at his sides.

"This is me not being a coward."

"What-"

My back was to the tile before I could finish my thought,

168

his hand around my throat, eyes focused on mine. My breath *whooshed* out of me, arousal heating my blood, my cock hardening between us. Hell below...

His mouth crashed against mine, hard and unforgiving. I froze, shock holding me still, until he caught my bottom lip between his teeth and bit down, *hard.* I gasped at the pain. He took the opportunity to slip his tongue between my teeth, tangling with mine. I groaned, meeting his lips, losing any ability I had to deny this. Gods, he kissed like a starving man. All teeth and tongue and intent. His fingers flexed against my pulse, a low noise of satisfaction in his chest.

"Fuck, Ez," he murmured, trailing hot, open mouthed kisses down my neck as I fought to gain any form of composure.

"Conan," I tried, but his name came out broken. Tears streamed from my eyes, mixing with the water as I rested my head against the tile, revelling in the way his lips felt against me. I was on fire as he moved his hand down my chest, his other pressed against the wall, trapping me between him and it.

He glanced up at me, nipping the crook between my neck and my shoulder with his teeth. I moaned, hot arousal pouring through me.

"Are you crying?" he asked quietly, frowning, concern bright in his eyes. "Do you want me to stop?" But he didn't move away, didn't so much as pull his lips from my skin. His kisses softened though, gentle and soft on my shoulder. It only made me cry more, chest shuddering beneath his touch.

"No." I wasn't sure of fucking anything right now except if he stopped touching me, I might die.

"Talk to me," he asked, stroking his thumb over my collarbone.

"I don't understand," I admitted, the words breathless and quiet.

"How can I make it more clear?" he said, sounding confused as he pulled back to look at me. I watched in awe as he sank to his knees before me. "Does this help?"

I was dying. That was the only explanation for the frantic pounding of my heart in my chest, and the unbearable *need* coursing through me.

The image of Rory flashed through my mind, but I didn't have it in me to feel guilt. Considering the way she'd shared Darius and I earlier, something told me she wouldn't object to this. Not that I should care. But I did.

Fuck, I did. I cared. About her. About him.

And I wasn't sure I'd ever seen anything as holy as Conan on his knees.

"Conan," I gasped, his name the only sound I was currently capable of making. He waited, stroking burning trails up the inside of my thigh, not enough to cool the ache, only drive it higher.

"Ezra," he said, voice gravelly. "I won't ask again." His tone took on a demanding tone, sending a thrill through me. "Does this make it clear?" To punctuate his question, he leant forward, opening his mouth and dragging the flat of his tongue along the length of my cock.

"*Fuck*," I hissed, cock twitching, the feel of his tongue driving me insane. He didn't repeat the motion, simply sitting back on his heels as he waited. Even on his knees, he was in control.

"Use your words," he urged, voice dark and dangerous. I shuddered, fighting for control over my own body.

"Yes," I bit out, desperate for him to give me what I knew we both wanted. Needed.

"Good."

His mouth closed around me, and I cursed, hand flying to his hair and tangling in the wet locks. He groaned, teasing the head of my cock with slow flicks of his tongue. I bucked my hips, needing more, needing *him.*

Without warning, he gripped my hip and took me deep in his throat, swallowing around me. I moaned, helpless to the bliss he was torturing me with.

He groaned around me, his own dick hard as steel as he sucked me. I itched to touch him, taste him, unravel him completely until I got to the centre of his feelings.

Conan wasn't the kind of man to talk. His fucking motto had always been *actions speak louder.*

And his actions were loud as fuck.

I never wanted him silent again.

30

Conan

I had been in love with Ezra Hutton since I was seventeen. The day I realised, we were covered in blood and dirt. A dead man lay between us, a hole in his chest and the scent of charred flesh heavy in the air. It was our third job, our second kill, and the first time I identified the hammering in my chest that had begun to happen whenever he turned those dark eyes on me.

It was also the day I resigned myself to never fucking telling him. To never upset the steady balance of trust and friendship between us.

We cleaned up the body, shoving it into a black bag and driving it to the farm with the pen of pigs that were far fatter now than the first time we'd seen them. We both knew the owner was dodgy as fuck, doing Hell only knew what and disposing of the evidence the same way we did. But he let us use his animals, so we didn't care.

I washed the evidence from the ground, summoning water from deep in the soil to drain away the stain of blood. When we got back to the shitty, dirty motel - the only room we could afford after using the pay from our first job to cut all ties from our previous life - I turned to Ezra, taking in the messy cut of his hair, the dark circles under his eyes, the small spatter of scarlet across the dark skin of his arm.

"Are you scared?" I'd asked him. The killing didn't haunt me the way I thought it did him. I felt nothing but a calm sense of justice after burying the bastards we were hired to dispose of, knowing the heinous crimes they'd committed. A part of me had always craved violence, the tinge of blood, the hopeless, choking begging of a person knowing they're about to die.

But Ezra had always been softer than me. I wanted to protect him from it all, despite the fact that this had all started with him. I didn't want to watch the spark in his eyes dim. I didn't think I could survive that.

"No," he said, turning to me, a smile on his lips that spoke nothing of the horror we'd just committed. "Why would I be scared? I have you."

That was the exact fucking second I decided that he'd always have me. And yet, just hours ago, I'd broken that silent promise, smashing apart all that trust in fear. *Fear.* I hadn't felt scared in years.

This man could ruin me.

I didn't think I'd mind as long as it meant I got to hold him while he did it.

I looked up at him, resisting the urge to take him the way I craved - hand around his throat, bent over the nearest available surface, claiming him until he forgot everything but my name. I wanted to mark him, make him beg for me, submit for me.

But I knew that would be too much, too soon. And after the

shit show of a day we'd had, I couldn't handle anything else going wrong.

I pulled back a little, savouring the taste of him on my tongue before I took him deep again, satisfaction fuelling me as he groaned and squeezed his eyes shut. It was like he couldn't help himself, the way his hand flew to my head, fingers tight in my hair. It hurt, the pressure on the now nearly healed wound, but the pain did nothing but drive me on. He tried to shove me back down again, bucking his hips against me, and I smirked around his dick before pulling back.

"You seem to be under the illusion that you have control here," I murmured, shaking my head. "Rory might submit to you, let you do what you want. But I won't. Make no mistake, Ezra. You're *mine.*"

He made as if to protest, eyes wide, and I shut him up by choking on his dick. I was under no illusions that we needed to actually talk about this, about us, about *her,* but now all I wanted to focus on was making him fall apart for me.

"Fuck, Cee," Ezra gasped, fighting to keep still as I held him in place, grip tightening on his hip. "*Fuck.* Don't stop."

As if I could. I was fucking addicted to the ragged breaths flying from his parted lips, the barely restrained groans rumbling in his throat, the taste of him driving me insane.

"Conan..." he moaned, voice dark and desperate. I thought I could've come from the sound of my name on his tongue alone. I knew he was close, and I chased his orgasm with him until he shattered, filling my throat.

I swallowed, cleaned the remnants of his release off his length with my tongue, then stood, facing him. He was breathing heavily, staring at me like he'd never fucking seen me before. Like, finally, after all these years, he'd opened his eyes.

"Ez," I mumbled, reaching for him. I grasped the back of his neck and sealed our mouths together so he could taste himself on my lips, relishing in the way he opened so easily for me now, kissed me back with hungry abandon. I was so fucking turned on it hurt and when he slid his hand between, wrapping it around my hard cock, I swore. He stroked his fist up and down my length, nipping my bottom lip between his teeth and soothing the sting with his tongue. I wasn't going to last. Not when I could still taste him, not when, after all these fucking years, he was finally touching me. His lips trailed down my neck, canines scraping across my skin.

"Shit," he mumbled against me, grip on me tightening.

"What?" I was shocked I managed to speak at all, pleasure clouding my mind.

"I want to bite you."

Fuck. Hot lust shot straight to my dick and I groaned.

"Then bite me," I urged, angling my neck. I wanted his teeth, his soft brand of violence, every fucking part of him.

"No, Conan," he said softly, his breath hot against my neck as his hand worked faster, driving me rapidly towards the edge. "I want to *bite you.*" The tension in his voice was clear, like he was fighting something within himself.

Finally, I understood what he meant. He wanted to claim me. *Bond* me. Fucking shifter. The idea should have had me running for the hills but instead, all I could feel was red hot *want.* I wanted to be irreparably his, I wanted the bond, I wanted to fucking own him.

But he'd regret it. I knew, without voicing it, that this was pure instinct riding him. Years of pent up emotion and tension uncoiling messily between us. The second he was down from

175

this high, he'd regret it.

I didn't want him to regret me.

"Soon, love," I promised him, leaning into his touch and closing my mouth over the pulse on his neck. A mock bite, a placeholder, a test. I bit down, sucking, until I tasted blood. He pulled me closer, his body pressed close to mine, the feel of him against me too much to bear. I came violently, head pressed against his shoulder, breath escaping my lungs as pleasure took over my body. He groaned at the reaction, easing me through the orgasm until we were both wrung out and silent.

Reluctantly, I pulled away from him, the sight of my release coating his stomach sending pure satisfaction through me. He opened his mouth to speak but I pressed a soft kiss to his lips, shutting him up, and encouraged him under the spray. The water was hot and he hissed slightly as it met his skin.

I washed him reverently, memorising every line of his body, every scar I'd seen before, vowing to trace every inch of him with my tongue. He let me, watching me with hooded eyes glued to my hands as I swept soap over his skin.

Eventually, the water was turned off, and we exited, Ezra leaving with the towel wrapped around his waist to retrieve another for me.

Maybe I could avoid admitting my cowardice and just suck his dick until he fell for me. The thought of telling him how I'd felt for ten years made my teeth grind together. Surely, he understood after what had just happened.

The bathroom door swung open again and I turned, expecting to find him with a spare towel in hand.

Instead, Rory stood in the doorway, lips parted in shock.

31

Rory

Conan was naked.

Very naked. And for some stupid fucking reason I couldn't look away.

The room was warm and steamy, water droplets clinging to his skin, flushed from the heat, and dripping from his hair. His body was lean but muscular, the soft hint of abs on his stomach practically fucking begging me to run my hands over. My mouth went dry when my gaze trailed down. He didn't even try to cover himself, just watched me, eyes hard and head cocked like he was surveying prey.

Heat pooled in my core under that gaze. I chastised myself, hating the way it affected me. Hating *him* for turning my body against me.

"What are you doing, princess?" His voice was dark and rough. I blinked, forcing my eyes back to his.

I cleared my throat. "I didn't realise you were in here." I'd only come in to grab the hairbrush I'd left on the counter, intending to head to the bathroom attached to my bedroom to shower there. I'd seen Ezra exit, so jumped in - "Oh fuck."

He raised a dark brow at me, watching me reel back a little in surprise. I recovered quickly, a short laugh bursting from my lips. "In my shower, really?" I joked, covering my mouth with my hand so he couldn't see my grin.

"Why, never tried it?" he shot back, leaning against the counter, shamelessly showing off his body. I refused to give him the satisfaction of lowering my gaze again.

"Oh, honey," I drawled sarcastically, fighting for composure. "You think you're the first person to fuck in here? I was bent over that counter months ago when you were still pining over Ezra pretending you didn't want to fuck him."

He glowered at me, though I saw his fingers tighten on the edge of the grey counter top.

"How long?" I asked, tilting my chin back in defiance. It had hit me with the force of a truck earlier when Ezra had relayed their fight to me. It was obvious, painfully so, and I had no idea how he hadn't noticed by now. Honestly, I was almost relieved they'd finally fucked. Although, a sting of bitterness hit me when I imagined them together. Had I lost Ezra before I even fucking had him? What the fuck was I thinking? I didn't want to *have* him. I didn't want any of them.

Liar.

"What?"

"How long have you wanted him?" I asked. He only shook his head and tutted, tongue clicking against his teeth.

"Rory?"

I jumped as Ezra entered, a towel tied around his waist, another in his hand. My eyes darted between them, wide and startled. Stuck between them, in a room that still smelled faintly of soap and sex, while they were both fucking naked, was causing havoc on my heart.

178

"I can explain-" Ezra started, but I turned to him and shook my head.

"You don't need to," I said, forcing a smile onto my face. "We're not together or anything. I'm glad you worked it out between you two."

I turned before this situation could fuck with me any more, knocking Ezra's shoulder with mine as I retreated, forgetting about the stupid hairbrush as I darted into my bedroom.

Only to find the third of my fucking problems waiting on the bed.

"Fuck off, Dare," I said immediately, patience thin as fuck. I was exhausted after searching for Conan for bloody hours, not to mention the image of the blood soaked flowers burned into my brain. And however the fuck Darius knew what the colours meant.

"Sit, little thief," he insisted, patting the bed beside him. I stiffened, blood simmering at his tone.

"No. Please leave."

"We both know I won't."

Frustration bolted through me. Today was beginning to wear me down to nothing. I didn't even want to think about the shit with Ezra and Conan. I was happy for them. I was. So why did it feel like someone had punched me in the gut?

"Little thief," Darius soothed, standing and reaching for me. I was trapped between him and the door, unable to turn and run without meeting the others in the hall. "Tell me how to help."

"I don't need your fucking help!" I screamed, unable to contain it any longer. "I don't need *any of you to fucking help me!* Do you hear me? I finally, finally, had a fucking shot at fixing everything! And then you all came and fucked it up!

179

Just leave me alone."

"Ro-"

"No, Darius! I didn't ask for any of you. I don't want any of you. I just want my fucking revenge. I just want *peace.*"

He stepped closer to me, eyes soft, hands open at his sides as if surrendering. "Don't lie to me, little thief."

"I'm not fucking lying, you asshole."

"Did you forget what I am?" His laugh was humourless. I tensed. "I could pluck the truths from that pretty little mind with three words if I wanted to."

"You can't," I reminded him.

"You know what I think?" He grinned, biting his lower lip. "I think you wish I would. I think you're begging for someone to take the control out of your hands. To quiet all the noise."

I wasn't breathing. I didn't want to acknowledge his words, or the cutting, raw truth of them.

"Let me," he said smoothly, reaching out to tug on a strand of my hair.

"No." My voice trembled as I fought to swallow the emotion in my throat.

"Tell me what's wrong."

"You already know."

"Ezra?" He asked. My silence was answer enough. "There's more."

There was. So much more. These men were ruining me, tearing me apart piece by piece. I wanted them in my bed as badly as I wanted them gone. I wanted Darius to follow through on his threat. I wanted him to take the weight of it all, to see the dark, haunted parts of me and want me anyway.

I wanted him to erase the memory of Ezra's hands on me, his cock inside me. I wanted to not feel this sick, stupid jealousy at the thought of him and Conan. I wanted to be wanted, to be someone's first fucking choice.

I wanted to not feel as broken as I always did.

"Dare." His name was a soft, begging sound falling from my lips. His arms were around me in a second, wrapping me in his warm embrace. I wouldn't cry. Not in front of him.

"Don't be scared," he whispered, taking a deep breath as he ran his hand up and down my spine in soothing strokes.

Seconds later, the oddest sensation of someone prodding inside my mind surprised me. It wasn't *unpleasant* and felt distinctly like Darius, but I still recoiled, instinctively trying to distance myself. But he held me tight as his magic curled around my thoughts, as if asking for entrance.

Before I could second guess myself, I let him in. I was exhausted. And maybe it was ignorant and misplaced, but I trusted him.

I hoped to all the false gods that he didn't make me regret it.

Slowly, I let him see the hurt, not all of it, but enough. Let him feel the confusion and hurt and bone deep anger. Let him see the fucked up things I craved to escape the Hell of my memories, to feel at home in my body again. Things I knew I shouldn't want. Things I wanted, anyway.

I watched his face go from curious to heated, his eyes narrowing.

The tendrils shaped like him retreated and my mind felt empty in his absence. For a minute, neither of us so much as breathed too loudly. I was still clutched to his chest, his grip on me tight. I didn't want to admit how much I liked the contact. Somehow, it felt more intimate than when his tongue had been inside me.

Fuck, now I was thinking about his tongue inside me.

181

"Go shower," he said softly, kissing my hair and releasing me. Shocked, I stumbled back.

"Oh," I muttered, the hurt like a knife in my chest. This is what I was scared of. He was disgusted, no longer interested in the fucked up girl he'd accidentally got involved with. I clenched my jaw and turned. "Right."

Loneliness crept into my chest as I closed the door to my bathroom behind me. Tears stung the back of my eyes, threatening to spill. An ache bloomed beneath my ribs as I stumbled to the shower and turned it on. I blinked, clearing my blurry vision, seeing flashes of blood and green eyes every time my eyes closed. My stomach turned. I didn't want to think of Eryx. Of his hands and his teeth and his touch.

I showered quickly, rebuilding myself as I did. I wasn't that girl any more. Wasn't scared or weak or relying on men.

I was the only person I could rely on.

32

Rory

I expected the room to be empty when I reappeared. Exhaustion weighed me down, and I stumbled, swearing under my breath as I caught myself on the edge of the doorway. Maybe I'd get lucky and wake up to an empty house.

Apparently I couldn't even get my own room to myself.

Darius was perched on the edge of my bed, toeing the floorboard that hid the grimoire. I watched him, his light brown skin glowing under the stream of moonlight entering the room. His dark hair was tousled around his shoulders, his golden gaze fixed on the board. He was fucking stunning.

He looked up, hearing me enter, and watched as I closed the curtains, plunging the room into darkness and shutting out any prying eyes. Silence stretched between us as I met his gaze.

"I just want to sleep, Darius," I mumbled, sighing. I'd dressed in my usual pyjamas - Grace's old t-shirt and silky shorts. My hair was wet, and I shivered in the cold air, crossing my arms over my chest and tucking my hands under my arms.

"Come sleep then," he answered smoothly, standing and

pulling the duvet back. I stared at him, unmoving. "Do you want to be alone, Rory? Really?"

I knew he knew the answer. He'd seen. I was too tired to argue.

I was really fucking tired of being alone.

"No," I whispered, swallowing the lump in my throat. I crossed to the bed quietly, crawling onto the mattress and slipping under the duvet. He must have left at some point, because he was dressed in loose fitting cotton joggers, and stripped his t-shirt off before he climbed in beside me. "What are you doing?" I asked as he grabbed me and tugged me towards him, my back pressed flush against his chest, my ass against his crotch. He was hard, but made no move to do anything about it.

"Being here," he said simply, sweeping the damp locks of hair off my back and high onto the pillow so he could get closer to me, his lips pressing softly against my neck. I fought the urge to shiver at the closeness.

I wanted to pull away, to put distance between us, to make the smart choice and leave, now, before this could get any worse.

But I couldn't. He was warm and drawing soft circles with the pad of his thumb on my stomach as he held me close.

"I don't want to-"

"That's not what this is, little thief," he soothed, tugging the duvet closer around us to trap out the chill. I breathed a slow sigh, the tension in my muscles relaxing as his warmth seeped into me. I wanted to hate this, hate him, but fuck it was so *nice* to just be held. "Just sleep."

"I can't," I answered, tensing again. Sleep usually came after long hours of rolling back and forth trying to convince my body that we were safe. It had been years since I got out, but the memories alone were enough to wake me screaming in the middle of the night. Occasionally, I spelled myself so I'd sleep, but that didn't feel safe now. Sometimes, Grace would stay over and play with my hair, hum lullabies in her soft, warm voice until I fell asleep. I had a sneaking suspicion that she'd left her shirt here on purpose, knowing I needed the comfort. She was the only person I'd allowed myself to trust since Eryx and his brothers.

"Why?"

"I don't want to talk about it," I mumbled, shuffling further against him, seeking the comfort of his body. "You can sleep though."

"Let me help," he offered, turning me over to face him. It was dark, but I could make out the soft pinch between his brows, the worry in his eyes. My heart clenched.

"You don't have to."

"I want to," he argued, slipping his hand around my waist, the other coming up to cup the back of my head. "Close your eyes."

I obeyed mindlessly. It's not like he could make anything any fucking worse. The odd, comforting feel of him in my mind returned, like nails dragging down my spine - not uncomfortable, but slightly sharp.

Slowly, he faded the memories to black. The memory of sharp teeth and laughter, of raw bleeding, of bitten tongues and clenched fists, silenced and pushed to the back of my mind.

My breathing softened as my mind emptied, Darius plucking the horrors from my brain one by one until I couldn't hear them any more.

For the first time in six years, I fell asleep with ease.

I woke up alone.

I washed the bitter taste of disappointment from my mouth with toothpaste. It was still dark outside, but I had no chance of falling back asleep by myself. Still, it was the best sleep I'd had in months, and I couldn't decide whether to be grateful or pissed off about it.

He'd left.

Of course, he'd left.

I cursed myself for thinking otherwise. I didn't have time for this sappy shit. Two weeks, that was all, and then I could move on. I didn't think Ezra and Conan would turn me in now, but I'd been wrong before. I gripped the edge of the counter and looked myself in the eye in the mirror. My hair was tangled but my hairbrush was still in the other bathroom, and I'd rather shave my fucking head than go in there so soon.

They were making me hate my own house. Resentment curled around my throat like a fist.

I shoved my hair on top of my head in a lopsided bun and swiped concealer under my eyes. One night of good sleep didn't remove the weeks of broken nights from my body. I painstakingly drew on eyeliner, nearly giving up and throwing the fucking thing in the bin when I couldn't get the wings to match.

I dug out the tinted lip balm from a drawer, smudging a layer onto my lips.

I couldn't let them know they'd hurt me. I'd look good until I felt good. And torture them while I was at it.

Hence the low cut black shirt and skin tight jeans that made my ass look amazing. Not that anyone would be awake at this time to see me yet, but still.

Finally, I left my room, the need for coffee fuelling me as I padded through the hallway, holding my breath past the guest bedroom and the sofas. My eyes wandered anyway, dreading seeing the man who'd left my bed sound asleep by himself.

But the sofa was empty.

I blinked, pausing in my walk to stare at the furniture. I glanced around, eyes narrowed as my heart stuttered in my chest. Retracing my steps, I checked the bathroom door wasn't locked, and circled the living and kitchen space.

The scent of him was faint, strongest in my room and by the front door.

I scratched at my arm absently, a nervous habit I'd had since Eryx, a way of reminding myself that I was still alive, could still *feel.* I stared at the front door like it would give me answers. The sun was beginning to crawl over the horizon lazily, but the sky was still grey and cloudy. I leant closer to the kitchen window, bracing my hands on the counter by the sink to balance.

A shadow moved across the ground, so quick I nearly missed it. I choked on my heart as it leapt into my throat, my pulse loud in my ears.

Someone was out there.

I grabbed the dagger from the bookshelf I'd left it on, holding it tight in my fist before creeping to the front door and leaning my ear against it. I breathed slowly, trying to keep as silent as possible.

I strained, a quiet, incoherent murmur meeting my ear. The voice was familiar, and male, and my stomach flipped.

187

Darius.

A lilting female voice answered, again too muffled for me to make out the words. A cold shiver trickled down my spine, fear mingling with cold suspicion in my blood.

Who the fuck was he talking to?

And why had he left my bed to see her?

33

Darius

"Leave, Rosa," I growled, anger burning across my skin. She stood in front of me, nostrils flaring, teeth bared like a cornered dog. Like the bitch she was.

"You summoned me," she snapped back, tilting her head and eye fucking me as if she had the right to. I wanted to rip the fucking smirk from her face.

"You summoned yourself and you fucking know it," I argued, sick of this, sick of her, sick of the life I'd left in the Underworld. "Come back and I'll rip the black heart from your chest."

She laughed, grinning like it was the best thing she'd ever heard. The sound set me on edge, memories of the first few months of our relationship flashing through my mind. Why I'd ever let her into my bed in the first place was beyond me. She was attractive, physically - long black hair, deep brown eyes, breasts that strained the fabric of her shirt.

Now, when I looked at her, all I felt was repulsed.

"Oh, Darius," she tutted, pouting dramatically. "Always such a drama queen." She shrugged one shoulder, giving me

189

another long, heated look before she started to fuzz around the edges.

"I'm warning you, Rosa," I hissed as she faded, returning, no doubt, to her scheming father's side.

"I know," was all she said before she was gone, leaving nothing but the scent of smoke and caramel in the air.

"Fuck," I muttered, forcing air into my lungs as my body burned with the need to chase her down and make damn sure she never fucking left her realm again. *"Fuck."*

I'd left Rory's bed for this. She'd been sound asleep, curled up beside me, her breathing soft and heavy. It had been nearly impossible to tear myself away from her, the way she nuzzled into me, seeking contact in her sleep.

I'd tried to be kind when easing her mind. Tried not to look too closely, tried not to see things she didn't want me to see despite how fucking tempting it was to find every person who'd ever hurt her so I could hunt them down and remove their heads from their bodies.

I'd controlled myself. But still, her mind was a fucking graveyard of innocence. I hadn't seen their faces, but I'd seen their fangs, smelt the salty tang of blood, watched the scrape of their fingernails across her flesh.

I didn't know how she'd survived it. Never mind surviving intact.

I wanted to wrap her up in my arms and never let her go. I wanted to stand by her side as she burned the fucking world down with vengeance

More, though, I just wanted to go back to her bed.

And I never wanted to see my ex's face ever again.

The only reason I hadn't killed her on the spot was because I was almost positive it would make things worse. I was lucky as fuck that she hadn't got to Rory. Conan would be fine. He was big enough, strong enough, powerful enough that he'd bounce back quickly. Besides, all Rosa had really done was fuck with me.

I knew most of Rory's hurt was because of Conan and Ezra. She'd fucked him first, much to my anger, but considering the shit she'd pulled with him and I, I hadn't expected her to be hurt by Ezra and Conan's connection.

And, if she'd actually talk to him about it, I was pretty fucking sure he wouldn't mind sharing.

I wouldn't, either, if it meant I got even the smallest part of her. She was a fucking addiction. Had been since the second I'd caught her stealing that fucking book. My little thief.

And, after she'd shown me what she really craved, the addiction was only worsening. I wanted to ruin her. I wanted to break her apart, to fulfil every fucked up desire in her mind, until she was nothing but a shaking mess beneath me.

I hadn't even been inside her yet and she'd already brought me to my fucking knees. The memory of her taste on my tongue, the image of Ezra's cock choking her as she fought to stay still under my onslaught, had me groaning.

I moved from the spot I'd been standing in, making to go back to her bed and bury my face between her legs.

The door opened before I even touched the handle, and I came face to face with her. I knew before she even opened her mouth that she was pissed. I steeled myself, raising a brow at her and trying not to make it obvious that, seconds before, I'd been imagining her coming on my tongue.

The look of red hot rage on her face sent a bolt of pleasure through me, my dick no doubt visible through my thin sweatpants.

191

"Good morning," I drawled, narrowing my eyes and examining her stance. *Holy fuck.* Her tits were practically falling out of her shirt, and she'd darkened her eyes with black liner that made the green stand out. I wanted to make it run down her face.

"Is it?" she asked, raising a brow and looking me over, pausing her gaze at my crotch before she caught herself and raised her head. I laughed, wondering if she knew how fucking easy she was to read.

"Are you angry at me, little witch?" I asked, dropping my voice as I stepped towards her. To her credit, she stood her ground, though I watched her throat work as she swallowed.

"Why would I be?" she snapped back, biting her bottom lip as if stopping herself from saying more. I reached her before she could move, leaning down to pry that lip from between her teeth and trap it between my own.

"You tell me," I said, releasing her and delighting in the way she stepped back. *Run all you want, little thief.* "How did you sleep?" I asked before she could answer, walking towards her with slow, measured steps.

"Fine."

"Fine," I repeated, dragging the word out. "Any more... dreams?" I knew she got my reference by the way her cheeks heated. The desires that played in her mind, that she'd tucked away and hidden in darkness.

"None that you need to know of," she answered primly, tilting her chin back to spear me with a look that would make a sane person turn and run. But fuck I loved playing with fire, especially when I knew she'd burn so damn good.

I watched her back herself into a corner, trapped between me and the kitchen counter. It was the perfect height to bend her over. Her black nails clicked against the counter top as she stared me down. I needed to borrow her polish and fix my own. The house was quiet, the two others still deep asleep judging by the closed door, not that I'd have given a fuck if they were here. They were beginning to grow on me.

"Have you told Ezra what it is you really need?" I asked her. The need to take her, to strip her and fuck her until she was sobbing for me, pounded through me. I clenched my fists at my sides to stop myself reaching for her. Hot tension was thick between us, tinged with her indecision. It tasted sweet as fuck on my tongue. We both knew she wanted this, despite how much I knew she'd tell me otherwise.

She'd shown me.

"I don't need anything from you."

"Strike one," I murmured, shaking my head. She froze, hands gripping the counter top. "Tell me the fucking truth, Rory. Or you won't like the consequences."

"No," she gritted out. "I haven't told him anything."

"Does anybody know how badly you wanted to be fucked until you're screaming?" I advanced on her, trapping her with my arms on either side of hers, refraining from touching her at all. "How badly you need to be taken until you're an aching, shaking mess? How much you want to be degraded, told what a little fucking slut you are, how much you want it to hurt?"

"Stop it."

"Do they know, little thief? How even now you're fucking soaked thinking about me holding you down while I drive inside that tight little cunt of yours?"

"Don't."

"Such a fucking liar," I hissed, moving so my hands were circled around her wrists, pinning them against the counter.

193

"Will you fight me, Rory?" She said nothing. "Or will you spread those pretty thighs for me and beg me to fuck you like the whore you are?"

"I don't want to fuck you," she spat, struggling in my hold. *There she is.*

"Strike two."

"What the *fuck?*" she squealed as I spun her, holding her hands behind her back as I shoved her down onto the counter until her face was pressed against the surface.

I reached around, using my free hand to unbutton her skin tight jeans and yank them down, keeping them around her thighs so they acted as soft restraints.

"Hell below," I cursed as I stared down at the black lace thong fucking begging me to tear it off. She yelped as I brought my hand down on her ass, *hard*, the skin pinking under the impact. Fuck she was gorgeous.

"That fucking hurts, you asshole!"

I chuckled, spanking her three more times until she stopped swearing at me and her breathing became heavier. Unable to help myself, I slipped my hand between her legs, pressing my fingers against the wet fabric of her thong.

"Little liar," I hummed as I teased her through the fabric, grinning as she squirmed. "Stay still and I'll let you come before I make it hurt."

Her intake of breath was audible and I grinned as I released her wrists and knelt behind her, gripping her thighs and forcing her to part them. She wobbled on her feet but I steadied her, digging my fingers into her soft skin to hold her in front of me. My mouth watered but I forced myself to go slow, dragging one hand up her inner thigh to yank her panties to the side. Slowly, I dragged one finger over her, light

194

enough that I did nothing but piss her off as she attempted to buck against me, asking for more.

"What did I fucking tell you?" I growled, pinching the inside of her thigh as a warning. "Remember, little thief," I hissed as I rose to my feet and planted my hand flat against her back, forcing her further forward so she was flat against the counter top. I reached down with my free hand to release my dick, cursing at the sight of her, wet and waiting. "This is your fault."

I lined myself up with her entrance, grinning as she writhed in my grip, like she couldn't decide whether she wanted to run away or get closer. I didn't give her the option. I rammed into her in one thrust that had her crying out and her hands scrabbling against the counter. *Fuck.* She tightened around my cock as she whimpered, and I had to close my eyes to keep from embarrassing myself. The taste I'd had of her yesterday hadn't been nearly enough. I was jealous as fuck of the shifter for knowing what it felt like to be inside her.

"Gods, Rory," I groaned. "You feel like fucking heaven. Such a perfect little slut for me, aren't you?"

I withdrew slowly before burying myself deep again. She was so fucking wet, I met no resistance as I took her with short, brutal thrusts that pressed her hips against the edge of the counter. She choked on her whine as I reached around with one hand, pinching her clit hard between my fingers.

I knew it hurt her. I wanted it to fucking hurt. More, I knew *she* wanted it to hurt. I gritted my teeth to regain control as she ground her hips against me, soaking my cock with her arousal. *Hell below.* I kept up the pace, quick, hard thrusts designed to drive us both close to the edge as quickly as possible.

I reached for my power, extending my mind to hers, not

enough that she'd notice, but enough that I could sense her pleasure, checking that she hadn't changed her mind. Next time, I'd take it further.

For now, I'd teach her a lesson.

"Feel how fucking soaked you are, little thief?" I taunted, grabbing a fistful of her hair and pulling her head off the counter. "You're going to come for me. Again. And again. Until it fucking hurts, do you hear me?"

Her lips parted in what I assumed was meant to be an objection. I released her hair, and she jolted as I dragged her wetness up to her clit with my other hand, circling the swollen bud with teasing strokes. She gasped, arching into me as I increased the pace.

"Dare, fuck-" Her words were breathy and short, and the sound of her nickname for me shoved me closer to the edge. She tightened around me, biting her bottom lip between her teeth to silence herself as her orgasm ripped through her. I swore, unable to stop myself from following her as she clenched around me, bracing myself against the counter as I came inside her, pleasure overtaking me.

I withdrew, both of our releases dripping down her thighs. The sight was fucking godly. Before she could recover, I swung her into my arms, ignoring her soft protest, and took her into the bedroom, throwing her on the bed and bracing myself over her.

"Dare-" she started, eyes wide as I slid two fingers inside her, groaning at her slick heat. She squirmed as I found the spot that made her eyes flutter shut, objections dying on her lips. Did she know how easy she was to read?

"This time, when you come for me," I instructed as I added another finger, stretching her. "You come *loudly*."

I was pissed as Hell that she'd silenced herself when I was inside her. I had half a mind to put her fucking throat to better use. I watched the furrow appear between her brows with amusement.

"I'll do what I want," she answered, but the edge to her voice was dulled by lust.

I rolled my thumb over her swollen clit, memorising the way the sheets fisted in her palms. "Show me how good you look when you come for me, sweetheart," I urged, needing her to know how much I wanted this. She released the sheets and threw her arm over her face, hiding her reaction as I felt her orgasm begin to crest, drenching my fingers.

This fucking witch.

The second her breaths returned, I threw my magic at her, entering her mind so fast she had no time to fight back. This out of her mind, her body still recovering, she was easy to influence.

Don't fucking move, I commanded, watching the anger spark in her eyes when she realised what I'd done. I only grinned at her, rich satisfaction coursing through me. I left her there, legs parted, hair wild, cheeks flushed as I darted into the living space. I returned a minute later to Rory glaring at me like, had she been able to, she'd have driven those sharp nails of hers right into my heart.

I kept her there, under my control, as I tied her wrists together with the rope we'd used to bind Dumb and Dumber when they'd broken in. I smiled at the protest burning in her eyes, looping the rope around a rung in her wooden headboard and securing her arms above her head. *Try to hide from me now, little thief.*

"I'll keep going until you learn how to listen," I warned her,

197

gripping her thighs and forcing them further apart. I lowered myself between her legs, mouth watering at the scent of her arousal, the sight of her perfect pussy swollen and soaked with both of our orgasms. The second I relaxed the hold I had on her mind, she began to swear at me, fighting against the restraints around her wrists.

"What the fuck, Darius? What in Hell's name is wrong with you, let me fucking go-"

I ignored her, answering her objections by sealing my mouth over her sensitive flesh, licking her release from her. I wasn't slow or kind or teasing. No, I devoured her, my tongue deep in her cunt, scraping my teeth over her clit, coating a finger with her need and pressing it against her ass.

"I swear to all the fucking gods, Darius, I will drive a fucking dagger through your chest-"

"Sure thing, sweetheart," I mumbled, turning my head and biting her thigh, *hard*. She screamed at me, but I felt the want rippling through her. I returned to my task, savouring the taste of her. I could spend hours with my face between her thighs, making her shake and scream and curse while I rode her higher and higher until she forgot her own fucking name. I teased her ass with my finger, sucking her clit into my mouth and groaning as she came again, her orgasm fast and hard.

She obeyed me better this time, but I knew she was holding back. Her legs shook with the effort it took her to stay still, even as she tilted her head back, moaning loudly.

"Where do you keep your toys?" I asked her, releasing her and rising to my knees. Her eyes widened at me.

"I don't have any."

I slapped her pussy, shaking my head at her. She gasped, trying to move away from me, thighs pressing together as if to ward me off. I laughed. "You never fucking learn, do you?"

"Maybe you're just a shit teacher," she shot back, indignation darkening the green of her eyes. Her dark hair was fanned out around her, her chest rising and falling fast.

But she wasn't crying yet, or begging me to stop.

So I kept going.

34

Darius

"Stop, please, stop," she cried, thrashing in her restraints to try to move away from me. She'd come five times, and I knew she had to be sore but I didn't give a fuck.

"Tell me where they are then," I answered, trailing my wet fingers along her thighs. She was dripping, the sheets beneath her damp, and wispy strands of hair were stuck to her forehead. Her pussy was swollen and glistening with her cum, her thighs pressed together the second I moved.

But her makeup was still intact. I clicked my tongue.

"No more," she begged, groaning as she watched me stand and lean over her. I brushed my lips against hers slowly, speaking my next words onto her mouth.

"One more for me, sweetheart," I told her, reaching to yank her top down and expose those perfect tits. I rolled her nipple between my thumb and forefinger, watching the way she fought the pleasure with pure fascination. "Tell me where your vibrator is."

Indecision flickered on her face. I hardened my expression, reaching down to cup her pussy, a warning in the narrowing of my eyes. Her throat worked as she swallowed.

"Night stand."

I'd guessed that much, of course, but that was beside the point. I wanted her to tell me, to submit enough to give the control willingly. I knew she craved the fight, but I craved her trust. I wanted her stripped bare in more ways than one.

"See? That wasn't hard, was it?" I teased as I opened the cabinet and reached in, a grin on my lips. "Do you fuck yourself with this?" I asked. The toy was pale purple, long and thick, with two small buttons along the side. I pressed the first and it began vibrating in my hand. I smirked, looking up from the toy to find Rory wide-eyed and shaking her head.

"No," she whispered as I approached her again, the soft buzz of the toy filling the air. "I can't."

"You can and you will," I promised her, easing her knees apart and exposing her pussy to me once more. "You were warned, little thief. This is me taking it easy on you."

I dragged the toy through the centre of her, slicking it with her desire before bringing it to her oversensitive clit. She hissed at the contact, a small whimper falling from her lips as she tried and failed to move away. Tears leaked from the corners of her eyes, smudging her makeup in watery black streaks down the side of her face. My dick twitched in my trousers as I fought the urge to groan at the sight.

She jumped as something clattered in the kitchen, two familiar male voices exchanging low words. She tried to close her legs again, shaking her head and biting her lip. I only grinned wider and pressed the second button, increasing the vibrations and wringing a low, pained moan from her.

"Dare, please," she gasped, face pinched in pain and pleasure. Her back arched off the bed as I pressed the toy harder against her clit, a loud gasp falling off her tongue.

"Look me in the eye and let them fucking hear you," I demanded, shifting and bracing myself on one hand beside her stomach and leaning over to scrape my teeth along the side of her neck, pressing open mouthed kisses to the skin to ease the sting.

"Fuck!" My little witch bucked her hips against me, pressing the toy closer to her as she fell apart, tears streaming down her face, lips parted and choked cries carrying through the air. I raised my head and met her eyes, cock straining against my zipper as she held my gaze as she rode out her orgasm.

I immediately removed the vibrator from her, turning it off and throwing it down to the end of the bed. I reached up and released her wrists, throwing the rope down to join the toy, and rubbing the marks on her skin with gentle pressure.

I pulled back to take her in, heart stuttering in my chest.

She was a fucking mess. Teary, makeup smudged, legs shaking, cunt swollen and weeping.

I'd never seen anything more perfect.

35

Rory

I felt like I was floating, weightless, not quite in my body properly.

Dare slid down beside me in bed, scooping me into his arms and tucking me tight against his chest, pressing slow kisses to my throat, my cheeks, my forehead as I fought to control my breathing again. He rubbed his hands down my arms, my spine, my legs, ensuring I was okay.

"You did so well," he murmured, tucking my damp hair behind my ear and tracing his thumb over the line of my jaw. "So perfect, Rory. So good for me." I sighed, body relaxing under his touch. The metal of the ring on his pinkie finger was warm against my skin, and I focused on the soft sensation of it as I came down from the high he'd given me. His praise kicked my heartbeat up a notch, and I shuffled closer to him. "Wait here for me, sweetheart."

I nodded as he extracted himself from me and stood, ducking into my bathroom. I watched the easy grace with which he moved, unable to tear my gaze away. The muscles in my legs were shaking and the ache between my thighs deepened as I rolled over onto my back, the movement aggravating the swollen, sensitive flesh.

It scared me, the way he'd broken me so carefully. I knew he had gone easy on me, testing my limits, seeing how much I could take. The thought sent waves of warmth through me, and I gritted my teeth against the feeling. When he'd seen the thoughts I'd been harbouring for years, I hadn't expected him to act on it.

The year I'd spent with Eryx and the others had left a permanent scar on me. In more ways than one. Since them, I'd only had one night stands - quick fucks with strangers in bars that did nothing to satisfy the depraved needs settling in my chest. I wanted to be dominated, hurt, broken down. I wanted to reclaim the body that had been so brutalised, to escape the shame weighing on my shoulders, to allow myself to want what I wanted without being scared of it.

Darius reappeared, a damp cloth in his hand, and rejoined me on the bed, cleaning me up with shocking softness.

"What are you doing?" I asked him, resenting how thick my voice sounded.

"Making sure you're okay," he answered simply, throwing the cloth into the laundry bin and urging me close to him again. I frowned at him, blinking as he tucked me close to his chest.

"Why?"

"It's called aftercare, Rory," he growled, chest vibrating with what I assumed was anger. I only nodded, clenching my fists against the wave of shitty memories flashing behind my eyes.

"We should get up," I told him, despite the fact my body was relaxing against his, my head tucked tight to his chest. He'd pulled the blanket up around us, his chin resting on my hair, his arms tight around me. I studied the ring on his finger, the raised design of a crown surrounded by roses, as though if I didn't focus on the softness of this moment, I wouldn't have to process it. I couldn't remember the last time, before him, that I'd been held like this.

Had I ever been held like this?

"Just let me care of you," he mumbled, tugging my hair slightly to make me look up at him. "Trust me."

I swallowed my complaints, the deep gold of his eyes holding me in place. "Okay."

We stayed like that until my stomach was rumbling and the smell of toast and bacon was wafting under the door, signalling that either Ezra or Conan was cooking. Darius chuckled, releasing me and drawing back the covers.

"Let's go get you some food, little thief," he laughed, tilting my chin up for a kiss. I groaned when I stood, the sting between my legs worsening with the movement. I caught the smirk on his lips before he turned away, rummaging through the pile of clean clothes beside my dresser to find new panties and jeans.

I changed, flipping him off when he bit his lip to stop from laughing when I winced, trying to hide my own smile behind my hair.

We left the room, and I braced myself for the inevitable dirty looks from Conan. I refused to cower in their presence, to show any sense of hurt, to let either of them see that I was anything less than okay. *They're not on my side,* I reminded myself. I'd thought Ezra was, but after whatever happened between him and Conan, I wasn't sure of anything any more.

"Is there a reason that the kitchen smells of sex?" Ezra asked, turning from the sizzling pan on the stove to cock his head at me.

I tensed, pulling my bar stool up to the centre island and keeping my eyes on Darius as he began fixing me coffee.

"Is there a reason my bathroom smelled of sex last night?" I replied, leaning on the counter. Conan was standing at the toaster, refusing to look at me, and my stomach clenched tightly.

Darius snorted, nearly spilling my coffee as he returned to my side, handing me the cup. I thanked him, sipping the contents slowly. The strained tension in the air was nearly palpable, and the relaxed warmth that I'd felt tucked up in bed beside Dare was rapidly dissipating.

"Are we going to talk about yesterday or continue to pretend it didn't fucking happen?" Dare asked smoothly, wrapping his arm around my waist and staring at the other two men. I forced my muscles to relax, focusing on the hot cup in my hands to ground myself.

"Talk then, demon," Conan answered, plating the toast. It was unnerving seeing him and Ezra so domesticated, moving around the kitchen like they belonged here.

But they didn't belong here. They couldn't.

"So what, you and Ezra fucked and made up?" Dare asked, an edge to his voice that made me tense. "After throwing a fucking tantrum and getting *kidnapped?*"

Conan visibly tensed, turning slowly to face us. I peered at him over the rim of my mug.

"What happened between me and Ezra is none of your business."

"Actually, it is," I spoke up, slamming my cup down and

shaking my head. "None of this works if you try to hide shit. This house is not big enough for secrets, Conan."

"Is that so, princess?" he asked, voice low and dangerous. I fought the urge to shiver. "Why don't you tell us what happened to you then? What those fuckers did that was so bad you want to murder them?"

Anger flashed through me, hot and sharp. "You want to know?" I asked, pushing to my feet and leaving Darius' embrace. "The last member of my family was *burned*. I was alone and broken and needed something, *someone*, to live for. And then I met him. Eryx." I fought the urge to gag at the rotten taste of his name in my mouth. "He was a vampire. A *leader*. Promised to make me feel so much better if I'd let him help me."

"Help you?" Ezra cut in, sliding the pan off the hot stove and fixing me with his dark glare.

"By feeding," I snapped, closing my eyes briefly to collect myself. "Have you ever given blood to a vampire?" A collective shake of heads, with Darius looking ready to snap someone's neck. He'd seen the snapshots of it all in my mind. He knew, but he let me tell what I needed to. His solidarity strengthened me. "It makes you feel high. Like nothing matters but them and you. Like you're dreaming." I paused, shrugging to shift the weight this story was putting on my shoulders. "And that's what I needed, at first. But then they brought in more girls, more vampires, and suddenly he wasn't my boyfriend any more. I was just a walking blood bag. He'd tell me how good witch blood tasted, how I was his favourite. I didn't feel alive for the entire year I was with him. And then they killed one of the girls. Her name was Lila. She was seventeen fucking years old."

"Rory-" Ezra stepped forward, hand out, and I immediately stepped back.

"I woke up, I started fighting, refusing to lie down and let them feed from me and rape me," I was shaking now, hands fisted at my side. "It took a month for me to get out after her death. They chased me for the first six months. When I finally found a grimoire with the protection spells I needed, I bought myself enough time to hide. I was safe here for four years until they tracked me down again and left that fucking body on my couch. Another victim." I took a shaky inhale, forcing myself not to scream. "That was when I knew I had to kill them."

Nobody spoke for a few seconds, until Conan opened his fucking mouth.

"Why the grimoire, though?" he asked, dragging his teeth over his bottom lip as though considering. "Why not just hunt them down and murder them the good old fashioned way?"

"Because I can't have it tied to me," I answered. "I have a life here. People I care about. A job I like. I refuse to ruin my life again if someone discovers it was me. The magic in that book is dark and ancient and leaves no fucking trace. They'll suffer and they'll die and I'll finally be free. Unless you fuckers turn me over and let Eryx and his fucking cult continue destroying girls like me."

Guilt flashed across Ezra's face, and Conan's jaw ticked.

"Nobody is turning you over, little thief," Dare said softly. "And nobody will be taking you again."

His words were both a threat and a promise, and I shuddered.

"He's right, Ro," Ezra echoed, coming to stand in front of me. I moved away quickly, escaping his outreached hand.

"Don't, Ezra," I said quickly, shaking my head. "Tell the dicks that hired you to fuck off. And get out. Both of you. I don't owe you anything just cause I fucked you." I spat the words at him like venom, suddenly disgusted with their presence.

"You don't mean that."

"I won't be used and thrown out again!" I yelled, fury burning through me like a living flame. Ezra looked like I'd slapped him in the face, and Conan bared his teeth. He pushed past the shifter to corner me against the cupboard, eyes hard.

"Don't fucking insult him," he hissed. "Don't insult any of us like that."

Before I could analyse what the fuck that meant, a loud knock rattled the front door, cutting through the thick air. I took the others' pauses as an opportunity to duck away, leaving all three frozen in the kitchen as I darted to the front door.

"Grace!" I greeted far too enthusiastically, her pretty face contorting in confusion as I pulled her in for a hug. I wasn't usually this affectionate, but the comforting scent of coffee and cakes she always carried wrapped around me, soothing my ragged nerves.

"Ror, what's wrong?" she whispered, returning the hug. Her body was soft and warm against mine.

"Everything," I answered as I pulled away, opening the door wider for her to step inside. Truthfully, I'd forgotten we'd planned to hang out today. I'd forgotten nearly everything in my life except the three men driving me insane and the revenge plan constantly in my mind. I was lucky as Hell that Grace was my boss, or I'd have undoubtedly been fired for calling off work on such short notice.

"Do you need me to get you out?" she offered without

209

hesitation, voice low. "I can call-"

I shook my head immediately, stomach twisting. Grace's past was as dark as my own and what she was offering would only bring it all back to her. I loved her endlessly for being willing to do that for me, even if there was no way I'd ever accept the offer.

"I can't leave," I sighed. "I don't want to. But uh...I guess you should probably meet the root of the problem."

She frowned, red brows knitting together as I walked into the kitchen, my best friend hot on my heels.

The guys were all in the same position I'd left them in, but the low murmurs I'd heard ceased entirely when we entered the space. I frowned at them, crossing my arms over my chest and forcing my body to remember to breathe.

As much as I wished I could keep them and Grace apart until they left, it seemed impossible. She was too much a part of my life to hide this from. I was already hiding the revenge plot and thievery from her, for her own damn good.

"Uh, Ror, who the fuck are the three men in your kitchen and why does it smell like sex in here?"

Fuck me, this was going to end in disaster.

36

Conan

Rory's friend was nice but I wished she would fuck off so we could finish what we'd started. I wasn't done with her.

Grace sat next to the witch on the sofa, glaring fucking daggers at me as she ate the toast Ezra had piled up next to the bacon and sausages on the little table. I was sitting on the edge of the sofa, Ez beside me and Darius beside him, being interrogated by the red-headed feline.

"So why are you here?" she asked for what felt like the tenth time. I left the talking to the other two, focusing instead on Rory who was purposefully avoiding my gaze.

Ezra had made me listen to him last night. We hadn't so much as kissed since the shower, in fact he'd distanced himself from me again, and it hurt like a bitch. Not that I was about to let him see that. I'd put myself on the fucking line for him, got on my damned knees for him, which I never fucking did for anybody, and instead of opening up he'd closed himself off. I itched to take him into the other room and make him see my fucking side, preferably with my dick.

But I knew his issue. If I was being honest with myself, I understood, despite the fact I hated her for it. He wanted her. He wanted me. And I was damn sure she wanted the same thing.

I didn't like sharing my possessions. But maybe I could break the rule.

If she'd stop fucking yelling at us for a second and listen.

The witch was on my last fucking nerve. I wanted her almost as much as I hated her, and the combination was deadly. I knew for a fact the demon had made damn sure we heard them this morning, and the subsequent hurt on Ezra's face made me want to bash Darius' skull in.

We needed to talk. All of us.

After this fucking feline shifter had left. The sooner the better.

I listened to Ez lie about our circumstances. That Rory had offered us her spare room while we finished a job here, in return for protection after the bloody door incident, since it appeared Grace somehow already knew about that.

I knew by the shimmer in Grace's silvery eyes that she didn't believe him. Her hand was around Rory's in a vice as she nodded and smiled, sipping tea and acting like nothing was wrong.

Finally, two hours later, she got up to leave. Ezra elbowed me hard in warning. Clearly, my relief had shown. Not that I cared. I'd stopped giving a fuck what people thought of me years ago. Ezra was the only one whose opinions I wanted to hear.

Except that wasn't strictly true now.

"I'll see you at work tomorrow?" Grace asked Rory, an edge to her voice that hadn't been there earlier. Rory nodded, dipping her head to whisper something to her friend before waving her off and closing the door behind her.

She moved to push past us, all three of us having followed the girls to the door, and made for the kitchen. I blocked her path, glaring down at her.

"Couch. Now."

"Move, Conan," she answered, voice hard. "I'm not in the mood for your shit right now."

"Tough fucking luck, princess," I answered, patience snapping all together as I threw her over my shoulder and carried her over to the sofa, tossing her onto the cushions. "We're talking whether you fucking like it or not."

She stared at me, clearly shocked by my outburst. I stared right back, unrelenting.

"I didn't peg you for a talker," she snapped, shaking her head as the others came to stand beside me. We'd discussed this while she was answering the door earlier, all of us in agreement for once. For better or worse, she'd ensnared us in this fucking web, and we better learn to live with it.

"He's not, little witch," Darius spoke up, sitting beside her and pulling her close to him. She refused, though he dragged her woodenly onto his lap and wrapped his arms around her, making it clear she didn't have a choice in this matter. "But we are." He nodded to Ez, who sank down with me on the opposite sofa, staring at the others over the empty plates and coffee cups.

"What the fuck is going on?" Rory asked, struggling in Darius' embrace.

"You need to listen to me, hellhound," Ezra said, shaking his head as his gaze darted from me to her.

"I don't fucking need anything from any of you," she spat

213

back, anger visible in the whites of her knuckles as she tried to pry herself from the demon's arms. I had to give him credit, he was far stronger than he looked.

"Do I need to tie you up again?" Darius threatened, voice low. I stilled, images of her tied up at our mercy flashing through my head with unnerving clarity. Fuck.

She froze, glaring at him with such darkness I thought she might curse him then and there. "Don't you fucking dare."

He chuckled, but she stopped struggling and reluctantly stayed still in his arms. She turned back to me, venom on her tongue when she spoke. "Talk then, you fucking asshole. Tell me all the shit you've been wanting to say since you discovered I was fucking the man you've been in love with for how long? Years, right? Go ahead, I guarantee you I've had worse than whatever the fuck you're about to throw my way."

The urge to wrap my hand around her neck and show her who was in charge was agony in my bones. I resisted, barely, Ezra's hand on my arm the only thing tethering me in place.

"Be very fucking careful what you say, princess." A cold calm seeped into my voice, like a killer before the final strike. "Or I'll make you regret opening that filthy little mouth of yours."

Her intake of breath was audible, and I grinned. So easy. Ezra's hand tightened on my arm, and I sat back, pinning her with my stare.

"I don't want what we had to stop, baby," Ezra piped up, soft and soothing as ever. He was always the calm to my chaos.

"We didn't have anything, Ezra," she hissed, shaking her head. "You can fuck him if you want. I don't care."

Darius visibly tightened his hold on her. "Little thief, what have I told you about lying?"

She swallowed whatever retort she had, though the violence in her gaze didn't dim.

"I don't want to choose, Rory," he repeated steadily. "And I don't think you do, either."

Her mouth dropped open as she took his words in.

"None of us want you to choose, little witch," Darius echoed, tucking her hair behind her ear so he could skim a kiss along her neck. I clenched my fists at the action, and by the way Ezra's lips twitched, I knew he noticed.

"I don't understand," she stuttered, looking between all of us before finally settling her eyes on me. "You're okay with this? With sharing him?"

Ezra barely restrained his laugh. "Oh, baby, he wants you, too."

I said nothing as Rory laughed, shoulders shaking. "Right," she drawled, dragging out the syllable with blatant sarcasm. "Conan can't even fucking talk to me. He hates me, Ezra."

She was talking like I wasn't in the room and it infuriated me. I stood quickly, striding to her and pulling her from Darius' grip and slamming her back against the wall beside the fireplace so hard her breath flew from her lungs and her eyes widened, the bright green boring into me.

I pressed her against the wall, yanking her head back with my grip on her ponytail so she could look me in the eye when I spoke to her.

"Look me in the fucking eye when you talk about me," I warned her, satisfaction pouring through me as her breath came back in quick gasps.

"Or you could talk to me yourself without going through your fucking boyfriend," she hissed back, gritting her teeth. "Tell me exactly what you want to my face, you coward."

215

I was going to ruin her. She tested every fucking limit I had, rendered my patience non-existent. Did I like her? No. Did I want to know what she felt like around my cock more than I wanted my next fucking breath? Yes.

"You want me, Conan? You want both of us?" her eyes darted to Ez, watching us with barely disguised lust in his eyes. "Tell me. Say it! Say *Rory I want you.* Say it, you fucking asshole!"

I threaded my hand through her hair and clenched my fist, tugging on the strands so hard she flinched. She was pushing me too far.

She was right. I wanted her. I wanted him. I wanted them both on their knees for me.

But I couldn't say it.

"You will submit to me," I growled instead, barely controlling my need to feel her as she pounded her fists against my chest. "Make no mistake, you will be mine. There's no getting away, no running. The second you drop to your knees, that's it. I don't do half measures, princess. I'll have every fucking piece of you or none at all." She was breathing heavily, lips parted, cheeks flushed like she couldn't decide whether she wanted me or wanted to kill me. That made fucking two of us. "This is your only warning. When you accept that, you get on your hand and knees, crawl to me and beg at my fucking feet for me to take you. Do you understand?" I punctuated my question with a tug on her hair when she didn't answer. "Do. You. Understand?"

There was nothing but her narrowed eyes and struggle for a moment, the room fading until there was nothing but us, the unspoken, red hot flame of *potential* burning between our bodies. Her eyes were glazed over and her voice strained and gritty when she finally said, "yes."

Nodding sharply, I released my hold and turned, leaving her swaying on her feet as I left the room and slammed the door shut behind me.

She wasn't ready yet. And as much as I ached to dominate her, I didn't want to harm Ezra by harming her. Hurt her, yes, see how pretty she looked with tears streaming down her face, how good she sounded begging for me, how long she could hold out before I drove her over the edge.

But I would sooner die than hurt her the way the assholes in her past had, force her into something she didn't want. Even the thought of what they'd done to her made me want to set the fucking world on fire to rid the planet of them.

So I would wait. I could only hope she made her choice before it drove me insane.

37

Rory

I t was barely noon, and I already wanted the day to be over.

After Conan's outburst, I'd been unsteady. Darius hadn't left my side and was curled up to me on the sofa reading one of my favourite books and playing with my hair.

I'd tried to focus, to make a list of all the shit I still needed for the spell and push all thoughts of whatever relationship they were all proposing from my mind. We had far more pressing matters at hand. For one, figuring out what the fuck the bloody heart and flowers were about, who had hurt and taken Conan, and where the hell Eryx had moved his shitty little cult to. And that girl Darius had left me to talk to, the knowledge of which made me wince. I suspected she was from his past, but I knew he wasn't ready to talk about it. And, as much as I hated to admit it to myself, I was beginning to trust him, despite it all. She hadn't reappeared, and he hadn't mentioned it again. I forced it from my mind.

My head *hurt* with the stress of it all. I didn't doubt that Grace would be on my ass at work tomorrow about it, not to mention that leaving the grimoire here all day would no doubt stress me out even more.

In short, my life was a fucking mess and, despite all the rest of the shit I needed to deal with, all I could think about was *sharing*.

"This is insane," I murmured, throwing the notebook that was still fucking empty thanks to my wandering mind down on the table.

"What's wrong, sweetheart?" Dare asked, folding down the corner of the page he was reading before setting the book down. I debated chastising himself for damaging it but decided I only had the energy for one fight today.

"I just don't understand," I said slowly, shifting away from him a little. He was intoxicating, and it was fucking with my mind.

"What don't you understand?" He frowned, dark brows furrowing.

"Any of this!" I said, exasperated. "Whatever the fuck is happening with all of you. I can't, I don't-" Fuck, I was spiralling. My breathing picked up, my skin suddenly feeling far too tight.

"Hey, little thief," Darius said softly, reaching for me. "It's okay. You don't have to do anything-"

I wanted to scream.

"That's not-" I broke off, shaking my head. "This is fucking insane."

"Hey, baby, what's-" Ezra's voice broke through the chaos in my brain as he entered the room from the guest room he'd been in with Conan.

"Don't call me that!" I yelled, rubbing my temples to stave off the migraine. I stood, determined to get a fucking grip and make the herbal tea I knew would clear my head. It had been so long since I'd got caught up in this fucking rip tide of emotions threatening to drown me. I'd been doing so well.

I watched hurt flash across Ezra's face but I couldn't find it in myself to go to him.

I stumbled into the kitchen and gripped the counter to steady myself while searching for the herbs and flowers I needed for the blend in the ingredients cupboard I always kept stocked.

"Fuck," I cursed as one of the glass jars tumbled from the shelf. I caught it before it hit the counter, clenching my fist around it to stop the shaking.

It had been worse at the start, the panic, the fear, the flashbacks. They'd got less and less frequent over the years, though my nightmares persisted. Every time this happened, every time I felt the swelling wave of terror build beneath my skin, I wanted to collapse. I felt *weak*. Like no matter what I did, I'd never escape what had happened to me.

I squeezed my eyes shut tightly for a second, focusing on the empty blackness behind my eyelids. I got a few seconds of reprieve before I opened them to find Ezra looking at me.

"It's okay," Ezra said again, his deep voice washing over me. I began to protest - to tell him that he was wrong, none of this was okay - but he continued. "You're allowed to want us all."

I stopped, body stilling as I reached for a teapot. "What?"

"You're allowed to want us all, Rory."

I swallowed thickly, trying to stop the shaking. "I don't know what you mean."

"Stop it," he snapped, stalking over to me and looking down at me, dark eyes gleaming. "Stop beating yourself up over it. I'm not fucking choosing."

I blinked at him. "But you and Conan-"

"Yes," he cut me off, snatching the mug from me and slamming it on the counter so I didn't drop it. "Wanting Conan doesn't mean I don't still want *you.*"

"I just need a minute," I answered tensely, unable to look at him. I waited until I felt the space clear out and the buzz in my brain receded enough that I could combine the ingredients, mutter the simple soothing spell to enchant the tea with and pour myself a cup without burning my hand. As a dark witch, I was limited to the green spells I could pull off, but if they were simple enough, I could manage. It wasn't in my nature, didn't call to me the way the dark arts did, but it was still witch magic. Green witches, if they lowered themselves off their high horse, could perform little dark magic tricks too - perhaps reanimating a dead mouse, or placing a quick hex on someone they disliked.

I turned and left Ezra and Darius, seeking the space of my bedroom.

I changed my bed sheets so they no longer smelled of Dare and sat on top of the bed, tea in hand, staring unseeingly at the grimoire.

Ezra's words kept replaying in my mind, no matter how hard I tried to shake them off. *You're allowed to want us all.*

Why the fuck was I so torn up about this? I'd had a threesome with him and Darius for Hell's sake. Why did this feel different?

I knew why, of course. I hadn't felt anything for anyone, aside my friendship with Grace, since I'd escaped Eryx. Feelings were dangerous, fickle things that had never done anything but hurt me. I didn't trust them. I didn't trust myself.

The fact that I wanted more than sex with any of them was

terrifying. The fact that I wanted it with *all* of them made me want to run.

But I wasn't a coward. Eryx's influence over my life needed to end. I couldn't let what he and his *friends* had done to me make my decisions for me. Darius, Ezra, and Conan were different. I didn't doubt that the first two had at least some feelings for me. Dare had made it perfectly clear he wanted me, and Ezra had outright said it. Conan, on the other hand...

I knew he wanted to fuck me, and there was no point denying that I'd thought about it. He needed control, and I understood that. It would be nice, I thought, to hand over the control to someone else for a while. I'd had such a tight grip on the reins for years that my body was starting to ache with it.

I wanted the memories of the vampires wiped clean from my skin by new ones. Maybe it didn't have to be more than sex, at least right now. My body wanted them, all of them, loved the idea of being *shared*.

My mind still seized up at the thought. They wouldn't hurt me like Eryx and his friends had. Wouldn't use me and gift me to each other. They might be assholes, but they weren't evil.

I had never been fully convinced by monogamy, though for a while I'd thought Eryx would be it for me. I expected the idea of sharing Ezra with Conan to send jealously through me, and while there was still a hint of the bitter feeling, all I could feel was the desperate want to be included in it. I'd seen how Conan softened for the man, how Ezra managed to tease some form of emotion from him. I wanted to be the one to pull him apart, to help Ezra tear away the wall Conan had built around himself. Not that I thought he'd let me, at least not until I *submitted*.

The idea sent heat through me, despite the residual soreness from this morning. Darius, I knew, had no qualms about any of this. He was so laid back, easy going, calm and collected and warm. He centred me, Ezra challenged me, Conan fucking infuriated me.

I still didn't know what I'd overheard with Darius this morning, but I knew that until he told me, I shouldn't trust him with my emotions. Shouldn't trust any of them with anything more than my body.

So we could start there. I wanted to fuck them, and I was sick of denying myself.

I breathed in deeply, letting the decision calm me before digging the point of my nail into the palm of my hand and dripping the blood onto the grimoire. Regardless of what did or didn't happen between the three of us, I'd felt how angry all three of them had been when they heard what Eryx had done. I wasn't alone in this, not any more. I opened the spellbook, licking the blood off my nail and grinning as I imagined the Hell I'd rain down on the fucking vampires that refused to stop hurting other people like me.

It wasn't just me they had to reckon with now.

It was them, too.

38

Ezra

"I'm going to fucking kill them," Conan muttered, pacing in front of me. Rory had taken her tea to her room to *think*, and despite the fact that the space was making me fucking itch, I'd let her go.

I shook my head, looking up at Conan and trying to focus on what he was saying. "Who are we murdering?"

"The fucking blood suckers that convinced her she was worth nothing!" he answered through gritted teeth, hands balled into fists.

While every atom in my body agreed with him, the anger radiating off him confused me. "Careful," I said slowly, cocking my head as I tried to understand what had pushed him to this point. "Someone might mistake this for caring."

"I don't care," he immediately countered, glaring at me. The look had my dick hardening and my heart pounding. "But pieces of shit like that deserve to be wiped off the face of the earth."

"I know, Cee," I soothed, standing but keeping distance between us while he paced. "But we're not exactly the good guys here. We've done some fucked up shit. And she doesn't want heroes in shining armour. She needs to do this herself."

"She shouldn't have to do any of it by herself!" he yelled. My eyes widened.

"And she won't," I answered, shaking my head at him. "But you can't kill them. She'll never forgive you if you take this from her."

The room was silent as he took in my words. I was right, and he knew it. If he ever wanted her on her knees for him, he had to stay back. Conan was never one for staying out of things. He was at his best covered in blood and vengeance.

The image nearly made me groan. How the fuck had I convinced myself we were just *friends* for so long? How was there ever a time I didn't want him naked and undone before me?

"What are you thinking?" he asked, noticing the shift in me.

"Nothing."

He tutted, mock disappointment crossing his handsome face. "So many liars in this house," he admonished, reaching for me and sliding his hand into my hair at the back of my neck. "I won't ask again."

I swallowed, relishing in seeing this shift in him. Conan was dominant to his core, I knew that. And Hell, I'd submit to him every fucking day of the week if it meant he wouldn't stop touching me. Some part of me craved it, the rough edge to him.

"I was thinking you should have way less clothes on," I said honestly, grinning as surprise flitted across his clear blue eyes, followed quickly by something much darker.

"Is that so?"

I nodded happily, reaching for him. He let me work my

hands under his shirt, tracing my fingers over his lean stomach and chest, releasing me to allow me to pull it over his head. When I reached for his belt, he wrapped his hand around my wrist to stop me, squeezing slightly as if to remind me who was in charge here.

"How do you feel about a little revenge of our own?" he whispered, voice low and dark. I shivered, nodding despite having no fucking clue what he meant. I trusted him, blindly, and yet no part of me had ever doubted that it was the right thing to do. He nodded once, letting go of my wrist and urging me back a few steps. "Stay here."

I watched him leave, confusion mixing with the haze of lust in my head. What the fuck was he up to? Nervous anticipation coiled around my bones, leaving me jittery with the need to know what was happening. He wasn't gone long, and when he returned he wasn't alone.

"Princess has a lesson to learn," he said roughly, dragging Rory behind him. She was glaring at him, though hadn't removed her arm from his grip. I smirked. She was stubborn as fuck, but deep down she knew what the answer to all this was. I suspected she'd already decided.

But she needed a push.

Fuck. Conan grabbed a chair from the corner, sitting her in it while she glared at him like she was imagining putting a dagger through his skull.

"What the fuck are you doing?" she asked him as he pulled her arms behind the back of the chair. "What the Hell is that?" She tried to move, but something was holding her hands and ankles in place. I laughed, unable to help myself. Fuck, she was cute when she was angry.

"A little magic to make sure you stay still like the good girl I know you desperately want to be," Conan purred. Her eyes widened and her lips popped open in shock. Heat shot straight to my cock at his words and tone, and her subsequent reaction. "Watch. If you're good, I'll let you join in."

Holy fucking Hell. I was going to combust with the heat roaring through me. I gaped at Conan, who turned away from Rory with a nonchalant shrug, pinning me with his bright stare. My breathing hitched as he walked towards me with slow, deliberate steps, pausing just out of reach in front of me.

"Strip," he demanded. I blinked at him, trying to clear the fog in my mind.

"Uh, what?"

"You want me, Ez? You fucking got me. Now strip."

My body began obeying before I'd made a conscious choice to, pulling my shirt over my head and undoing the buttons of my trousers.

"See, princess?" he said to Rory without ever taking his eyes off me. "Look what obeying gets you."

Another time, I promised myself, I'd challenge that statement. But all I could think about right now was him and her and having his hands on me as she watched. Finally, I was naked before them, and Conan's sharp inhale had warmth flowing through me freely.

"What the Hell are you doing?" Rory hissed, struggling in her chair. I raised a brow at her.

"Tell me something, Ro," I spoke before Conan could get the chance. So much for obeying. Oops. "Do you want to leave?" I crossed to her, leaning over her and bracing my hands on either side of her. "Look at me and tell me you don't want to sit here and watch him fuck me. Tell me you don't want to be a part of it." I didn't want her to go, quite the opposite, but I wanted her to realise she wanted this as much as I did. She said nothing, just stared at me with those green eyes, silent protests burning in them. I grinned. "Go on, baby. Tell me you're not dripping at the thought of watching."

My taunts were met by yet more stubborn silence and a fresh wave of desire washed over me. I didn't even hear Conan cross to us until his hand landed on my shoulder and he was pulling me away.

"You don't talk to her," he warned, hand around my throat. "Bad girls don't get rewarded," he said to her before returning his attention to me. His hold on me tightened, and I gasped, even as my dick ached with need. "Eyes on me, love."

He must have seen the submission in my eyes because he nodded and walked me back to the bed, shoving me down on it. I blinked up at him, still half dressed and towering over me from this angle, making my role in this very clear. I didn't sub for just anybody. The power imbalance went straight to my head, emptying it of any logical thought.

"Touch yourself," he commanded, eyeing my cock with hard eyes. "Show us how much you want me."

I didn't hesitate, propping myself up on one hand and fisting my cock with the other. I felt her eyes on me as I slid my hand up and down my shaft, gritting my teeth against the urge to beg Conan to touch me instead. Fuck I was out of practice if I was contemplating begging so fast. Or maybe it was just him, just *them*, that drove me this insane.

Conan watched me for a few seconds, as though he was as caught up in it as I was, his eyes burning with lust that fed my own. He snapped out of it, raising his eyes to mine as he slowly undid his belt, his gaze darting to Rory's as he slid it free of the loops and gripped the leather in his hands.

"Be grateful that I'm not reddening your ass with this right now," he told her.

My hips bucked at the idea of it, a low groan escaping my mouth. Her eyes darted to mine and narrowed, though she said nothing in response to Conan. He dismissed her again, refocusing on me as he shoved the rest of his clothes off, freeing his hard cock. My mouth watered instantly, my hand freezing on my own cock as I took him in. I didn't think I could ever get tired of looking at him. He maintained the cold self controlled facade that made him so intimidating, but it only reinforced his dominance in the scene.

"Get on your knees."

I slid off the bed without thought, the carpet soft beneath my knees as he fisted my hair and pulled, forcing me to look up at him.

"Open."

My jaw dropped open, too desperate to taste him to think about disobeying. Without a second thought, he thrust into my mouth, giving me no time to prepare for his size. He was long and thick and hit the back of my throat as he shoved my head down on his shaft, groaning as I took him without complaint. I hollowed my cheeks as he fucked my face with brutal, quick thrusts, his hand tightening in my hair to the point of pain. I moaned as he met my gaze, dragging my tongue along his cock as he pulled out of my mouth, lapping up the drop of precum coating the head.

"Up. Now," he ground out, stepping back and reaching for something out of my line of sight. I stood on slightly shaky legs, my eyes darting to Rory. I could hear her soft panting as she tried to control her breathing, and I grinned. Her eyes were glassy with want, and I could scent her arousal as I breathed in. She met my gaze, running her tongue over her bottom lip, chest rising and falling in time with my own. The air in the room was thick with arousal and lust, and all three of us were under its spell.

"On the bed on your hands and knees," Conan ordered as he turned again, catching the silent looks Rory and I exchanged with a slow smirk that spelled trouble. Fuck if it didn't have my pulse sky rocketing.

Keeping my eyes on the witch, I crawled onto the bed, positioning myself so I was facing her. My whole body was tight with anticipation, my dick painfully hard with the memory of Conan's cock choking me.

The soft rustle of a bag opening filled the air and then the mattress dipped as he joined me, Rory's eyes fixed on us as I felt him move behind me. Her eyes widened as the sound of a cap being popped open broke through the tension. Conan leant over me, hard cock pressed against my ass, running his hand down my back before reaching around to hold my throat and forcing me to hold Rory's gaze.

"Watch her watching us," he said lowly. "Watch how she squirms as I fuck you. Let her know how good it feels, love." He dragged his teeth over my pulse point, sending my instinct to claim him barrelling into me with such ferocity I groaned. He knew what he was doing. He always fucking knew what he was doing.

He returned to his position behind me, gripping my hip with one hand to steady me as he spread lube over my ass. I shivered under the cold slide of his finger, resisting the urge to push against him.

"Eyes on our girl, Ez," Conan reminded me, his voice dark and decadent as it slid over my skin, as he slid a finger inside of me, readying me for him.

A gasp flew from my mouth as he added another, fucking me with his fingers slowly. I saw her shiver as she watched us, the burning desire in her eyes only strengthening the pleasure coursing through me.

"I can't fucking wait any longer," Conan mumbled, pulling his fingers from me and quickly replacing them with the head of his cock.

I forced my body to relax as he pressed inside me, the delicious stretch of him knocking the breath from my lungs. I pressed my head against the bed as he added another inch, the slight sting of pain heightening the perfect fucking feel of him. Gods, I needed him. Needed him unrestrained and fucking me until he lost control. He stopped, holding himself still as his fingers threaded in my hair once again, pulling my head up forcefully.

"I told you to keep your fucking eyes on her," he growled. "Do I need to remind you whose you are, love? Is that what it is? Have you already fucking forgotten who owns you?"

I had no time to answer before he pulled back and thrust fully inside of me, sheathing himself in my ass. He groaned, fingers flexing on my hip, as I moaned, panting at the feeling of him.

"You feel fucking amazing," he praised, pulling back and thrusting inside me again, slower this time. I made an incoherent noise of agreement, far too caught up in the pressure and pleasure of him, unable to look anywhere but Rory. Our witch was staring at us like she'd never seen anything she wanted more in her life.

"Conan," I panted, his name rolling off my tongue like I was always meant to be moaning it.

231

"What do you need?" he asked, continuing to fuck me agonisingly slowly, despite me moving my hips against him, urging him to speed the fuck up.

"You," I answered as he released my hair to grip my cock. *"Fuck."*

"Say please."

I froze, fighting the urge to look away from Rory to glare at him over my shoulder.

"Beg for my cock, Ezra," he said, slamming said cock inside of me and holding me flush against him. I gritted my teeth, holding Rory's dark gaze as Conan's words hung between us.

She nodded, near imperceptibly, and I cursed, grinding my ass against Conan, feeling him try to still himself from fucking me the way I knew he wanted to. Fuck it. I wanted this, he wanted this, *she* wanted this.

"Please."

39

Rory

I couldn't decide whether I was pissed as Hell or turned on. Or both.

Nope, definitely both.

Ezra's eyes were fixed on mine, dark and filled with unrestrained lust, his fists clenched in the bed sheets as Conan fucked him. Despite the hurt still lingering from Darius' torture earlier, my panties were fucking soaked as I sat watching them, held to the chair by Conan's magic. Fucking elementals and their air powers.

I clenched my fists against the urge to struggle to get to them, not willing to let either of them know how much this was affecting me. Fuck, all I could think about was being between them, knowing how it felt to have both of them, pressed against me, inside me.

I had no doubt Conan had brought me in here to torture me. And I fucking hated him for it, but it was working. I was burning, my body begging me to get the fuck up and go to them. Regardless of the fact that I was definitely not in a fucking state to attempt a threesome right now, watching the two men I was already stupidly attracted to fuck was driving me insane. Ezra moaned as Conan gripped his hips and pulled him back onto his cock, looking up from the shifter to narrow his eyes at me in challenge.

I squeezed my thighs together, swallowing the moan in my throat when Ezra groaned, swearing and meeting Conan's thrusts with his own. They moved together like they were made for this, their bodies in sync, Conan's hand moving from Ezra's hip to grip his dick, pumping it with long strokes in time with his thrusts.

"Fuck, Conan," Ezra cursed, fighting to keep his gaze on mine so Conan didn't punish us both.

"Doesn't he look good taking my dick, princess?" Conan groaned, pleasure clear on his face. I dug my nails into the palm of my hands to try to curb the white hot desire scalding me. "So fucking good," he groaned again, and Ezra fought to catch his breath as Conan upped his pace.

"Oh gods," I gasped, unable to stay silent any longer as Ezra cursed under his breath, his orgasm stealing his control as he bucked back against Conan, cum coating his stomach and Conan's hand.

"Hell below, Ez, *fuck*," Conan growled, burying himself deep before following him over the edge, head pressed to Ezra's back as he came.

My heart was still racing as I watched them come down, Conan collapsing next to Ezra on the small bed. My chest squeezed as I stared at the way he held him, both their breathing patterns still uneven, Ezra's stomach and chest still painted with his release. I felt like I shouldn't be watching them, despite the fact I'd just watched them fuck. This felt so much more intimate.

The jealousy was far worse than it was before.

"Conan," I spoke up, voice thick. "Let me go."

His head raised, one brow raised as he looked me over. "Oh, Rory," he admonished, a smirk on his lips. It was unfair how attractive it looked on him. "I took your restraints off the second I started fucking him."

Heat flooded my cheeks as I realised he was right. There was nothing holding my hands in place except their grip on each other. I stood quickly, blinking and swallowing the excuses in my throat. Why was I trying to explain my desire away? They were unashamed. I could be too.

"If you're quite done torturing me," I said, crossing my arms over my chest and meeting his gaze unblinkingly. I could feel Ezra's eyes on us, could picture the smirk I knew he'd have on his lips as he watched the exchange. "I have work to do. People to kill and all."

Conan's eyes hardened as he took in my words, and I tried to hide the effect it had on me. He looked ready to murder, too, despite being naked and wrapped around Ezra.

"Give us a minute," Ezra said, stretching as he stood. I looked away instantly as every delicious inch of him came into view. "Shy?" he joked, grinning.

"I think I've seen enough of both of you to last me a while," I shot back, the lie bitter on my tongue.

"Oh, little witch," Dare's voice came from the doorway, amusement colouring his low voice. "We all know that's a lie."

I flipped him off as I stormed out, leaving their laughter behind me. I snatched the grimoire from my bed and made it to the front door, one shoe on, before one of them stopped me.

"Enjoy the show?" Darius asked, the sunlight streaming in

through the windows illuminating his brown skin and lighting the gold of his eyes on fire. I had to remind myself to breathe. My panties were fucking ruined from the *show,* but there was no way I was letting any of them near me again today so I'd resigned myself to suffering. Not that he needed to know that.

"Did you?" I asked back, curiosity piqued. I had no idea what, *who,* he was into. I had no idea about a lot of things when it came to him. "I assume you could hear it all from the lounge." After all, he'd laughed as Conan dragged me past him earlier. There was no way he didn't know what was going on.

"I only want you, if that's what you're asking," he said softly, reaching out to cup my cheek. "But I don't mind sharing you. Especially now I know how wet the thought of it gets you." He chuckled as my eyes widened, and I shoved his hand away from me. "But if you're asking which way I swing, gender has never mattered to me." I nodded, smiling up at him. I understood that. "Where are you going?" He looked pointedly at the one shoe on my foot and the book clutched in my hand.

"The shed," I told him, sliding my other shoe on. "To get to work."

"Can we come?" Ezra's voice joined in as he and Conan reappeared, Ezra's clothes slightly rumpled, Conan's spotless as usual. I flushed as I saw them, unable to stop thinking about the way they'd looked together.

How the fuck was I supposed to hate him when I knew how he fucked?

"Uh, sure," I muttered, looking away from them quickly. Conan waved his hand through the air, unlocking all the locks on my door without so much as a hint of effort. I glared at him. "Fucking elementals."

He pinned me with a stare that had me fighting not to look

down. I wouldn't give him that satisfaction. Not yet.

"One of us should run a perimeter check," Ezra was saying as I stepped out into the afternoon sun, basking in the warm glow. I heard Conan murmur an agreement, and then the sound of clothes hitting the stones and the distinctive *crack* that came with shifting.

I spun, immediately met by Ezra's wolf. Last time he'd shifted, he'd barely let us near him, he was so determined to find Conan. His determination made sense now that I knew he was in love with him. Something warm sprouted in my chest at the thought, and I quickly pulled it up at the root. There would be no thoughts of love. It was a fool's game, one I'd lost before. I didn't plan on putting myself in the running again.

The wolf was so tall I could hold his gaze without so much as bending my head. His fur was deep grey, the colour of a storming sky just before the rain breaks, and his eyes were a deep brown, so dark they were almost black. I had to remind myself to breathe as he moved closer to me, nudging my hand with his head like a house dog asking for pets.

"What the fuck is the overgrown mutt doing now?" Darius snorted, looking down at the beautiful wolf like he'd really rather be anywhere but here.

I rolled my eyes at him, shaking my head, before running my fingers through the wolf's coarse coat, scratching him between his ears. I knew from talking to Grace that shifters' animals were like half of their soul - both their own entity and inextricably linked to their human side. So I assumed Ezra could hear me when I said, "hey there, beautiful."

Conan laughed, a short, humourless sound, raising his brow at me. Immediately, I wanted to punch him in the face, despite the connection I was sure we'd had earlier.

"The wolf's a sap," he said, but I knew I hadn't imagined the fondness in his voice. "But only for the right people. I've seen him rip a man's intestines out with those claws."

I blinked at him, the mental image running through my mind, and glanced down at the wolf's paws. They were massive, the claws long and thick. I grinned. "I'm sure he deserved it."

Ezra's wolf, as if proving Conan's point, turned to Darius and snarled, hackles raising. I released him from my grip, slapping my hand over my mouth to keep my laughter inside at the horror in the demon's eyes.

"Don't tell me the demon from Hell is scared of dogs?" I teased as the wolf bared his teeth.

"I'd just rather not get fur all over me," he snapped back, putting distance between him and the animal. The wolf turned away, heading for Conan and happily nuzzling against his waist. I watched as the normally serious asshole of a man softened, stroking the wolf without hesitation and smiling at the happy rumble coming from the animal's chest.

"Come on, little thief," Darius said, hand on my shoulder as we turned away. I led him around the back of the cottage to the little shed I'd built when I re-erected the property. It was small, built with wooden slats I'd painted lilac, with a sloped roof and a door that was hanging on by its hinges.

I entered, lighting a candle with a pinch of my fingers and a quick spell, illuminating the little room with a warm glow. It smelled of dew and moss, a comforting, reassuring scent that soothed my nerves. A workbench took up most of the space, with shelves above holding jars and herbs and torn out book pages with spells I'd used.

"That thing gives me the fucking creeps," Dare muttered as he picked up the jar containing the heart, holding it up to the light and cringing.

"Don't touch it then," I told him, snatching it back from him and returning it to the table.

"Do I want to know where you got it? Or why the fuck you need it?"

"You tell me," I answered, grabbing a few of the jars off the shelf and sitting in the rickety chair. Dare stood behind me, watching as I unscrewed the lids and peered at the contents. "Do you want to know? Or would you rather keep picturing me as some good girl gone bad who needs three big, strong men for protection?" I coated my words with a heavy dose of sarcasm, focus honed on the rusty nail I extracted from a jar.

"I have never thought of you like that," Dare said, voice low and dark. I swallowed. He grabbed the back of my chair and spun me around so I had no choice but to face him. "I'm under no such illusions that you need us, little witch. The problem is, I think we fucking well need you."

40

Darius

My little thief was so fucking cute when she was surprised. It amused me, the widened eyes, lips parted, hands clenched in her lap. I thought I'd made it clear enough when I'd told her I didn't mind sharing her. But apparently not.

"What the fuck is that?" Conan interrupted, his tall frame filling the doorway, staring at the heart on the desk.

"You're just in time," I said, smiling down at Rory. "Our girl was about to tell me."

I caught her inhale at the use of *our*, warmth spreading through my chest. Fuck. I could spend weeks watching her reactions, learning all the things that made that delicious blush creep across her cheeks. Although, Conan and Ezra had beat me to that, I supposed. I hadn't minded him dragging her through to watch them fuck. In truth, it had been hilarious, the stubborn anger on her face despite the utter *want* I could feel radiating off her.

I'd fucked men before, been in bed with multiple people on many drunken nights after the parties my parents were obsessed with throwing. It was different here. Above. Hell was where every emotion, desire, sin was heightened. On the surface, they weren't much different, the human realm and the mythic. My father, with his crown and castle and gold, spared no expense on his balls and celebrations and alcohol. Or the weddings he meticulously planned.

I couldn't find it in myself to feel bad for fucking up those plans. I was young and already tired of the meaningless power games. There was only so many times I could get drunk and fuck the same people before it all lost its sparkle.

So I'd left.

"I took it from the first man they sent to get me back," Rory was saying, snapping me out of my thoughts. I blinked at her, clearing my head. "He was human. I almost pitied him. No doubt they'd told him they'd give him eternal life and power in exchange for me or some such bullshit. In reality, they'd have drained him the second he returned. They don't like leaving a trail."

For a second, neither Conan nor I spoke. It shouldn't have surprised us, the calm, detached way she talked about murder. A dark sort of need washed over me, the image of her standing above the dead man, blood on her hands and a satisfied glint in her eye had sparks shooting through my veins.

Conan, apparently had the same thought process as I did, judging by the way he was staring at her like he wanted to devour her whole.

"How many people have they sent?"

"Oh, just him and the dead girl," she hummed, weighing out what looked like ashes on a set of old, silver scales. "But they've made their presence known in other ways, like the door. A dead crow once." I winced on her behalf, knowing

241

the connection dark witches had to the birds. Subconsciously, I rested my hand on her shoulder, though I couldn't decide whether it was for my benefit or hers. The urge to reach out and see what was going through her mind was nearly impossible to ignore, but I didn't want to piss her off right now. Not when I knew she was going to try to murder me the second she found out why I'd left her bed.

"You've lived with this for how long?" Conan growled, blue eyes hard with anger.

"I left them six years ago."

I noticed the tick in his jaw, the tenseness in his shoulders, even as Rory continued filling a small bag with the ashes she'd weighed, tying it off with twine. Once I focused on her, I couldn't tear my eyes away from the ease with which she moved, black pointed nails tapping against the worn wood of the table.

"What is all this for?" I asked, just to clear the tension from Conan's anger that was polluting the air in the small space. It was crowded enough in here without his overgrown emotions.

"Spell."

I snorted. "No shit, little witch."

She sighed, putting down the bundle of herbs and shooting me a withering glare over her shoulder. "Ashes, rusty nails, heart," she listed, pointing to each. "For punishment, suffering, and death." She picked up the bundle of scented herbs and a long blue candle. "Ash leaves for protection. Blue for anonymity."

"Protection?" I repeated, frowning.

"To stop the spell coming back on me," she explained, shrugging. "Unlikely but possible if they've upped their defences. The grimoire is pretty brutal in its violent efficiency though so I'm not too worried."

Too worried. I didn't want her worried at all. I stopped myself from reaching for her.

"What will the spell do to them?" Conan butted in, voice near a growl.

Rory paused, gathering the supplies into a small pile and standing again. She turned to face us, face hard with determination, head tilted so she could look us in the eyes.

"They'll purge themselves of all the blood they've consumed," she began, a gleam in her eye that called to a deep hunger in me. "Until they're husks. Unable to move or run. They'll feel like they're burning, their bones breaking, skin flaking, screams silenced as their tongues are ripped from their heads." She was grinning now, as though the image of it was the most delicious thing she'd ever imagined. "Finally, their hearts will explode in their chests. And Eryx and his legacy will be wiped from the face of the earth entirely. Reduced to ashes."

"Fuck, little thief," I breathed, unable to stop my power reaching out to caress the edges of her mind, to feed on the blood lust there. "You're stunning when you're murderous."

She turned to me, her smile softening a little at the edges, sending molten heat through my veins.

"Here," she said to Conan, eyes still on me, reaching behind her to grab the jar with the heart. "Carry this in for me."

The look of disgust on his face had laughter spilling from me, Rory immediately following me, doubling over and clutching her stomach as the man held the jar out from his body like he thought the heart would bite him if it got too close.

"What the fuck have you done to him?" Ezra's voice came from the door, amused and curious. "And why are you acting like you've never seen dead things before?" he asked Conan, snorting at the twisted expression on his face.

"It's fucking disgusting," was all he said, voice dark and unamused.

"Oh, 'cause your hands are totally clean of blood," the shifter teased, raising his brows. He was naked, obviously having just shifted back, but Conan was too busy glaring at him to make any comment on it.

"I don't keep souvenirs," he shot back, nose wrinkled. Rory was still trying to catch her breath, and I looped my arm around her waist and tugged her close to me, relishing in the feel of her against me.

"Little thief has you beat," I told him, enjoying the glare it received me.

"I think you need a lesson, princess," he replied, eyes fixed on her as she collected the rest of the stuff and sauntered out of the shed, pausing to take in the very naked Ezra. I chuckled at the blush on her cheeks, the not so subtle way she stared.

"I'm sure you want to punish me," she drawled back, looking him up and down pointedly. "But not as much as you want my submission."

He growled, shoving the jar at Ezra and advancing on her, snatching her from me and grabbing her hair to make her look up at him. "You're fooling nobody," he hissed, teeth bared. "You want my cock. You want to earn it. You know, deep down, how much of a fucking slut you are for us."

He shoved her away, turning and heading into the cottage without another word.

Rory stood still, chest rising and falling quickly with each breath, eyes wide and glassy. I narrowed my eyes at Conan's back. Despite the brutality of his words, I could tell she was fighting the urge to obey him. She may dislike him, but he was right. She wanted this, him, us. I grinned at the renewed determination, barely disguising the lust in her eyes.

She wouldn't last long.

41

Rory

"Cappuccino two sugars?" I called out, sliding the takeaway cup across the counter. The woman on the other side smiled as she took it and dropped a few coins in the tip jar. When she opened the door, a stream of cold air flew in, and I recoiled back into the warmth of the kitchen. It was still early, and not particularly busy, and I had been half way through making batter for muffins when the customer had arrived.

As usual, Grace was all smiles, dressed in a bright orange dress that was definitely not made for the cold.

"So…" she began, drawing out the world conspiratorially. "It's a no on the escape plan?"

I groaned, dumping sugar into the bowl and mixing with perhaps a little too much enthusiasm. "No. And, regardless, I'd rather die than let you call them."

By *them* I meant the ghosts from Grace's past. The ones she'd left behind five years ago. She'd just opened the cafe when I moved here, back when we were just two strangers running from shit neither of us could put words to. We'd bonded instantly, though neither of us ever divulged the details of the horrors we'd dealt with.

I knew the barest bones of her story. That she'd been sold just weeks before she turned eighteen. How she'd run before her *owners* could move her into their house. The thought turned my stomach. But she was irreparably linked to them by the pack bond forced on her, the bite she kept covered by high collars and foundation and carefully selected hair styles. I'd burn before I let her ever open up that communication again. She was younger than me but you'd never know judging by the darkness she kept thoroughly concealed by the bright smile and brighter clothes.

"I'd resurrect you just to kill you again if you did that, you bitch," she shot back, rolling her eyes at me.

"Good luck with that," I snorted.

"You're right," she sighed, bumping me out of the way before I could ruin the muffins by beating them half to death. "You'd probably be just as stubborn dead as you are alive."

"You love me like that."

"I do," she conceded, smiling. "Okay fine, no rescue mission. But for the love of all the false gods, why haven't you murdered those men yourself? No sex is good enough to put up with their shit. And please tell me you don't expect me to believe the bullshit about you needing protection."

I choked on my laugh. "Okay but the *sex*…" I tilted my head back, groaning. Grace laughed, the sound instantly lightening my mood. "Killing them would be pointless. They're leaving in a week." I paused, resigning myself to telling her the real story. "And, no, I don't need their protection. I just needed to convince them not to get me arrested."

"What? Why?"

247

"I might have accidentally stolen something." I winced at the look Grace pinned me with.

"Accidentally," she repeated, hands on her hips. "I'm not convinced you've ever, in your entire twenty six years on this planet, done anything by accident."

She was right. "Fine. I totally on purpose stole something. And I so nearly managed to pull it off."

She was silent as I explained the whole ordeal, leaving out the more gruesome parts of the revenge plan, her blue eyes narrowed as she chewed on her bottom lip.

The muffins were in the oven by the time I was done.

"You should've told me," Grace said softly, voice thick with emotion. My heart jumped in my chest, guilt slithering through me.

"I'm sorry," I told her, glaring at the kitchen door when the little bell above the entrance rang to let us know a customer had arrived. They could wait. "I didn't want to drag you into-"

"You're my best friend for fuck's sake, Rory!" She fought to keep her tone low, practically shaking with anger. "I don't want you to be doing this shit alone."

"Everything's okay, Gracie. I know how to handle myself," I tried to reassure her. She rolled her eyes and shook her head a little.

"I know you do," she said, wiping the flour off her hands on her apron and turning to the door to the cafe floor. "But you don't have to do it all alone."

I was drained by the time I got back home. Grace was hurt, understandably, by my omissions for the last few months, but she was also far too nice to curse me out about it. I'd have felt better if she'd just yelled at me. Instead, she'd taken deep breaths and gone back to work, trying her godsdamned hardest to pretend that she wasn't hurt.

As a shitty sort of apology, I closed up for her and told her to leave early. I knew we'd be fine, we always would be, but that didn't help the guilt that weighed me down. I should've known she'd be dragged into this one way or another. I should never have tried to hide it at all. But it was too late now.

I was exhausted. Not physically, because I'd slept like the dead last night after all the shit the guys had pulled, but like my bones were heavy.

I wanted this whole thing to be over with. I'd wanted it for so long and now that I was so close to ending this, ending *them*, ending *him*, it was painful to wait another minute.

"Hey, little thief," Darius greeted me, looking up at me from the couch. I blinked at him, offering a smile I knew came out shaky and unconvincing. He stood quickly, cocking his head as he took me in. "What's wrong?"

As the words left his mouth, Ezra and Conan looked over from the kitchen, eyes narrowed.

"Who do we need to kill?" Ezra asked immediately, crossing to me and wrapping me in his arms. I sank into his embrace gratefully, soaking in his strength. He released me just for my demon to grab me and tuck me close to him, my head pressed against his chest. I savoured the close contact, even as I knew, deep down, what I really needed now.

There was no point in lying to myself, to any of us, now. The only conflict I had the energy for was murdering the men who'd abused me, and countless others, for years. I may not have *needed* these three men at my back, but I wanted them there.

Fuck it, I wanted them *all* there.

I pulled away from Darius, who pinned me with a look that told me he knew exactly what I intended to do. Before I could say anything, he grabbed Ezra's shoulder and pulled him towards the door, muttering something about checking the woods to make sure we weren't being watched again.

Ezra looked like he didn't believe the excuse for a second, but went with him nonetheless, curiosity in his dark gaze as he glanced back at me before the front door swung shut behind them.

"Princess," Conan said finally, blue eyes darkening as he narrowed them on me.

I swallowed heavily, throat tight. I needed him to break me, ruin me, so I could feel whole again. The idea of giving up control, just for a little while, felt like heaven.

Conan scared me in a way that made me want to know more. Like a fire I'd happily be burned by if it just meant I could get a closer look at the flame.

I exhaled slowly and turned, giving him my back, and walked into my bedroom. I heard his quick intake of breath, like he was physically restraining himself. Finally, his footsteps followed mine when I left the door open and waited for him to enter.

The room was clean, despite the small pile of fresh laundry on the chair in the corner, thanks to the tidying I'd done yesterday evening while trying to sort through everything in my mind. It hadn't helped, really, but at least now the floor was clear.

"What are you doing?" he asked, voice deep and ragged as I pushed him onto the bed. He didn't resist, though I assumed that was out of shock alone, and sat on the edge of the mattress. He was wearing dark trousers, fixed with a black leather belt, and a grey shirt, the collar undone. His hair was loose around his shoulders, the front strands tucked behind his ears so it didn't fall in front of his face.

I forced myself to stop staring at him, stepping back and steeling myself. Fuck, I wanted this, but that didn't mean some part of me wasn't fighting me on it. Purposefully, I held his gaze before dropping my eyes to the floor. A signal of trust, of compliance. Of submission.

And then I dropped to my knees.

42

Rory

The carpet was soft beneath my knees as I fought not to shake. I'd worn a skirt and knee high socks and boots to work today, knowing it would be warm inside the cafe, but now I was wishing I'd worn jeans. I felt exposed, kneeling before him, a chill sweeping over me. Conan didn't move, though all I could see were his legs and feet. His low, satisfied sound of approval sent heat through me, anticipation and a tinge of fear causing me to squeeze my thighs together.

"Crawl."

Later, I promised myself, I would fight him on these demands. But right now, we both knew what I needed. I lowered myself onto my hands, looking up at him through my lashes and forcing myself to breathe when I saw the undisguised lust in his bright eyes. *Fuck*.

The thick tension between us grew almost unsurvivable as I crawled towards him until I knelt at his feet. I sat back on my heels, hands on my thighs, head bowed. There was a strange sense of relief that came with such submission. Like finally, *finally*, I didn't have to be anything but his.

"What do you need, princess?" he asked, voice dark but not demanding, not yet, as though he was testing the waters with me. I'd seen him with Ezra, I knew what *he* needed. And I wanted that, him, everything he had to give me.

"You," I whispered, the word a prayer as it slipped off my tongue.

"Then beg."

His self restraint was fraying as he looked down at me, his hands fisted at his sides as though he was forcing himself not to reach for me. I wanted to take that restraint between my teeth and snap it.

"Please," I managed, voice breathy and broken. "Please, Conan."

"I know you can do better than that," he snapped, shaking his head. I shuddered, searing lust burning through me. "You want me? You want my cock? Beg like the good little slut you are."

Something between a cry and a whimper broke from my lips at his words, desire pooling between my legs and soaking my panties. Gods, what was happening to me? I felt like I might die if I didn't get to touch him soon. I wanted him to own me.

"Please Conan-"

"Sir," he corrected, tutting like he was disappointed. I bit my lip to hide my shame. "You address me as *sir* when you're on your knees for me, is that clear?"

I nodded. "Yes, sir."

"Better." The praise warmed me, my heart pounding against my ribs so hard it hurt.

"Please, sir, I want to touch you," I told him, clasping my fingers together so he couldn't see my shaking. "I want you

253

to fuck me. Please." When he was silent, I raised my eyes to find him analysing me. *"Please."*

"Such a needy little slut," he said darkly, running his tongue over his bottom lip. His hands slid to his belt, undoing it slowly as he stood. "Bend over the edge of the bed. You haven't earned me yet."

I blinked, shock rippling through me. *What?* "But, I begged."

He laughed, but it was cold and humourless. "You kept me waiting. I'm not in the habit of letting my pets disobey me."

Too stunned to argue, I did as he asked, standing only to fold myself over the edge of the bed, hands in front of me, cheek pressed to the duvet, knees on the floor. He moved behind me, until he was at my back and all I could see was the empty bed beside me. Quickly, he yanked my skirt up and my panties down, baring my ass to him.

Oh fuck. I heard the snap of the leather before I felt it.

Stinging pain spread across my ass from the impact of the belt, and I yelped. I didn't have a chance to recover before he did it again, harder this time, and I shifted, trying to get away.

"Stay," he demanded, his hand pressing against my lower back, both dominating and oddly reassuring.

"It hurts," I gasped as he ran his hand over the place he'd hit with the leather, biting back a moan. It *did* hurt, but I was also so fucking wet. The pain only heightened the need burning through me, until I was wiggling my hips against his hand, desperately trying to get him to touch me.

"So fucking needy," he murmured, withdrawing and bringing the belt down again. And again. And again. Until I was arching my back with the sting, tears at the corners of my eyes, panting as I tried to catch my breath.

The pain made my legs weak, and I slumped against the bed,

blankets clutched in my fists. The sound of the belt hitting the floor broke me out of my stupor, and I blinked the tears back, gathering my strength to rise on my elbows and look over my shoulder at him. He was staring at my intently, gaze fixed on the red marks on my ass, his trousers doing nothing to hide how badly he wanted me.

"You took it so well, princess," he praised, raising his eyes to meet mine. I whimpered, shivering under the warmth of the words. This is what I needed. To be broken down to my barest needs and then pieced back together. The second he saw the relief in my eyes, his hardened again, the dominating, cruel mask falling back into place. "Kneel."

I obeyed without a word, eagerly lowering myself back to the floor, wincing as I sat on my heels. Fuck that hurt.

He moved to sit in front of me again, snapping open his fly and freeing his cock. I shifted, mouth watering as he lounged on the bed, still fully clothed.

"Open," he said, leaning forward to run his thumb across the seam of my lips before gripping my jaw. I opened my mouth quickly and he groaned. His grip moved to my hair, and he urged me towards him, until my lips brushed the tip of his dick. "Suck."

He didn't have to tell me twice. I wrapped my lips around him, eagerly running my tongue along his cock, moaning at the feel of him. He restrained himself long enough for me to get used to his length, testing how much he'd let me tease. I ran the point of my tongue across the head of his dick, satisfaction flooding me as he groaned. I managed to replicate the move again before he took control, refusing to let me adjust to his dominance before he tightened his hold in my hair and thrust into the back of my mouth, making me choke. He pulled out,

255

expression hard as he slammed back down my throat. I fought to swallow around him, saliva dripping down my chin as he continued to fuck my throat.

"Fuck, princess," he groaned, movements becoming more erratic as he neared the edge, his grip on my head forceful. "That's it. Take all of it."

I obeyed as best I could as hot spurts of cum shot down my throat, swallowing as he groaned, cursing under his breath as he rode out his orgasm. He withdrew as he came down, drool and cum coating my bottom lip as I gasped for breath.

"Such a good girl," he murmured, falling back on the bed and dropping his gaze to me. I inched forward, ignoring the need between my legs, desperate for his touch. "Are you ready for your reward now?"

"Yes, sir."

43

Conan

"Did you make Ez crawl to you, too?" she asked, head resting against my thigh. She was still kneeling, slouched against me as I played with her hair. I felt the tension release from my shoulders as the silky strands sifted through my fingers. She always carried this strange sort of calm with her, and though my instincts begged me to turn and run the fuck away, I couldn't make myself move.

"No."

She straightened, and I immediately mourned the loss of her. I placed my hand back in my lap, careful not to let my disappointment show. She frowned, those pretty, swollen lips forming a perfect pout. I reached out before I could stop myself, tugging her off the floor and into my lap. She let me, though I caught the confusion flash in her eyes. Still, she settled against me, her fingers trailing slow circles on my chest.

I regarded her with a tilt of my head, raising a brow. "Why? Would you like me to?"

Her hand fell as she started, reeling back a little. I caught her, hands wrapped around her waist to steady her. "What?"

I pressed my fingertips into her sides, dragging her forward until her tits were pressed against my chest. Slowly, I leaned down, trailing my tongue along the exposed column of her throat. "Do you want to see him crawl?"

Her breath hitched, a combination of my teeth on her pulse point and my words. I stopped, sitting back, away from her. She frowned, chest rising fast and hard as she fought to keep her breathing steady.

"Answer me." It wasn't a question. It was a demand. She nodded. I shook my head in answer. "Use your words."

"Yes."

"Yes, what?"

"Yes, I want to see him crawl to you."

"Such a little slut," I murmured, resuming kissing her neck, taking all my self control not to sink my teeth into her skin and make her cry out. She moaned, shifting her hips against me. I stopped again, ripping myself away from her. I'd heard the front door open again a while ago, not that I'd given a single fuck if they'd heard us. "Ezra!"

She stilled, eyes widening. "What are you doing?" she hissed.

"Granting your wish." The corners of my mouth twitched up when I heard the telltale footsteps.

Seconds later, Ezra stood in the doorway, brow furrowed and stance tense. "What is it?"

I eyed him, letting my gaze linger on the way he'd un-buttoned half his shirt and already taken his belt off. I'd caught him in the middle of changing. Good. "Rory here has something to say to you."

Quickly, my girl spun round, nearly knocking herself off

my lap in the process. I chuckled, catching her and holding her flat against my chest, her back pressed against me so she could watch Ezra.

"No, I don't!" she protested, wiggling in my grip. I tutted, dipping my hand lower to stroke along her inner thigh.

"You're telling me you're not wet as fuck thinking about him on his knees for you?" I asked her quietly, mouth grazing her ear as I whispered. She stopped her struggling instantly, the small gasp that left her lips telling me all I needed to know. For good measure, I let my hand wander higher, between her thighs to tease her over her panties. Hell below, I could feel her arousal through the fabric.

"Are either of you going to tell me what you wanted or am I just supposed to stand here and watch you finger her?" His voice was gruff and low, laced with annoyance and his own arousal. I laughed, stroking the top of Rory's thigh lightly with my thumb as I met his gaze.

"Don't act like you're not drooling at the thought of joining in," I replied coolly, relishing the way both of them reacted. Neither were as subtle as they liked to believe - though Ezra rarely managed to hide anything from me at all.

His eyes narrowed and he shifted on his feet, and Rory whimpered on my lap as I cupped her over her clothes. Fuck, I wanted to strip her naked and have her displayed for me, for *us*, to do what we wanted with.

"Conan…" Ezra began, tone warning and short. I scoffed, staring him down, knowing he'd crumble eventually.

"Ezra," I answered easily, licking my lips. He quietened, rolling his eyes but never removing his gaze from mine. Warmth bloomed in my chest but I pushed it down. I'd deal with that later. Now though… "Ask him."

She tensed for a second against my command but softened easily when I pressed a kiss to her throat. Ezra was eyeing us with suspicion and blatant lust and, despite the fact I'd come down Rory's throat minutes before, I was already hard again beneath her.

She cleared her throat, tilting her head to meet my eyes. I nodded once, reassuring her. Yes, I wanted to control her, ruin her, break her down to her basest desires but never, not once, did I want to make her feel like she couldn't trust me in this.

She exhaled quickly, before turning back and resting comfortably against my chest. I tightened my hold on her, inhaling the sweet scent of lust filling the room.

"Crawl to me," she whispered, voice quiet but strong as she met Ezra's eyes. His widened almost comically, flicking between me and her in shock. Finally, he settled on me, questions visible in his expression. I set my jaw and cocked my head, settling into my role as their dominant in this scene we were building.

I knew the second Ezra noticed the shift. Rory did too, by the way she shifted against my hand.

"*Crawl to you?*" Ezra repeated, in disbelief.

"Yes," Rory answered, her voice strong now. I smiled, relishing their interaction.

"What the Hell?"

"It came to my attention that I was the only one made to beg at Conan's feet," she continued sweetly as Ezra stared on, though the growing bulge in his trousers didn't go unnoticed. "So I thought we'd remedy the issue."

Ezra groaned. "You're a terrible fucking influence," he told me, but he didn't say no.

"Maybe I'm the bad influence," Rory shot back before I could answer. I sincerely doubted that, but this was far too amusing for me to step in. Her tone hardened when he stared at her, mouth open, "now get on your fucking knees."

Hell save me. The pure demand and lust in her tone threatened to have me throwing this whole fucking thing out the window and slamming into her right then and there. I restrained myself, barely, digging my fingers into the soft flesh of her thighs so hard I knew she'd have bruises. She moaned quietly in response, grinding her ass against me in encouragement. She liked the pain.

I watched, rapt, as Ezra finally obeyed her demand. The breath left my body in a rush, watching him sink to his knees, a mix of determination and awe on his face. Rory rested her head against my chest, eyes fluttering closed as her breathing kicked up. I grabbed her chin between my thumb and forefinger, forcing her to look forward.

"Watch him," I told her, though my eyes never left him. Slowly, like the fucking brat he was, he crawled towards us, anticipation building in the air. "See how good he looks obeying you?"

Rory nodded, apparently beyond words, and I didn't blame her. Ezra was dangerous and dark and wild and fucking *breathtaking.* By the time he rested obediently on his knees before us, I was painfully hard and clenching my teeth to try and remain unfazed. Rory had no such concerns.

"Fucking hell, Ez," she breathed, blinking at him.

"Tell him what to do now," I told her, controlling her controlling him. It was heady, this power exchange, and the pleasure it gave me having them both submit to me was nearly too much to bear. Rory swallowed, adjusting herself on my knee.

"Touch me," she said softly, near begging. "Please."

I smiled, loving the way she looked to me for confirmation. Ezra growled, low in his chest, as I gripped each of her thighs and pulled so her legs were spread wide. Without warning, I hooked my finger in the thin material of her panties and ripped. Rory moved to complain, but I slid my hand from her chin to her throat in warning before hiking her skirt up further, fisting it and raising a brow at the man at our feet.

"You heard her," I told him, holding her still. "Put that bratty mouth of yours to good use."

He glared at me for a second longer before gripping her thighs and leaning forward, groaning as he descended on her.

"Fuck, hellhound," he murmured, fingers flexing on her legs, as she shifted her hips to try to get closer to him.

I chuckled, tightening my hold on her waist and throat until she stilled again, gasping as her breaths came short and fast. I watched Ezra trace slow circles around her clit with his tongue as she whimpered in my lap. I released her throat to reach for Ez, tugging on his hair hard enough to make him look up at me.

"Stop teasing her," I warned as he narrowed his eyes at me. Gods, these two were going to destroy me. "She wants her reward. Give it to her."

I saw the spark of defiance light up his dark eyes before Rory lifted her head from my chest and pinned him with a glare. "Ez…" she said, her voice breathy with need.

His resistance immediately crumbled. Gods, he was as lost to her as I was. He thrust two fingers inside her, grinning at her immediate moan, before returning his mouth to her clit, chasing her orgasm with single minded determination.

"Gods," Rory panted, turning her head so she was pressed against my shoulder, practically shaking under Ezra's attention. My own control was thinning, close to snapping completely, and the second she came on his fingers, I knew I was fucked.

She cried out, back arching, as Ezra drew every second of pleasure from her until she was limp in my arms. He eased his fingers from her, dripping with her release, and sucked them clean as I fought the urge to fuck them both until this stupid tightness in my chest eased.

I was worried it would only make it worse.

Fuck it.

"On the bed," I told Ezra, who looked up at me with a soft smirk on his face. He stood and I immediately pulled him closer, kissing him and tasting Rory on his tongue. "You too, princess."

She blinked at me, still firmly trapped in the haze of pleasure Ezra had left her in. She stood on shaky legs, and I followed, undressing her quickly and cursing as she shuddered under my touch.

"You look so fucking good obeying me," I told her, tracing the soft curve of her waist with my hand as I pressed her backwards, her thighs hitting the edge of the bed. "Now get on your hands and knees and show Ez how good you can be."

She shivered, glancing back at Ezra waiting on the bed, and obeyed slowly, making eye contact with him as she fell to her hands and knees on the mattress.

Ezra reclined against her pillows, watching her with a heat that suggested he needed her as badly as I did. I needed them both. They were mine. I wasn't sure at what point this had gone beyond needing to fuck her, but now the thought of ever

263

letting either of them go made me want to tear the fucking world apart.

I shook my head, focusing on her as I knelt behind her, and using a finger to drag her release from her cunt to her ass, satisfaction flooding me when she gasped.

"Has anyone ever taken you here, princess?" I asked, Ezra watching us with hunger.

I didn't miss the soft intake of breath, or the pause before she answered in a small voice, "Yes."

Anger pierced the lust surrounding us, the hint of fear in that one word readying me for murder. I ground my teeth together, fighting to regain control.

"Do you trust me?" I asked slowly, meeting Ez's eyes over her head. He nodded once, slowly, understanding my intent without me having to say anything out loud.

Rory exhaled slowly, body relaxing as I stroked up and down her spine.

"Yes, sir."

"Good girl," I murmured against her skin, trailing kisses down her back as Ezra slid off the bed.

"Lube?" he asked her, cocking his head to gauge her reaction. She nodded to the side cabinet without hesitation, and my heart immediately picked up pace in my chest.

I'd go slow, with this, the first time. We'd have time, I told myself, to push her, break her.

Now, I just wanted to stop the fear in her voice.

Ezra was quick to pass me the bottle and undress, sliding back into his place in front of her, dragging her up his body so he could kiss her. I watched them, unable to look away, need pulsing through my veins. His hand was in her hair, hers splayed on his chest, their kiss deep and hungry.

264

I let them continue, knowing she'd need the distraction, as I uncapped the lube and slid it over her ass. She yelped against Ezra's mouth when I pressed into her, slowly at first, preparing her.

"Ez," I said, voice low, as I added a second finger and she began shifting against me.

He pulled away from her long enough to whisper, "Come here, baby," and reach between them to line himself up with her. Rory pressed her face into the crook of his neck as she sank onto his length, moan muffled.

"Ride him," I told her, groaning when she obeyed instantly. She sat up straighter, hands flat against Ez's chest, fucking herself on his cock and my fingers. The ache to be inside her was painful. "Make yourself come, princess. Show me how well you take his dick."

Her nails dug into Ezra's chest as she picked up speed, one of his hands on her hip to help her, the other moving to play with her tits. He rolled her nipple between his fingers, and she gasped, grinding herself against him.

I made eye contact with Ezra over her shoulder, watching pleasure dance over his features.

"Don't you fucking dare come yet, love," I warned him, narrowing my eyes as Rory swore, nearing her release. I reached between them with my free hand, finding her clit.

"Fuck-" Rory swore, head tipping back as she came around his cock, Ezra's fingers digging into her hip as he fucked her through it.

"Gods, hellhound," Ezra said through gritted teeth, watching her with heavy lidded eyes.

Fuck they were perfect.

Before she'd recovered, I pushed her forward so she was

lying on his chest again, slipping my fingers from her ass and replacing them with the head of my dick.

"Conan-" she gasped, tensing slightly. She didn't move away though, just pressed herself closer to Ezra.

"Relax for me, princess," I urged, restraining the urge to slam into her until we were both ruined.

"I'm fucking trying," she muttered, ignoring Ezra's chuckle.

"We'll make it feel good, baby, I promise," he told her, tilting her head up to press a kiss to her mouth. "So fucking good."

She moaned slightly at the promise, grinding herself against him. I clenched my jaw, pressing further into her before withdrawing and repeating the process. I held myself there as she began to move against us, desire washing away her trepidation.

"Conan," she panted, pushing herself up on her hands and looking over her shoulder at me. "Move."

"Princess-"

"Fucking *move*," she repeated, voice breathy with need. "Please."

I was helpless to her when she asked so fucking sweetly.

44

Rory

I was too out of my mind with need to be worried any longer. Conan moved slowly at first, both of them giving me time to change my mind. I wasn't going to, but it was touching that they were giving me the opportunity.

Right now I just wished they'd stop holding back.

The pressure was intense, but it didn't hurt. I felt full, stretched but not sore. I just wanted *more.*

"I swear on all the false god's stupid names, if you don't both start fucking me properly, I will kill you," I told them, though the words were less demanding and more pleading.

"You need more, baby?" Ezra answered instantly, grinning in a way that made my stomach flip. I nodded, digging my nails into his chest as he grabbed my hips and impaled me on him, simultaneously shoving Conan's cock deeper.

"Fuck!"

"That's it, princess," Conan said behind me, scraping his teeth along my shoulder, "let us hear you scream." He nipped the side of my neck at the same time he upped his pace, both of them moving in sync. It was all I could fucking to do hold on to Ez. *Gods.*

It was too much, the pleasure so intense I forgot how to breathe. Already, I could feel my orgasm barrelling towards me, the feel of both of them inside me together, their thrusts unrestrained now, unlike anything I'd ever felt.

I came quickly, so fast it took me by surprise, screaming something that might have been their names. Pleasure flooded me, both of them cursing as I tightened around them, damn near seeing fucking stars.

"Fuck, Rory," Ezra cursed beneath me, thrusting deep as his own release hit him.

Conan followed closely, grabbing my hips as he bottomed out, cursing as he came. I collapsed against Ezra, Conan bracing himself over us, hands braced on either side of me on the bed.

We stayed like that for a few seconds, all three of us trying to catch our breaths, me trying to find the strength to hold myself up without shaking. I still hadn't recovered enough to leave Ezra's chest when Conan eased out of me, lying down beside us and stroking his hand down my spine.

My eyes were closed, my breathing shallow, my body still reeling with the aftershocks of the orgasm they'd given me. I ached in the best way, exhaustion washing over me as I soaked in Ezra's warmth.

"Come here, princess," Conan murmured, lifting me off Ezra to tuck me between them on top of the covers. Ezra immediately turned to wrap himself around me, my back pressed to his front, while Conan grabbed my chin and tilted my head, his lips meeting mine with shocking softness.

That, more than anything we'd just done, scared me most.

I kissed him back slowly as I came back into my body,

savouring this side of him, the way I felt so fucking treasured tucked between them both. He pulled away, and I protested, a sleepy whimper falling from my lips before I could stop it. I was too undone to try to hide how I felt.

How did I fucking feel? Cosy and satisfied and horribly open. This was supposed to be about submission, sex and nothing else. Why the fuck was I lying between the two men who'd been planning my fucking downfall just days ago, *cuddling*.

Why the fuck couldn't I bring myself to move?

"What are you thinking, hellhound?" Ezra asked, shifting so he was propped up on his elbow.

I sighed, desperately trying to figure out where the fuck my defences had gone. "I'm scared."

I didn't mean to say that out loud. Fuck. It wasn't a lie, though, and no matter how badly I wanted to, I couldn't take it back.

"Of what?" my shifter urged, turning me onto my back so they could both pin me with their gazes. Ezra's dark eyes were worried but Conan's blue stare was hard, like he wanted to find whoever had scared me and murder them.

"You."

Ezra looked like I'd slapped him, but Conan just tilted his head, inspecting me. "Why?" he asked, voice low and suspicious.

I looked away from him, suddenly feeling horribly vulnerable. Ridiculous, really, considering I'd been getting fucked by both of them mere minutes ago.

I reached for a blanket, attempting to cover myself, but Conan's hand stopped me, ripping it away and leaving me exposed.

"No," he growled, shaking his head. "You don't get to hide from us. Not now, not ever."

Ever? Panic spiralled through me, closely chased by a keening, giddy desire.

"What do you mean ever?" I breathed, voice shaky. I started to sit up, to get away from whatever this was, but Ezra wrapped his hand around my waist and held me still.

Conan narrowed his eyes at me. "No running, either. Are we fucking clear, Rory?"

"What the Hell?" My voice rose with anger and panic. "I can do what I want!"

"Baby, calm down," Ez murmured. I tensed. "And you -" he pinned Conan with a pointed stare - "stop speaking in riddles and just tell her."

"What?" I asked, confusion fuelling the panic rising in me.

"We're not letting you go," Conan said, tone flat and leaving no room for argument. "Nobody but us will ever touch you again. I don't know what the fuck you've done to me but I can't let you go. Ever. So, no hiding, no running, no not telling us shit like why you're scared."

I froze, brain refusing to process his words. "This. This is why I'm scared. Don't I get a say in this?"

"No," Conan answered at the same time Ezra said:

"Yes, of course you do."

"I can't…I don't know what's happening, this is too much-"

"Look me in the eyes and tell me you want to leave us," Conan said, voice still deadly calm. I blinked at him, breath caught in my throat.

"You don't even like me," I heard myself say.

Ezra snorted but Conan shrugged. "True," he acknowledged, eyes raking my naked body pointedly. "But I'll dismember any fucker who tries to touch you."

What the fuck?

"You're insane."

"You like us that way," Ezra grinned, leaning down to run his teeth over my pulse point. My breathing hitched regardless of my anger, my body responding to him so fucking easily it was embarrassing. "Tell him you don't want us, hellhound. Tell him your body isn't aching for me to claim you right now. Go on, baby."

I didn't get a chance to answer.

"She can't," Darius' voice came from the doorway. "She's a shit liar."

Conan raised a brow as the demon entered the room, closing the door softly behind him.

"I'm offended," Darius drawled, reaching the edge of the bed and staring down at us. "Nobody told me we were cuddling now."

"We're not-"

"Sshh, little liar," he soothed, stripping his shirt off and smirking at me as I watched. "Make room for me." He grinned, not giving me a second to process before he was on the bed, forcing the other guys to move so he could wrap his arms around me.

I wanted to protest. Really, I did. At the intrusion, at Conan's declaration of ownership, at Ezra's teasing about biting me. I'd never put any thought into being bonded to a shifter, given that the only one I knew was Grace, but the idea of being linked to him, and I assumed, to Conan...

No. I couldn't think like that. Stupid, idealistic thoughts.

"Stop thinking so hard," Darius whispered, running his hand through my hair, clever fingers untangling the knots.

Conan and Ezra had indeed moved to make room for him on the bed, though it was a tight fit now. Conan was now beside Ezra on the other side of me, giving Darius and I a moment as he kissed the shifter. I was fucking hypnotised by them, the way they seemed to fit so fucking perfectly together. More, the way that none of this felt odd, or awkward. It should have. I barely knew them, and I didn't understand why Ezra and Conan weren't complaining about Dare joining us.

Maybe they, like me, just sensed that this felt...

Right? Normal? Like nothing else fucking mattered except the silly little fairytale I was letting myself believe.

Darius' magic curled at the corners of my mind, gentle but probing. I frowned, but didn't push him out.

Stop thinking and just feel, little thief, he spoke into my mind, voice gentle and soothing.

I don't know how, I told him truthfully.

You're tired, he said.

Permanently.

I felt him laugh, his chest shaking as I gave in and leaned into him.

Shouldn't this be weird? I asked him silently, even as I tucked myself closer, seeking the calm warmth I knew he'd provide.

Why?

It was my turn to laugh. This was all ridiculous.

Because I have three men in my bed and none of them are objecting to it. I'm not objecting to it. What the fuck is wrong with us?

He rolled me off his chest, sitting up. The others immediately broke apart, Conan upright in an instant, eyes wary. Ezra furrowed his brow, reaching for me and threading his fingers with mine.

"Little thief," Darius began, staring down at me. "We're not like them."

I bit my bottom lip, the sting centring me.

Conan growled low in his throat. Ezra squeezed my hand in reassurance.

"That's what she's thinking?" Conan asked. "Gods, Rory." He sounded almost *apologetic*, like he was sorry for not seeing it sooner.

I couldn't blame him. I hadn't even known that was what I was thinking. Clearly, Darius had seen it in my mind, shoved somewhere dark and shadowy in my subconscious. But it rang true when he said it, made total fucking sense. The last time someone told me they wanted me, to keep, to share, to *own...*

Well, I still bore the fucking scars. Spelled them to invisibility but they were there.

Ezra was on top of me before I even registered him moving, hands braced on either side of my head. "Listen," he urged, leaning down so his mouth skimmed mine when he spoke. "We will never, *never*, hurt you like that. Leave you like that."

"But Conan said he wanted to ruin me, to *own* me -"

Ezra was gone as fast as he came, Conan in his place. "Not like that, princess. Never like that." His voice was so soft I wanted to cry.

"But you need control-"

"I want to own you, yes. To break you. But not irrevocably. Did it feel bad when you crawled to me? Begged for me?"

Darius narrowed his eyes at me. "Seriously? I missed that?"

I smirked, but ignored him. "No." I took a deep breath, steadying myself. "It felt...freeing."

"And when you cried for me?" Dare asked, joining in.

273

"Begged me to stop even though we both knew you didn't want me to? Did it ever feel wrong or bad or remotely like what those dead men walking did to you?"

I shook my head immediately. It hadn't. Nothing that they'd done to me had felt like that.

"See, baby?" Ez said slowly, kissing my shoulder. "Cee's an asshole, granted, but he's not like that. I've known him nearly my entire damned life and his only fucking fault is that he's managed to convince himself he doesn't feel anything. He doesn't damage his property." The last bit was said with a smirk and it was impossible to keep my own smile hidden. Immediately, I felt all three of them relax.

"I suppose *we're* the property?" I asked, turning to Ezra. He grinned at me, eyes sparkling. Fuck, that did things to my heart.

"Are you complaining?" he murmured, reaching for me and dragging me close to him. I smiled, leaning into his embrace and hovering my mouth over his when I whispered,

"No."

I kissed him then, running my tongue over the seam of his lips. He opened for me quickly, deepening the kiss and tangling his tongue with mine. I moaned against his mouth, unable to fucking stop myself. I'd not let myself let go like this with anyone since Eryx, and the desire I'd shoved down deep for those years of recovery was scrambling to be met now.

"Stop hogging her," Darius complained, wrapping his arms around me waist and practically tackling me onto the mattress.

"Hey!" I yelled, mourning the loss of Ez.

"From now on," Dare said, absently stroking his hand over my bare stomach. "No leaving me out of all the fucking fun.

274

It's not fair."

Guilt soured on my tongue. "I didn't mean…" I trailed off, unsure what to say. He smiled at me, shaking his head.

"I'm not mad, little thief," he reassured, bending his head and flicking his tongue over my nipple. Gods, I should *not* be so fucking needy for his touch after what Ezra and Conan had just done to me. "This doesn't work if there's jealousy like that. I do want to be in on this next time though," he clarified, narrowing his eyes at Conan and Ezra above my head. I grinned, the idea of having all three of them at once sending heat rushing through me.

"Such a needy little slut," Conan huffed, staring at me hungrily as I clamped my thighs together.

"Let her sleep," Ezra defended me, smacking the others' hands away and tugging me back against him.

"Okay," Darius agreed softly, pressing a chaste kiss to my lips and smiling at me before making to stand. My heart plummeted.

"No," I said, reaching for him before I thought better of it. I didn't want him to go. Any of them. Just for tonight, I promised myself, I could give in to the fantasy of us. "Stay."

His mouth opened then closed again. He looked past me to Ezra and Conan, and I felt Ez nod against the pillow.

"Just get in bed, demon," Conan huffed, arms around Ezra, hand splayed across my stomach protectively. I tugged on Darius' hand, eyes pleading.

"Please, Dare," I whispered.

He nodded once, something flashing in his golden eyes. It was gone before I could analyse it, and the next second he was pulling the covers back and sliding in beside me. Ezra, Conan and I were still naked but he didn't seem to give a fuck. He was in baggy pyjama bottoms and nothing else and I tucked my head against his chest as he lay down beside me.

"Do you want me to help you sleep, little witch?" he asked quietly as Conan and Ezra's breathing evened out in the darkness.

I nodded against him, exhaustion rolling over me in waves. Some part of me wanted to stay awake, to savour the quiet warmth of them all, the sense of utter security I had in that moment. But Dare's magic curled around my thoughts, silencing the ever screaming part of my brain with a thick blanket of power that felt so distinctly like him, I hummed in satisfaction.

"Sshh, little thief," he whispered, stroking his hand over my stomach. I was squished between him and Ez, Conan's hand still resting on my hip over Ezra's body, and I savoured every point of contact as my eyes drifted close. "Sleep. I'll keep the memories away for as long as you need."

I tried to say thank you, but I was too sleepy.

I hoped he knew, anyway.

45

Darius

"Fuck!"

All three of us jumped as Rory yelled from the kitchen, where she was sitting hunched over the centre island, the grimoire spread out in front of her. I'd *just* got to the good bit in the book I'd stolen from her shelf - where the hero and the main character finally fucking kiss - but I threw it down regardless, concern spiking through my blood.

"What's wrong, baby?" Ezra was at her side in an instant, having been closest to her, and Conan and I followed quickly. It was natural, all of us gathering around her, like we'd been doing this for years not just days.

"I thought I had everything," she groaned, glaring at the spellbook like it'd apologise for misleading her. "The heart, the ash, the protection candle...but no. *Shit.*"

"What do you need, little thief?" I asked at the same time Conan grumbled something about just finding the bastards and removing their heads from their necks. I didn't disagree. I wouldn't mind bathing in their blood. But regardless of our collective desire to tear the fuckers limb from limb, Rory was perfectly fucking capable of doing it alone. I understood her desire not to have it tracked back to her.

She had to do this herself.

That didn't mean we couldn't try to help.

"I need their fucking hair."

Silence encompassed the house for a minute as we worked to take in that information. Admittedly, I knew little about dark magic, and what I had learned only encouraged me never to get on the wrong side of my little witch.

"I'm going to regret asking this," Conan started, running his hand through his hair as Ezra leaned into his side. "But why?"

Rory propped her chin on her hand as she sighed. "Because I don't want to hurt any of the other people near them. Intention is all grand and well but the girls…" She swallowed thickly, shaking her head. "They'll have Eryx and the guys' scents on them. They'll have their DNA on them in some way or another. It would be far too easy for the magic to confuse them for the guys without the focus of a specific item or possession that the men would have on them. It's much easier to guide if it has some sort of root."

I repeated her explanation in my mind, sickness curling in my gut at the implication of the other girls. "So we go get their hair."

"If we're doing that, why not just fucking murder them while we're at it?" Conan snapped, throwing his arms up, unbalancing Ezra. The shifter glared at him.

"Did you miss the entire fucking point of it being untraceable?" Ezra shot back, narrowing his dark eyes at him.

"We'll just destroy the evidence," Conan argued through gritted teeth. "It's not like we haven't done it before."

"Stop!" Rory yelled, hands clenched into fists. "Just shut the fuck up for a moment." I stepped towards her instinctively, hating the panic colouring her tone, but stopped when she held her hand up. "The answer to everything is not always getting your hands bloody, Conan."

"Maybe not, but in this situation it is-"

"If you don't close your damn mouth I will sew it shut," she threatened, eyes dark with rage. *Fuck.* My dick hardened at the power and promise of violence in her voice. "We can't go charging in and slaughter them in front of the girls."

"They'd thank us," Conan continued, digging his own fucking grave. The urge to punch him in the mouth was difficult to resist.

"Cee," Ezra hissed, shaking his head.

"No they won't," Rory corrected, standing and slamming the grimoire shut so hard her teacup shook. "They think Eryx and the others are saving them. They *love* them. They're fucking addicted to the feeling of not feeling. You go in there and murder him and his groupies, the girls won't fucking hesitate to turn you in."

"But they're being *abused-*"

Rory laughed, the sound short and humourless. She turned on him, body tense as she tilted her head back to meet his gaze. He towered over her, but it didn't lessen the effect of her anger.

"You have no fucking idea what it's like," she hissed, slamming her palm against his chest. "They think it's *love!* I thought it was love!"

Conan stood stock still, our girl battering her hands against his chest, out of her mind with anger.

"For just one fucking second, Conan, *think,*" she screamed.

279

"*I* am going to make them suffer. *I* am going to make them pay. *I* will be the one to make them wish they'd never met me. You came here to *stop* me so don't you fucking dare act like you're my saviour." She paused, pushing away from him and meeting each of our eyes with a glare. "I don't need you. Any of you. I saved myself once before. I'll do it again."

She tried to push past me, but I caught her by the waist and lifted her off her feet, ignoring her protests and kicking legs. I moved quickly, carrying her to the couch and holding her in my lap as I sat, banding my arms around her as she fought to get free. She didn't get to run. Not from us. I thought we'd agreed on this last night but apparently she needed reminding.

Ezra and Conan followed without question, Conan sitting tightly beside us on the sofa, Ezra crouching in front of her so he could grab her face and force her to look at him.

"Look at me," he said, his voice hard. "*Look at me, Rory.*"

She stopped struggling for just long enough to glare at him.

"What Conan is *trying* to say is that he's worried," he began, glaring at Conan as he held Rory's chin. "Unfortunately he is an overgrown man child who is incapable of admitting his fucking emotions and instead acts like a fucking asshole."

I didn't miss the flash of hurt and shock on Conan's face, nor Rory's soft snort of amusement. I kept my mouth shut, happy to just hold her as I began to trace my power on the outskirts of her mind. She was no longer shaking with rage, though she kept her defences solid against my attempts to see what was happening in her mind.

"We don't want you to get hurt, baby," he continued, and I squeezed her tighter in agreement. She relaxed ever so slightly into my touch, so I increased the pressure again until she sighed softly.

Does it help, sweetheart? I asked silently, and she jumped, tensing again. I doubt she even realised she'd dropped her guard.

Get out of my head.

"I'm not stupid," she said out loud. "Stop fucking treating me like I'm made of glass."

Oh, little thief, be careful what you ask for. Along with my words, I sent an image of her tied up, shaking and gasping, surrounded by all three of us. And naked. Very naked.

"What the *fuck*, Dare?" she screamed, breaking free of my hold. I laughed, not bothering to hide the desire in my blood. We were talking in circles. We all knew Conan wasn't going to apologise, at least not with his words, and tensions were too high to do anything productive.

And I'd heard her with them yesterday, seen the aftermath. I was fucking sick of being left out of everything they were doing to her.

"What did you do?" Ezra asked me, eyes flashing wolf.

"Care to enlighten him, little witch?" I asked her, thoroughly enjoying the struggle on her face as she debated whether or not to tell him.

Conan growled beside me, pushing to his feet. I slapped a hand against his chest, stopping him as he rose. "Not yet, big guy. You have an apology to make."

"Get off me you demon fucker," he answered, breaking free and making to leave. Fucking typical. And here I was thinking we'd come to an unspoken truce. I rolled my eyes, releasing my hold on my power and snatching his mind in a harsh grip.

"I said not yet," I repeated slowly. Conan stood stock still, anger and shock on his face as he raged.

"What did you do to him?" Ezra asked, sounding both

281

fascinated and pissed.

"Rory?" I turned back to my little thief, ignoring the others. "Continue."

The look she gave me, filled with ire, made my cock twitch.

"Darius what the fuck did you do?" The shifter's voice was more urgent now.

"Relax, wolfie," I drawled rolling my eyes. "He's fine. Once Rory tells you the plan I'll let him go."

"That is *not* the plan, Dare!" she protested, throwing her hands up. Her gaze shifted between all three of us, indecision sharp in her green eyes.

"Hellhound?" Ezra urged, brows pinched together with concern.

"Fine!" she finally relented, shoving her head in her hands to avoid any of our eyes when she mumbled, "he wants to tie me up."

Ezra's frown deepened. He opened his mouth to press for more information, but I interrupted.

"Come on, sweetheart," I said, tone darkening as she took a sharp inhale. "Tell him everything."

I sent another image into her mind, grinning at the immediate rush of desire I felt before she remembered to slam up her walls again. She'd yet to redo the spell she'd cast on herself the first time she met me. It filled me with satisfaction.

She knew she was mine. Ours. Even if she wouldn't admit it yet.

"Dare what the fuck-" she hissed, shutting up promptly when I glared at her. Ezra looked ready to murder me if I didn't let Conan go but I wouldn't. Not until she told him how he was going to say sorry. "I'm naked and tied up and Conan's eating me out."

The words were forced through gritted teeth but, nonetheless, the shocked expression on the shifter's face was priceless.

"That wasn't hard now, was it?" I *tsked*, before releasing my hold on Conan. He stumbled, shaking his head to clear the sensation of my power lingering. His nostrils flared as anger radiated from him, his fists clenching. "I believe you have some apologies to make."

I turned, heading for her bedroom, as I spoke into Ezra's mind.

Get our girl ready.

46

Ezra

I had no idea what the fuck was happening.

I gaped after Darius, his words echoing in my head. *Get our girl ready*. What was he playing at? I knew demons had mind powers - abilities that allowed them to read minds, communicate without words, to rummage through someone's brain and find whatever they wanted if said person didn't have their defences built high enough. I assumed that was what happened but it was clear that both Conan and Rory understood more about it than I did.

Fuck it. I didn't need to know to agree. There was not a single part of me that objected to following his instructions. I was confused, not *insane*.

"You heard him," I told Conan, raising a brow at him. "I hope you're feeling very apologetic."

He said nothing, but I caught him flinch. He was wrong, and he knew it. I turned back to Rory, pinning her with a dark look as I stood. A shaky breath fell from her lips as I reached for her, sliding my hand under the hem of her shirt, her skin soft and warm beneath my touch.

"Up," I urged, sliding her shirt up her body and over her head as she lifted her arms for me obediently. Her eyes were wide, the anger that she'd been filled with earlier masked by her shock.

She blinked, and the rage returned, ramping up the heat between us. I grinned, grabbing her wrists and shaking my head as she bared her teeth.

"Feral little thing," I mused, nodding to Conan to come hold her while I stripped the rest of her clothes off. He held her wrists above her head in a punishing grip, neither of them saying a single word as I threw her clothes to the side.

"I hate you," she hissed, naked but no less furious. She was flat out ignoring Conan, not that I could blame her.

"You know I love it when you say that," I encouraged, standing again and taking her from Conan. She glared at me, eyes narrowed as I turned her, preparing to shove her back down and watch Conan fuck her with his tongue.

Before I could so much as encourage her back onto the cushions, she brought her knee up sharply, aiming straight between my legs. I spun out of the way quickly, avoiding the strike but letting her go in my haste. Free, she turned, sliding round the side of the sofa as she slipped on the wooden floor and running to the door.

She'd opened it before either Conan or I could stop her. We took off at once, my wolf driving me. I fought the animal, refusing to give in fully to the instincts of the chase. She'd not stopped to put shoes on and was barefoot as she darted into the forest, hair streaming behind her.

"What the fuck?" I heard Dare call distantly as I chased her, Conan by my side. The demon's footsteps joined ours quickly but my eyes remained on my hellhound, my pulse loud in my ears. Chasing her only heightened my need for her, every inch of my body begging me to tackle her to the ground and fuck her in the dirt.

I saw no reason to tell myself no.

"Run, hellhound," I called out, my pulse loud in my ears. We were close to her now, close enough that I could see the leaves caught in her hair, hear the way her breathing hitched when she heard my voice. Fuck. "You don't want to know what I'm going to do to you when we catch you."

I peeled off to the left, leaping over a fallen tree that she'd moved to avoid, changing the angle so I came at her from the side. One second she was running, panting with the effort of keeping in front of us, the next she was on the ground, screaming as I pinned her down.

"Go ahead and scream," I told her, voice dark. There was no controlling this need now, not after she'd run, not considering I could fucking smell the tell tale sweetness of her need. She wanted this. We both fucking knew it. "It won't save you."

Darius and Conan were there seconds later, Cee with danger written all over his features, Darius looking like he'd just been delivered a fucking prize. It was only then I noticed the rope slung over his shoulder.

Good.

I was on top of her, leant over her body, holding her wrists against the mossy forest floor to stop her escaping.

"Get the fuck off me you asshole!" she protested, trying her hardest to move under my weight. It was futile, but fuck if it didn't make me even harder.

"Rope." Darius grinned at the demand, sinking to his knees beside us and turning his gaze on our girl.

"Oh little thief," he teased, shaking his head as he unwound the rope. "Don't you know by now you aren't getting away?"

"Fuck you," she spat back.

Ignoring her, Darius nodded to Conan. "Hold her while I tie her up."

I shifted my weight off her just long enough to yank her into a sitting position, slapping my hand over her mouth to stifle her yells. She sank her teeth into my palm, hard, in an attempt to get rid of me. I withdrew my hand only to replace it with my teeth, nipping at her bottom lip as she yelped. Tasting blood, I drew back, licking it off her lip and fighting the urge to groan at her taste. My wolf was riding me, pleased as fuck we'd caught her, urging me to sink my canines into her throat and mark her as ours. I wouldn't, not yet at least. This would have to do.

The move stunned her long enough for Conan to hold her still as the demon tied her wrists tight behind her back. She wriggled against her bindings, and Conan tugged on her hair as a warning.

"Here's what's going to happen, sweetheart," Darius said, standing back and analysing his work. "Conan is going to apologise, but he's not going to let you come. None of us are. Punishment for running *naked* into the fucking woods where anyone could see you." He paused, crouching down in front of her. I moved out of his way so he could grip her chin in his hand and force her to look at him. "Anyone sees you like this, I'll fucking kill them, do you understand? You're ours. Nobody fucking touches this pussy but us, are we clear? Nobody so much as *looks* at you or we rip their fucking eyes from their head. *Do you understand?*"

Her jaw went slack, lust and fear glazing her eyes. Conan growled in agreement with Darius, clearly pissed at the idea

287

of anyone but us getting to see her like this, messy and naked and practically begging for cock. The easy going demon was long gone, replaced by a man with violence and dark promise flashing in his eyes.

None of us were complaining, though I didn't doubt Rory had seen this side of him before.

Darius shoved her back and stood, leaning casually against a tree and crossing his arms over his chest. Rory shifted in her bindings, complaint written over her face. I wrapped her hair around my fist and tugged, forcing her onto her back on the ground. It was no doubt uncomfortable with the way her hands were tied, but I didn't give a fuck.

"Teach her a lesson," I told Conan in a low voice, a spike of power shooting through me as he did as I said. He shot me a glare that made it very obvious I'd be paying for it later, but right now he was content to make it up to Rory long enough to let it slide.

I held her down by her hair as Conan gripped her hips and brought her to his mouth, drawing his tongue slowly through her pussy to her clit. I clenched my jaw to stifle my groan at the sight, the way she shivered in my grip, even as she writhed to get away from him. His fingers dug into her skin, and he turned his head, biting the inside of her thigh. She yelped, swearing and struggling in earnest.

"You want to fight, princess?" he asked against her skin, tracing his tongue over the bite. "You want to pretend this isn't exactly what you want? Go ahead. Fight me. You're fooling no one."

"Don't fucking touch me," she growled, Conan and I continuing to hold her still as he raised his gaze to meet mine.

"Shut up and take it," he told her, locking eyes with me as

he smirked and continued teasing her, tongue finding her clit easily and tracing tight circles around it. From where I knelt at her head, I had a perfect fucking view of him tasting her, my cock painfully hard. Watching the man I wanted fuck the woman I wanted would never fucking get old.

"Tell him when you're close, sweetheart," Darius instructed, still leaning against the tree nonchalantly.

In answer, Rory gasped, the noise betraying how much she was enjoying this.

"She's so fucking wet," Conan growled, pulling away just as she tried to buck her hips against his face.

"Conan, I swear to the gods-"

"They can't hear you, princess," he answered, his grip on her hips so hard I knew it had to hurt. He returned to his torture, sucking on her clit and scraping her sensitive flesh with his teeth until she was panting, arching off the ground.

"Fuck," she moaned, voice breathless.

"Are you close?" Darius demanded, pushing off the tree and strolling over to stare down at her. She didn't answer, closing her eyes. He bent down, curled his hand around her throat and squeezed as her eyes flew open. "I said, are you fucking close?"

She swallowed against his grip, eyes wide with shock. "No."

"Liar," Conan growled from between her legs, rising on his knees and running his thumb across his bottom lip to collect her wetness.

Darius tutted, hand flexing on her neck. "You want to be hurt? Is that it? You want me to choke you until you see stars?"

She opened her mouth to answer but no sound came out, a sharp look from the demon silencing whatever she was going to say. She blinked, her green eyes the colour of the mossy

289

floor beneath us, glassy with lust.

"Again," Darius said, without even looking at Conan.

"You don't give me orders, demon," Conan said, though he was staring at Rory as he spoke. "I'll fuck her pretty pussy with my tongue until she cries to come. But don't, for a second, think I'm doing it because you told me to."

I rolled my eyes at him. I knew he'd object to not being in total control, but he deserved it. He needed to be a team player, and if this was what it took then this is what we'd do.

"Look at me while he licks that needy little cunt," the demon told her, not once removing his hand or eyes from her. I would have been jealous if I wasn't content as fuck to watch Conan ruin my hellhound. I knew how good he was with his mouth. It didn't take long for Rory to be gasping again, pathetic little panting sounds falling from her parted lips.

"Stop," I told Conan, who glared at me as he rose. He strode over to me, grabbing me by the front of my shirt and yanking me to my feet, crushing his mouth against mine before I could so much as catch my breath. I kissed him back, tasting Rory on his tongue and groaning. I pressed closer, needing the contact, needing any form of release.

Rory's moan broke our concentration on each other, and I broke the kiss long enough to look over at her.

Darius was sitting against the tree, Rory's back flush against his chest, one hand holding her thigh and forcing her legs open, the other around her throat so she couldn't move.

"Watch them," he told her, though she didn't need encouraging. Her gaze was stuck to us, wild and needy. I could see how wet she was for us, how desperate she was for release.

I wasn't faring much better myself. It took every ounce of my strength to stop myself going to her and making her come around my dick. Instead, I held her gaze and dropped to my knees, reaching for Conan's waist band as she watched hungrily.

I smirked, watching as Darius squeezed her throat at the same second he coated two fingers with her need before sliding them inside her. Her eyes fluttered closed and she leaned into him, the look on her face driving me fucking insane. Conan evidently felt the same way, because his hand was in my hair and his eyes on mine before I could respond.

"Open your mouth so our girl can see how good you look choking on my dick."

47

Rory

I couldn't fucking move. Not that I was trying very hard because my gaze was glued to Ezra, on his knees in the dirt, Conan's cock in his mouth. It was a fucking effort to stay pissed off while watching them, and while Dare had his fingers buried inside me.

"Like the show, little thief?" Darius murmured in my ear, hand flexing on my throat. I fought to get air into my lungs. He crooked his fingers, adjusting the angle in a way that made me gasp.

"Fuck you," I tried to snap back, but the words came out like a request.

"Not yet," he said, stroking his thumb over my clit. My hips moved to meet his hand, body desperate for release. I'd been denied twice and I was already going out of my fucking mind. Instantly, he removed his hand, skimming his lips across my cheek before raising his fingers to his mouth and sucking them clean. I tilted my head back to watch him and he let me, his eyes dark and hooded.

"What if I ask nicely?" I tried. Desire for him, for all of them, was burning me, too much to bear.

"We both know it won't matter," he answered, flicking my peaked nipple with his thumb. "You can do better than that, little thief."

The torture started again, his hand sliding back between my thighs as I watched Conan take control of Ez, fucking his mouth in a way that made me ache for him. Ezra's eyes flicked to me, holding my desperate gaze as he swallowed around Conan's length.

"Fuck," Conan groaned, grip tightening in Ez's hair. I felt my own orgasm rise fast and bit my lip to stop the urge to moan. It didn't matter. Darius knew.

"No, please," I complained as he stopped, body tense and wound tight. Conan groaned Ezra's name as he came, the shifter still staring straight at me as he swallowed.

I was going to die. I swore to all the gods this would kill me.

"Dare, *please*," I begged, not giving a single fuck how pathetic it made me sound. Ezra stood again, walking over to us and looking down at me with a smirk.

"What's wrong, hellhound?" Ezra teased. "Need something?"

I squirmed in Darius' grip as Ezra grinned at me, running his hand down my chest, pausing to pinch my nipple. I ground my teeth together at the wave of pleasure it sent through me.

"Please," I breathed, looking between him and Conan, trembling in Dare's arms. Ez reached for me, but Conan shook his head once, halting him in his path. No no no -

"Touch yourself, princess," he said, staring me down. "Show us how much you want cock. How sorry you are."

I blinked at him, trying to process the instruction.

"That's it, little witch," Dare encouraged, releasing my throat to make quick work of untying the bindings. When my arms were free again, he banded his arm around my waist as I tilted my knees to the side, exposing myself fully. "Spread those pretty thighs for us."

Slowly, I dipped my hand between my thighs, gaze flicking between Conan, who was still standing staring down at me, and Ezra crouched before me, not even bothering to disguise how affected he was. I played with my clit as they watched, breathing short and fast. I was frustrated beyond belief, aching and empty and *pissed* that I was being forced to take matters into my own hands when there were three fucking men who could do the job for me.

"Can you stop torturing me now?" I gasped, squirming under the weight of their gazes. I was going to fucking scream if one of them didn't touch me soon.

"Does our dirty little slut need to be filled?" Dare asked, teeth grazing my ear as he whispered. I nodded frantically, fucking mindless with want for them. He chucked something that looked like a bottle at the others, but I was too slow to see exactly what it was. "Come here, sweetheart," he said, spinning me around and kissing me achingly softly, only worsening the frustrated need in my body. I nipped his lip, deepening the kiss and tangling my tongue with his, moaning against his mouth as he cupped my ass and lifted me onto him. I ground against him over his clothes, desperate for any sort of pressure.

The rustling of clothes broke through my foggy mind and then I was being yanked away from Dare into Conan's arms. I slammed against his chest as he brought me down to him on the forest floor, kissing me hard and fast in a way that made my head spin. I could kiss him for fucking ever and never get tired of it, I thought.

"Ride me," he demanded against my mouth, reaching between us to line himself up with me. "Take what you need, princess."

Impatience swept over me in a heady rush, and I didn't hesitate, slamming myself down on him so fast both of us let out a groan. I nearly fucking came from that alone, the all consuming relief at finally having him where I needed. He gripped my hips, steadying me as I rode him, hands braced on his chest as my orgasm neared.

"Good girl," he encouraged, sweeping a finger over my sensitive clit and making me buck against him. "Come for me, princess. "

I swore, pleasure coursing through me. Conan took over, controlling my movements while my orgasm ripped me to fucking shreds until I was a panting mess laying across his chest. He swept my hair off my neck and tilted my head to look him in the eye.

"Hold still," he instructed quietly, a teasing edge to his voice that had me instantly fighting against his hold. I managed to twist enough in his arms to see Ezra out of the corner of my eye. "Take her ass," Conan's voice was harsh and demanding, and Ezra grinned. "Her cunt's mine."

I tensed despite the excitement making me giddy. It wasn't like they hadn't done this before but I knew the stretch would hurt before it felt good. Darius appeared in front of me, one brow raised in an expression that promised trouble.

"Sit up, little thief," he said, voice quiet but demanding. All these orders would normally make me bristle but fuck if they didn't turn me on like this. I placed my hands flat on Conan's chest, using him to steady myself as my body shook with the aftershocks. He was still inside me, and I had to fight to hold myself still, wanting desperately to move. "Do you have any idea how fucking stunning you look taking his dick like that?"

I moaned, heat rushing through me at his words. I ground against Conan, unable to stop the urge, and was swiftly rewarded by him grabbing my ass and digging his fingers in *hard* to my flesh.

"He's right, hellhound," Ezra's voice came at my ear. "You'll look even more perfect filled with three though."

Without warning, he slid his finger to my ass, coating me with lube. I jumped at the shock, though I couldn't move as Conan tightened his grip to the point of pain. I didn't have time to even question his words before he started moving slowly inside me, and my head emptied of thoughts.

By the time he added a second finger I was whimpering, pleasure burning me as Conan loosened his bruising grip on me so I could fuck him.

The second Ezra replaced his fingers with his cock, sliding into me in one thrust, I shattered, screaming as he wrapped an arm around me to keep me upright.

They were going to kill me. I was sure of it.

48

Darius

I watched my little thief fall apart on their cocks, head tilted back and lips parted. Fuck she was stunning. I palmed my own dick through my trousers, so turned on I was aching with the need to fuck her.

I waited, barely managing to restrain myself, until she was limp against Ezra's front. Both the men had stopped fucking her long enough to meet my gaze, Ezra grinning and Conan propping himself up on his elbows to nod at me.

I moved towards them, standing in front of her so she could lean against Conan if she needed to. Slowly, while she watched, I shoved my jeans down and stroked my cock, noting the way she licked her lips as she fixated on me.

"Are you ready, little thief?" I asked, voice low. As much as I wanted to grab her and see if her mouth was as sinful as I suspected, I wanted to make sure she was as desperate for this as I was.

"All of you?" she asked, eyes widening. I grinned, anticipation setting my blood alight.

"You can take it."

Her answering intake of breath was enough confirmation for me, and I reached for her hair, wrapping it around my fist as she dragged her tongue along my shaft. I ground my teeth against her teasing, allowing her a few seconds to adjust to the slow rhythm Ezra and Conan began, timing their thrusts so that she had to dig her fingers into Conan's chest to stop from collapsing.

"Suck, Rory," I told her, refusing to wait any longer.

The others upped their pace, and she moaned, the sound fucking music to my ears. No longer hesitating, she opened her mouth wide and wrapped her lips around me, taking me deep and groaning around my cock as Conan released her hip with one hand to tease her peaked nipple.

"Gods, hellhound," Ezra said through gritted teeth, his breathing rough. "You feel so fucking good."

"You were made for this, weren't you, little thief?" I encouraged as she hollowed her cheeks around me. "Being fucked until you can't even speak. Such a perfect little whore for us."

She groaned at my words, shifting to try to meet the others' thrusts, making Ezra curse.

"That's it, princess," Conan murmured, reaching between them and drawing tight circles around her clit with his finger. "Make them come for you."

She shuddered, tears beginning to form in her eyes as the three of us fucked her ruthlessly. I lost my patience, moving my hips and fucking her mouth, groaning at how fucking good she felt around me.

"Sin, Rory," I said lowly, my orgasm approaching danger-ously fast. "That's what you are. That's what you were meant for."

"She's fucking strangling my cock," Ezra groaned as Rory fell apart under our hands, my own orgasm hitting me at the sight. I held her on my cock as I came down her throat, her cry muffled around me. I pulled out to let her breathe, nearly fucking dying at the sight of my release and her tears staining her gorgeous face.

"Fuck, hellhound-" Ezra leant over her, teeth skimming her neck as he came, holding her flush against him. Conan followed quickly, thrusting hard into her and swearing low under his breath as he emptied himself inside her.

She collapsed seconds later, panting and shaking, with a soft smile on her face that made my chest ache. I adjusted my clothes, bending down to take her from the others and lifting her gently into my arms. I sat against the tree, holding her close to me. She was wrung out, messy and limp.

She was fucking perfect.

"Hell, little witch," I breathed, holding her against my chest as Ezra and Conan regained their breaths and readjusted their clothes. "You're a godsdamned addiction."

She sighed, raising her head slightly to meet my gaze. "What a shame," she mumbled, the words sleepy. "Guess I'll have to stick around a while longer."

I smiled, pressing a quick kiss to her forehead before easing us both to our feet.

"Put this on," Ezra said, tugging his t-shirt off and throwing it at her. "As much as I'd love for you to be naked all the time, like fuck am I risking anyone seeing you on the way back. And my wolf's been dying to have you wearing my scent for days."

She rolled her eyes, but she was smiling as she tugged the shirt over her head, steadier on her feet now. It was massive on her, given that Ezra was about twice her damn size, and fuck if it didn't do something ridiculous to my heart.

I wanted to keep her in my arms, ease her down from the adrenaline rush with slow touches and reassurances, but she was likely to freeze if I did that here. When we got back to the cottage, I told myself, I'd run her a bath. Well, run us all a fucking bath considering the state of us, clothes and skin stained with mud. Rory was by far the worst off, cum running down her thighs, tear tracks on her face and twigs and dirt in her hair.

A wild thing. That's what she looked like. Wild and filthy and like the goddesses mortals always spoke of.

I'd never been inclined to pray to the fake gods, but fuck I'd make an altar to this witch if she so much as asked.

That thought was more dangerous than the fucking foursome we'd just had in a forest.

"Nice show."

The voice cut through the easy atmosphere around us, instantly turning the air icy with apprehension. I moved before I finished processing the new voice, shoving Rory behind me, and sending tendrils of my power out to figure out exactly where she was. It was her, I knew it was. Fuck. Fuck fuck fuck I'd fucked up this was bad -

"Ro…" Ezra's voice was low, his footsteps shockingly light as he moved to her side. *"RORY!"*

I spun, fear spiralling through me. My little thief was gone.

"Where the fuck are you, Rosa?" I demanded, panic sending ice through my veins. I couldn't fucking breathe. She was here. Why the fuck was she here, and what in Hell's name did she want with Rory? I'd warned her what I'd do if she ever fucking showed her face again.

"Darius what the fuck is happening?" Conan growled, bright hot anger on his face as he scoured the forest for Rory.

"You're so cute when you're scared," the female voice cooed again.

Finally, she came into view.

Rosa stepped out from behind a tree, Rory limp in her arms. Without thought, all three of us charged forward, reaching for her.

"I wouldn't do that if I were you," Rosa cooed, rendering Conan and Ezra immobile as her eyes hardened, concentration written in the line between her brows as she extended her power. My guards were up, they never fucking dropped, but I stilled nevertheless, fixated on the gleaming silver point pressed into my little witch's side. "It's coated in hemlock. Unless you want to test your girl's resistance, I'd hold off on the aggression."

"Rosa, let her go," I demanded through gritted teeth. Fuck. This was bad. So fucking bad.

"Oh, Darius," Rosa drawled, pouting exaggeratedly. "I'd have thought you knew better than to run like a coward. You ruined everything when you left. *Everything!*" Her voice rose suddenly with the last word, anger radiating off her.

Gods. "Rosa, just let her go and we can talk," I tried to talk her down, forcing some sense of calm into my words. "I'll even come back with you."

"I'm not falling for your bullshit again," she hissed, shaking her head. The air around her began to ripple as she narrowed her dark eyes and me and grinned, the smile a thinly veiled threat. Someone was fucking summoning her. "I'm sure her keepers will be very pleased to have her back. I hope you know you have no one to blame but yourself, babe."

301

She pouted her lips in a mock kiss and then fucking vanished, Rory disappearing with her.

Conan and Ezra started forward, shouting at me, shock and anger muddling the air around them. I couldn't hear them.

"No," I mumbled, staring at the space she'd just been. My little thief. "No. NO!"

"Darius!"

"Where the fuck did she go?"

"Who the fuck was that?"

I shook my head, panic driving me fucking insane. This wasn't happening. It couldn't be.

"*DARIUS!*" Conan's voice came again, then hands on my shoulders, shaking me until I snapped back into my body.

"Where the fuck is she, demon?" Ezra growled, eyes shifting rapidly to wolf and back.

The faint scent of ash hung in the air as anger settled in over the panic, dangerous determination tamping down all the things I couldn't afford to feel.

"Hell."

They stilled. "And who the fuck just took her there?" Heat radiated from Conan's body, so hot I swore it fucking singed my hair. I shook my head. I couldn't make the truth leave my lips.

"Answer the fucking question before I rip your tongue from your mouth." Ezra was more animal than person now, his eyes silvery, his voice gruff, body shaking as he tried to fight the urge to shift.

I forced air into my lungs, the fucking scent of her - caramel and ash - mixed with the cinnamon spice of Rory making my fists curl.

"Rosa," I said, looking Conan in the eye. "My wife."

302

Acknowledgements

To my partner who had to put up with my late nights and incoherent rambling about threesome positions, I love you. And to our son, I love you beyond words but I truly hope you never read this book.

To my beta readers for being the most encouraging and helpful group. I've never been more happy to be yelled at!

To the smut coven - the best group of spicy readers and writers that I could imagine. I love you all.

To the C2C team for being the best PA, cover designer and all round managers of everything to do with marketing and organising the release of this book. You're the best!

To Sin, who claimed Darius the second he appeared on the page. This is the official declaration that he's yours.

And, finally, to anyone who relates to Rory and her story. You are the strongest fucking badasses.

About the Author

Scarlet King is a bisexual twenty one year old university student. She lives in Scotland with her partner and toddler. She loves coffee, book stores and ignoring her responsibilities in favour of writing. She has a bad habit of falling in love with fictional characters and hopes someone out there will fall for the ones she writes, too.

If you liked this book, please consider leaving a review! A star rating and a few lines helps authors out massively. If you post a review on social media, feel free to tag Scarlet so she can say thank you!

If you want to yell at Scarlet about her books, chat with other readers and be the first to know about her upcoming projects, join her Facebook group, "Scarlet King-Dom."

Scarlet's Social Media Links
    TikTok: @scarletkingauthor
    Instagram: @scarletkingauthor
    Twitter: @ScarKingAuthor
    Facebook Group: Scarlet King-Dom
    Email: scarletkingauthor@gmail.com

Also by Scarlet King

The Runebreaker Trilogy
- Girl of Bone and Ivy (Book 1)
- Boy of Air and Ash (Book 2, coming April 2022)

The Revenge Duology
- Thieves and Thorns (Book 1)
- Revenge and Roses (Book 2, coming 10th June 2022)

Printed in Great Britain
by Amazon

75108680R00189